PLEASANT

CW00766097

ROBERT BLOCH was born in 1917 in (and Stella Loeb, both of German Jewi attended a screening of the Lon Chaney .... of the Opera (1925); the scene where Chaney removes his mask terrified the young Bloch and sparked an early interest in horror. A precocious child, he was already in the fourth grade at age eight and obtained a pass for the adult section of the library, where he was a voracious reader. At age ten, in 1927, Bloch discovered *Weird Tales* and became an avid fan, with H.P. Lovecraft, a frequent contributor to the magazine, becoming one of his favorite writers. In 1933 Bloch began a correspondence with Lovecraft, which would continue until the older writer's death in 1937. Bloch's early work would be heavily influenced by Lovecraft, and Lovecraft offered encouragement to the young writer.

Bloch's first short story was published in 1934 and would be followed by hundreds of others, many of them published in *Weird Tales*. His first collection of tales, *The Opener of the Way* (1945) was issued by August Derleth's Arkham House, joining an impressive list of horror writers that included Lovecraft, Derleth, Clark Ashton Smith, and Carl Jacobi. His first novel, *The Scarf*, would follow two years later, in 1947. He went on to publish numerous story collections and over thirty novels, of which the most famous is *Psycho* (1959), the basis for Alfred Hitchcock's classic film. He won the prestigious Hugo Award (for his story "The Hell-Bound Train") as well as the Bram Stoker Award and the World Fantasy Award. His work has been extensively adapted for film, television, radio, and comics. He died of cancer at age 77 in 1994.

Also Available by Robert Bloch

The Opener of the Way
The Scarf
Strange Eons
The Night of the Ripper
Midnight Pleasures

PLEASANT DREAMS

Nightmares

by

ROBERT BLOCH

With a new introduction by
JOE R. LANSDALE

VALANCOURT BOOKS

Pleasant Dreams: Nightmares by Robert Bloch
Originally published by Arkham House in 1960
First Valancourt Books edition 2025

Published by Valancourt Books, Richmond, Virginia
http://www.valancourtbooks.com

ISBN 978-1-960241-41-2 (trade hardcover)
ISBN 978-1-960241-40-5 (trade paperback)
Also available as an electronic book.

Set in Dante MT

Contents

Introduction

When I was starting out as a writer, when I turned to horror, I drew on my reading of Robert Bloch for how to do it. I reread all of his work that I owned, which was a lot, and studied his approach up and down, sideways and flipped over.

I read other writers as well, and had read a lot of them, including Bloch, growing up, but now I was reading and rereading in an attempt to learn how to do what they did my own way.

Something about Bloch's writing really hit me right, especially now that I was on a mission to become a full-time writer.

He was noted primarily for *Psycho*, his novel that became the acclaimed Hitchcock film, and he once said to me, "I'll be Robert Psycho Bloch until the day I die. But I've written other things."

He certainly has written other things. I would say that more than his novels, including *Psycho*, more than the many film scripts he wrote, his best work were his short stories, primarily those he wrote after breaking out of his Lovecraftian influence, striking out on his own to practically create modern horror and suspense.

Bloch was the forerunner of *Silence of the Lambs* and so many frightening stories that dealt with the unchartered recesses of the human mind. And in my view, I find that creepier than any supernatural tale. Those stories are the rough edge of reality rubbing up against everyday existence.

That's not to say he didn't write some great supernatural or otherworldly stories. This volume of short stories covers a lot of ground, and many of them are of the unearthly realm. My favorite being "That Hell-Bound Train," which also, deservedly, won the Hugo Award.

I even had the honor with Rick Klaw of purchasing it to be adapted to comic form for an anthology we edited years ago titled *Weird Business*. It was a fine adaptation. And if that wasn't enough, some years later my brother John and I adapted it to an IDW comic, and I openly admit I am proud of that adaptation. We also adapted "Yours Truly, Jack the Ripper." Entertaining, but less successful than "That Hell-Bound Train" in my view.

But nothing beats the original story, which is included here. It's not truly horror, as many of his stories were, it's odd, nostalgic fantasy beautifully written. That's not something that is as noted about Robert Bloch's work as it should be. He could be a fantastic stylist. His style was lean and yet driven by images as well as clever ideas. That was one reason his fiction was so perfect for film and much coveted by film makers.

This collection is one of many that he produced, for Bloch was prolific, to put it mildly. He also had a long career, starting out as a teenager and writing pretty much until his death. I used to get postcards from him, and he would take up the whole postcard writing little bits of this and that. I hope I still have them, or that they are in my library collections at Texas State or the library at A&M. I donated to both, but still have a few odds and ends I've yet to pack up and send off. They may still lurk in my ancient file cabinets, even though I fear they and so much else were lost in a house flood years ago.

Due to a change in those postcards I realized something was off with Bob when they became less covered in his handwriting and there was more free space on them. My fears were unfortunately correct. Bloch was dying. One of the best creative minds and one of the greatest contributors to popular fiction was ill and would soon pass away.

Bloch made it all look easy. And one of the things I liked best about his work, one of the major things I learned from him and have used in my work, is a sense of humor.

Horror and humor, flip sides of the same coin.

Cackling over the most horrible things one could imagine actually made them more horrifying. Bloch knew that. It wasn't something he kept secret, it was something he did that is easy to identify, but really hard to duplicate. He didn't have any real competition there. Many of us have been influenced by Robert Bloch, but none of us could do what he did. If there were a Mount Rushmore of popular fiction writers, he'd be on it, taking up a large part of the granite.

Here we have a very fine collection by Robert Bloch, and it is a sweet and sour taste of his wonderful storytelling ability. And there's so much more available. But let's start here, or if you've read these stories before, lets revisit.

Dip in. Oh, and of course, let me wish you Pleasant Dreams.

—Joe R. Lansdale
Big Bear Manor, 2024

Joe R. Lansdale is the author of over fifty novels and four hundred shorter works, including stories, essays, reviews, film and TV scripts, introductions and magazine articles, as well as a book of poetry. His work has been made into films, animation, comics, and he has won numerous awards including the Edgar, Raymond Chandler lifetime award, numerous Bram Stoker Awards, and the Spur Award.

His work has been made into films, among them *Bubba Ho-Tep*, *Cold in July*, as well as the acclaimed TV show, *Hap and Leonard*. He has also had works adapted to *Masters of Horror* on Showtime, Netflix's *Love, Death and Robots*, and Shudder's *Creepshow*. He has written scripts for *Batman: The Animated Series* and other animation.

He lives in Nacogdoches with his wife Karen and their pit bull, RooRoo.

Sweets to the Sweet

Irma didn't look like a witch.

She had small, regular features, a peaches-and-cream complexion, blue eyes, and fair, almost ash-blonde hair. Besides, she was only eight years old.

"Why does he tease her so?" sobbed Miss Pall. "That's where she got the idea in the first place—because he calls her a little witch."

Sam Steever bulked his paunch back into the squeaky swivel chair and folded his heavy hands in his lap. His fat lawyer's mask was immobile, but he was really quite distressed.

Women like Miss Pall should never sob. Their glasses wiggle, their thin noses twitch, their creasy eyelids redden, and their stringy hair becomes disarrayed.

"Please, control yourself," coaxed Sam Steever. "Perhaps if we could just talk this whole thing over sensibly—"

"I don't care!" Miss Pall sniffled. "I'm not going back there again. I can't stand it. There's nothing I can do, anyway. The man is your brother and she's your brother's child. It's not my responsibility. I've tried—"

"Of course you've tried." Sam Steever smiled benignly, as if Miss Pall were foreman of a jury. "I quite understand. But I still don't see why you are so upset, dear lady."

Miss Pall removed her spectacles and dabbed at her eyes with a floral-print handkerchief. Then she deposited the soggy ball in her purse, snapped the catch, replaced her spectacles, and sat up straight.

"Very well, Mr. Steever," she said. "I shall do my best to acquaint you with my reasons for quitting your brother's employ."

She suppressed a tardy sniff.

"I came to John Steever two years ago in response to an advertisement for a housekeeper, as you know. When I found that I was to be governess to a motherless six year old child, I was at first distressed. I know nothing of the care of children."

"John had a nurse the first six years," Sam Steever nodded. "You know Irma's mother died in childbirth."

"I am aware of that," said Miss Pall, primly. "Naturally, one's heart goes out to a lonely, neglected little girl. And she was so terribly lonely, Mr. Steever—if you could have seen her, moping around in the corners of that big, ugly old house—"

"I have seen her," said Sam Steever, hastily, hoping to forestall another outburst. "And I know what you've done for Irma. My brother is inclined to be thoughtless, even a bit selfish at times. He doesn't understand."

"He's cruel," declared Miss Pall, suddenly vehement. "Cruel and wicked. Even if he is your brother, I say he's no fit father for any child. When I came there, her little arms were black and blue from beatings. He used to take a belt—"

"I know. Sometimes, I think John never recovered from the shock of Mrs. Steever's death. That's why I was so pleased when you came, dear lady. I thought you might help the situation."

"I tried," Miss Pall whimpered. "You know I tried. I never raised a hand to that child in two years, though many's the time your brother has told me to punish her. 'Give the little witch a beating,' he used to say. 'That's all she needs—a good thrashing'. And then she'd hide behind my back and whisper to me to protect her. But she wouldn't cry, Mr. Steever. Do you know, I've never seen her cry."

Sam Steever felt vaguely irritated and a bit bored. He wished the old hen would get on with it. So he smiled and oozed treacle. "But just what is your problem, dear lady?"

"Everything was all right when I came there. We got along just splendidly. I started to teach Irma to read—and was surprised to find that she had already mastered reading. Your brother disclaimed having taught her, but she spent hours curled up on the sofa with a book. 'Just like her,' he used to say. 'Unnatural little witch. Doesn't play with the other children. Little witch'. That's the way he kept talking, Mr. Steever. As if she were some sort of—I don't know what. And she so sweet and quiet and pretty!

"Is it any wonder she read? I used to be that way myself when I was a girl, because—but never mind.

"Still, it was a shock that day I found her looking through the Encyclopedia Britannica. 'What are you reading, Irma?' I asked. She showed me. It was the article on Witchcraft.

"You see what morbid thoughts your brother has inculcated in her poor little head?

"I did my best. I went out and bought her some toys—she had absolutely nothing, you know; not even a doll. She didn't even know how to *play!* I tried to get her interested in some of the other little girls in the neighborhood, but it was no use. They didn't understand her and she didn't understand them. There were scenes. Children can be cruel, thoughtless. And her father wouldn't let her go to public school. I was to teach her—

"Then I brought her the modelling clay. She liked that. She would spend hours just making faces with clay. For a child of six Irma displayed real talent.

"We made little dolls together, and I sewed clothes for them. That first year was a happy one, Mr. Steever. Particularly during those months when your brother was away in South America. But this year, when he came back—oh, I can't bear to talk about it!"

"Please," said Sam Steever. "You must understand. John is not a happy man. The loss of his wife, the decline of his import trade, and his drinking—but you know all that."

"All I know is that he hates Irma," snapped Miss Pall, suddenly. "He hates her. He wants her to be bad, so he can whip her. 'If you don't discipline the little witch, I shall,' he always says. And then he takes her upstairs and thrashes her with his belt—you must do something, Mr. Steever, or I'll go to the authorities myself."

The crazy old biddy would at that, Sam Steever thought. Remedy—more treacle. "But about Irma," he persisted.

"She's changed, too. Ever since her father returned this year. She won't play with me any more, hardly looks at me. It is as though I failed her, Mr. Steever, in not protecting her from that man. Besides—she thinks she's a witch."

Crazy. Stark, staring crazy. Sam Steever creaked upright in his chair.

"Oh you needn't look at me like that, Mr. Steever. She'll tell you so herself—if you ever visited the house!"

He caught the reproach in her voice and assuaged it with a deprecating nod.

"She told me all right, if her father wants her to be a witch she'll be a witch. And she won't play with me, or anyone else, because witches don't play. Last Halloween she wanted me to give her a broomstick. Oh, it would be funny if it weren't so tragic. That child is losing her sanity.

"Just a few weeks ago I thought she'd changed. That's when she asked me to take her to church one Sunday. 'I want to see the baptism', she said. Imagine that—an eight-year-old interested in baptism! Reading too much, that's what does it.

"Well, we went to church and she was as sweet as can be, wearing her new blue dress and holding my hand. I was proud of her, Mr. Steever, really proud.

"But after that, she went right back into her shell. Reading around the house, running through the yard at twilight and talking to herself.

"Perhaps it's because your brother wouldn't bring her a kitten. She was pestering him for a black cat, and he asked why, and she said, 'Because witches always have black cats'. Then he took her upstairs.

"I can't stop him, you know. He beat her again the night the power failed and we couldn't find the candles. He said she'd stolen them. Imagine that—accusing an eight-year-old child of stealing candles!

"That was the beginning of the end. Then today, when he found his hairbrush missing—"

"You say he beat her with his hairbrush?"

"Yes. She admitted having stolen it. Said she wanted it for her doll."

"But didn't you say she has no dolls?"

"She made one. At least I think she did. I've never seen it—she won't show us anything any more; won't talk to us at table, just impossible to handle her.

"But this doll she made—it's a small one, I know, because at times she carries it tucked under her arm. She talks to it and pets it, but she won't show it to me or to him. He asked her about the hairbrush and she said she took it for the doll.

"Your brother flew into a terrible rage—he'd been drinking in his room again all morning, oh don't think I don't know it!—and she just smiled and said he could have it now. She went over to her bureau and handed it to him. She hadn't harmed it in the least; his hair was still in it, I noticed.

"But he snatched it up, and then he started to strike her about the shoulders with it, and he twisted her arm and then he—"

Miss Pall huddled in her chair and summoned great racking sobs from her thin chest.

Sam Steever patted her shoulder, fussing about her like an elephant over a wounded canary.

"That's all, Mr. Steever. I came right to you. I'm not even going back to that house to get my things. I can't stand any more—the way he beat her—and the way she didn't cry, just giggled and giggled and giggled—sometimes I think she *is* a witch—that he made her into a witch—"

Sam Steever picked up the phone. The ringing had broken the relief of silence after Miss Pall's hasty departure.

"Hello—that you, Sam?"

He recognized his brother's voice, somewhat the worse for drink.

"Yes, John."

"I suppose the old bat came running straight to you to shoot her mouth off."

"If you mean Miss Pall, I've seen her, yes."

"Pay no attention. I can explain everything."

"Do you want me to stop in? I haven't paid you a visit in months."

"Well—not right now. Got an appointment with the doctor this evening."

"Something wrong?"

"Pain in my arm. Rheumatism or something. Getting a little diathermy. But I'll call you tomorrow and we'll straighten this whole mess out."

"Right."

But John Steever did not call the next day. Along about supper time, Sam called him.

Surprisingly enough, Irma answered the phone. Her thin, squeaky little voice sounded faintly in Sam's ears.

"Daddy's upstairs sleeping. He's been sick."

"Well don't disturb him. What is it—his arm?"

"His back, now. He has to go to the doctor again in a little while."

"Tell him I'll call tomorrow, then. Uh—everything all right, Irma? I mean, don't you miss Miss Pall?"

"No. I'm glad she went away. She's stupid."

"Oh. Yes. I see. But you phone me if you want anything. And I hope your Daddy's better."

"Yes. So do I," said Irma, and then she began to giggle, and then she hung up.

There was no giggling the following afternoon when John Steever called Sam at the office. His voice was sober—with the sharp sobriety of pain.

"Sam—for God's sake, get over here. Something's happening to me!"

"What's the trouble?"

"The pain—it's killing me! I've got to see you, quickly."

"There's a client in the office, but I'll get rid of him. Say, wait a minute. Why don't you call the doctor?"

"That quack can't help me. He gave me diathermy for my arm and yesterday he did the same thing for my back."

"Didn't it help?"

"The pain went away, yes. But it's back now. I feel—like I was being crushed. Squeezed, here in the chest. I can't breathe."

"Sounds like pleurisy. Why don't you call him?"

"It isn't pleurisy. He examined me. Said I was sound as a dollar. No, there's nothing organically wrong. And I couldn't tell him the real cause."

"Real cause?"

"Yes. The pins. The pin that little fiend is sticking into the doll she made. Into the arm, the back. And now heaven only knows how she's causing *this*."

"John, you mustn't—"

"Oh what's the use of talking? I can't move off the bed here. She has me now. I can't go down and stop her, get hold of the doll. And nobody else would believe it. But it's the doll all right, the one she made with the candle-wax and the hair from my brush. Oh—it hurts to talk—that cursed little witch! Hurry, Sam. Promise me you'll do something—anything—get that doll from her— get that doll—"

Half an hour later, at four-thirty, Sam Steever entered his brother's house.

Irma opened the door.

It gave Sam a shock to see her standing there, smiling and unperturbed, pale blonde hair brushed immaculately back from the rosy oval of her face. She looked just like a little doll. A little doll—

"Hello, Uncle Sam."

"Hello, Irma. Your Daddy called me, did he tell you? He said he wasn't feeling well—"

"I know. But he's all right now. He's sleeping."

Something happened to Sam Steever; a drop of ice-water trickled down his spine.

"Sleeping?" he croaked. "Upstairs?"

Before she opened her mouth to answer he was bounding up the steps to the second floor, striding down the hall to John's bedroom.

John lay on the bed. He was asleep, and only asleep. Sam Steever noted the regular rise and fall of his chest as he breathed. His face was calm, relaxed.

Then the drop of ice-water evaporated, and Sam could afford to smile and murmur "Nonsense" under his breath as he turned away.

As he went downstairs he hastily improvised plans. A six-month vacation for his brother; avoid calling it a "cure". An orphanage for Irma; give her a chance to get away from this morbid old house, all those books . . .

He paused halfway down the stairs. Peering over the banister thru the twilight he saw Irma on the sofa, cuddled up like a little white ball. She was talking to something she cradled in her arms, rocking it to and fro.

Then there was a doll, after all.

Sam Steever tiptoed very quietly down the stairs and walked over to Irma.

"Hello," he said.

She jumped. Both arms rose to cover completely whatever it was she had been fondling. She squeezed it tightly.

Sam Steever thought of a doll being squeezed across the chest—

Irma stared up at him, her face a mask of innocence. In the half-light her face did resemble a mask. The mask of a little girl, covering—what?

"Daddy's better now, isn't he?" lisped Irma.

"Yes, much better."

"I knew he would be."

"But I'm afraid he's going to have to go away for a rest. A long rest."

A smile filtered through the mask. "Good," said Irma.

"Of course," Sam went on, "you couldn't stay here all alone. I was wondering—maybe we could send you off to school, or to some kind of a home—"

Irma giggled. "Oh, you needn't worry about me," she said. She shifted about on the sofa as Sam sat down, then sprang up quickly as he came close to her.

Her arms shifted with the movement, and Sam Steever saw a pair of tiny legs dangling down below her elbow. There were trousers on the legs, and little bits of leather for shoes.

"What's that you have, Irma?" he asked. "Is it a doll?" Slowly, he extended his pudgy hand.

She pulled back.

"You can't see it," she said.

"But I want to. Miss Pall said you made such lovely ones."

"Miss Pall is stupid. So are you. Go away."

"Please, Irma. Let me see it."

But even as he spoke, Sam Steever was staring at the top of the doll, momentarily revealed when she backed away. It was a head all right, with wisps of hair over a white face. Dusk dimmed the features, but Sam recognized the eyes, the nose, the chin—

He could keep up the pretense no longer.

"Give me that doll, Irma!" he snapped. "I know what it is. I know *who* it is—"

For an instant, the mask slipped from Irma's face, and Sam Steever stared into naked fear.

She knew. She knew he knew.

Then, just as quickly, the mask was replaced.

Irma was only a sweet, spoiled, stubborn little girl as she shook her head merrily and smiled with impish mischief in her eyes.

"Oh Uncle Sam," she giggled. "You're so silly! Why, this isn't a *real* doll."

"What is it, then?" he muttered.

Irma giggled once more, raising the figure as she spoke. "Why, it's only—candy!" Irma said.

"Candy?"

Irma nodded. Then, very swiftly, she slipped the tiny head of the image into her mouth.

And bit it off.

There was a single piercing scream from upstairs.

As Sam Steever turned and ran up the steps, little Irma, still gravely munching, skipped out of the front door and into the night beyond.

The Dream-Makers

I've got the right lead for it. That's easy. I can start out with all the usual blah—Hollywood is a crazy town, filled with crazy people, and the craziest things happen there. I can give this yarn the old build-up.

But there's only one trouble. It *isn't* a yarn, and it happened to *me*.

So let's just take it from the top, with me climbing into my car that afternoon and heading out Wilshire towards a place called Restlawn. It was just another assignment, and if *Filmdom* magazine wanted to do a series on *Grand Old-Timers of the Movies*, I was their man. Their hungry man.

I headed out past the Miracle Mile and into Beverly Hills, taking it slow and avoiding the Freeway. I didn't particularly care for this job.

Grand Old-Timers. That's what cooled me. I knew what I was getting into—nosing around the Actor's Home and Central Casting, following leads that ended up in cheap flophouses and the gutters of Main Street.

That's where the *Grand Old-Timers* were, most of them. The men and women who "grew up with the Industry" until the Industry outgrew them. Oh, Pickford, Cooper, Gable and a few others didn't have to worry. They'd survived or retired gracefully on their savings. Valentino and Chaney and Fairbanks didn't have to worry, either, because they died at the height of their success.

But what about the ones who weren't lucky enough to die while they were famous—Griffith, and Langdon, and Barrymore, struggling along until the all too bitter end? And what about those who hadn't died yet—Sennett and Lloyd and Gish and a dozen others? They'd be considered *Grand Old-Timers*, too.

I sighed, turning off Wilshire past Westwood Village and seeking the smaller side-streets. I knew all about the *Grand Old-Timers*. The "special awards" trotted out for them at Academy banquets, and the doors slammed in their faces the next day. The humiliating "bit roles" played in occasional way-back-when films; the overpublicized "comebacks" that puffed them up for one picture, then deflated them again to extra status.

It would be painful for them to be interviewed by me—and equally painful for me to do the job.

But a man must eat. And a man must dream . . .

They'd never be *Grand Old-Timers* to me, because of the dreams; the dreams they'd manufactured for my consumption thirty years ago. My dreams are still very much alive, and so are their creators.

Right now, riding down into Santa Monica, I found myself back in one of the great dreams—the great nightmare.

It's a warm fall Wednesday night in Maywood, Illinois. The year is 1925, and tonight is its climactic moment. Because you're eight years old, and you're going to the Lido, all by yourself at night, just like a grownup. Sure, there's school tomorrow but gee Ma, just this once, you promised, I won't be home too late, and I want to see it so bad.

You have eight blocks to walk, eight exciting blocks through autumn darkness, with the dime for the show in the right hand and the nickel for the candy-bar in the left hand.

The Lido is a Palace. Its doors are guarded by marble columns a hundred feet high, but you don't just go right in. First you must look at all the pictures outside—the big ones in color and the little ones that are like photographs. There's this beautiful woman with the long hair and the man with the mask. And here the woman is standing on top of a tall building with another man in a soldier's uniform. He's got a mustache—he must be the hero.

But there's the man with the mask, spying on them. You can't see his face. He's up on some big statue and he looks mad, even with the mask on. That must be him, all right. That must be him.

But it's almost seven, the show is going to start, so you go up to that glittering cage and give your dime to the pretty girl with the lovely costume on. She smiles, and punches some machine, and out comes your ticket. Then you walk in and give your ticket to the man at the door. He smiles, too. You've already bought your candy-bar at the store next to the show, and you're all set.

It's wonderful in the Lido, even the lobby is wonderful. All red carpets and fancy chairs and a big bubbler with the water running all the time—not like at home where you got to turn the water off on account of the water-bill being so high.

And it's even better inside, in the dark. Because there must be a thousand seats to choose from, all plush and soft, and when you sit down right spang in the center of the show and count the rows ahead and the rows behind and look to see if any of the kids from school are there to see you sitting all alone like a grownup, why then you just naturally look up at the sky.

Sure, they've got a sky at the Lido, just as blue as outside at night, and—it has stars in it! Honest, it has regular stars that twinkle! And all along the walls are statues, lighted up kind of dim, and the stars are shining, and it's more beautiful than any real place you've ever seen.

Then the light goes on up at the left side of the stage and it's the organ. A real pretty lady plays the organ; she has gold hair that kind of sparkles when the light hits it. But you don't look, now—you listen.

You sort of skooch down in your seat, all soft and snug, and look at the blue sky and the stars, and let the music just ooze over you. That organ must be just about the most wonderful kind of thing to play, and it plays everything, *Valencia* and *Blue Skies* and *Avalon* and that song, *Collegiate*, that they played when Harold Lloyd was in *The Freshman*.

But now the light is going out, except for the little one right over the keys, and the music is changing to a sort of loud exciting noise, and the curtain is going back, just like magic, and the side-lights blink off, and there is the movie, all lighted up.

And first off it's *Topics of the Day*, which is just a lot of grownup jokes one after the other, in writing on the screen. The organ makes fiddle-around noises but it isn't very interesting, not like pictures. But then comes *Felix the Cat* and that little mouse is in it and the old farmer guy with the bald head and the beard. Funniest part is where Felix chases him through the haystack with the pitchfork and he falls in the well and comes up and spits out the water and a fish comes right out of his mouth.

But the real comedy is even better. It's got Billy Dooley in his sailor suit—Billy Dooley is one of the best ones, better than Bobby Vernon or Al St. John, but not quite as good as Lloyd Hamilton or Larry Semon or Lupino Lane. This one is real funny and everybody laughs. Billy Dooley, he jumps up in the air and sort of wigwags his feet three times before coming down again. How do they do that?

Then the music pounds away and the comedy is over and they turn the lights blue for a minute. The big picture is coming—the one you've been waiting to see. You can tell by the lights and the kind of music that it's a real spooky picture. There's this man in the mask, and he wants to get the girl and he hangs this one guy in the cellar. Then he does get her, and takes her down to his secret hiding place where he sleeps in a coffin and plays the organ. He's sitting there playing with his mask on, and the girl sneaks up behind him, and you know what she's going to do now and you're waiting.

All at once she does it; she pulls off the mask. And the face comes up to fill the screen, rushes out of the screen and blots out everything until there's nothing else in the world but that grinning flesh-covered skull with the rotting fangs and the glaring eyes that you're going to dream about tonight and every night.

And that's the dream you got from Lon Chaney . . .

Oh, they made real dreams in those days. There's never been a monster since to equal Chaney, never a villain as arrogant as Stroheim, never a heroine as lovely as Barbara La Marr or a hero as rugged and determined as William S. Hart.

All of it came back from a million years ago, and then it was gone and I was riding down Caprice Drive and the sun was shining.

The sun shone on the *Restlawn* sign. I parked, walked up the drive, poked the buzzer. Chimes sounded.

The woman who opened the door wore a starched uniform. Her hair was starched and her eyes were starched, too. Stiff, sanatorium-face, stiff, sanatorium-voice.

"I beg your pardon. I'm from *Filmdom* magazine. To see Mr. Franklin."

"Have you an appointment?"

"I called this morning."

"Room 216. That's on the second floor, front."

I took the stairs. I walked slowly, not relishing this, dreading what I might expect to find. A white-haired old man, sitting at the window of a private hospital room; sitting and staring out at the living in the streets and then staring back at the pictures of the dead lining his walls. *To Jeffrey Franklin, the world's greatest director.* Signed—Mickey Neilan, Mabel Normand, Lowell Sherman, John Gilbert.

Well, supposing they were dead, and supposing he was sick, and old? He was still the world's greatest director. For my money and a lot of other people's money. Hadn't made a picture since that last floppola in '29, when sound really came in. But before that, he'd been one of the true dream-makers.

Let's see, that was twenty-four, almost twenty-five years ago. Hard to imagine him still alive. Must be older than God. This was going to be sad, very sad. But a man must eat . . .

I knocked discreetly on the door of 216. The voice called "Come in." I opened the door and entered.

And the new dream began . . .

2.

In the publicity shots I'd seen of him a quarter-century ago, Jeffrey Franklin had appeared as a tall, blackhaired man, smoking a curved-stem pipe. He was always pictured standing, legs apart, feet firmly planted, chin jutting forth aggressively.

Seeing Jeffrey Franklin in the doorway now was quite a shock.

He was a tall, blackhaired man, smoking a curved-stem pipe. He stood with his legs apart, feet firmly planted, chin jutting forth aggressively.

I guess I stared.

"Come in and make yourself comfortable," he invited.

It wasn't difficult to make myself comfortable—because 216 turned out to be a suite. There were at least two other rooms leading off the big parlor, and the parlor itself was more than spacious.

No hospital bed, no tattered clippings or faded photos on the walls, no institutionally uncomfortable furniture; instead, I found myself in a modern masculine *decor* that deserved to be called luxurious. The whole atmosphere was very definitely present-time. And so was Jeffrey Franklin.

"Get you a drink?"

"Here?" My voice implied the sanatorium surroundings, and he smiled.

"I'm a paying guest, not a patient. Little alcohol tones the system, I find. Keeps a man from getting old."

"It certainly seems to work." I blurted it out tactlessly, but he smiled again.

"Type-casting would put you down for scotch and water. Right?"

"Right."

"Speaking of type-casting, what did you think of Frisbie?"

"Who?"

"Miss Frisbie. The dragon who guards the portals. Isn't she perfect for the role?"

I nodded. Even before he placed the drink in my hand, I felt at ease.

I chose a lounge chair and Jeffrey Franklin made a gracefully self-conscious picture on the sofa across from me. He looked a bit like those man-of-distinction ads they used to run a few years back, and (as my thoughts grew still more remote) like one of the old-time Shakespearean hams. Come to think of it, hadn't he started out as a rep player in legit?

The question reminded me of my errand, and abruptly I felt embarrassed once again. He sensed it immediately; his perception was remarkable for a man his age. (Good Lord, how old *was* he? He had to be close to seventy. The whole setup mystified me.)

"It isn't easy, is it?" His voice, like his smile, was soft.

"What isn't easy?"

"Being a ghoul." He raised his hand. "I don't mean it unkindly, son. I know you're just doing a job, getting your story. But I wish I had a nickel for every inquiring reporter who has come out here, spade in hand, to dig up the remains during the past twenty-odd years."

"You've been here that long?"

He nodded. "Right here. Ever since *Revolution*."

"Your last picture."

"My last picture. The flop." There was no discernible emotion in his voice.

"But why—?"

"I like it here."

"But you're not sick, and if you'll permit me to say so, it doesn't look as if you're broke, either. And you could have had other pictures, there were contracts waiting for you, and—"

"I like it here."

He leaned forward. "I'm afraid I can't give you much of a sob-story. And neither can Walter Harland, or Peggy Dorr, or Danny Keene, or any of the other regulars in my old company. None of us was shoved out, none of us is on relief. You'll have a hard time forcing the tears for this scene."

It was my turn to lean forward. "Mr. Franklin, I'd like to set you straight on one thing. I'm not looking for a sob-story. I wouldn't write it if I found it. Believe me, nothing pleases me more than to know you're here by choice. I don't like anything to happen to my dreams."

"Your dreams?" He dropped the man-of-distinction pose. The long hands joined across his knees, and I noted with vague satisfaction that the backs were free of the tell-tale mottled markings of age. "What do you mean by dreams?" he asked.

So I told him, or tried to tell him. About Chaney in *The Phantom of the Opera*. The dream about Keaton in *The General*. Doug sliding down the drape in *Robin Hood*, Charlie eating the shoe, Renee Adoree stumbling after the truck in *The Big Parade;* half-a-hundred memorable moments that somehow stick in my mind with a greater sense of reality than the contemporary events of the childhood I lived through during the time I saw the pictures.

I guess I talked a long while. About the films, and the actors, and the directors of the silent days. About the effect of the organ music, the autohypnosis which was rudely shattered by the theatrical phoniness of sound. I wondered out loud whether or not I was alone in my experience or viewpoint; how many hundreds or thousands or millions of others (trending along towards middle age, now, and it's hard to realize that) who might share the illusions of the great days when the "silver screen" was really silver and shimmered with a strange enchantment.

And I tried to figure why it had changed. Was it that I was no longer a child, had grown up? No—because I've seen some of the films again, since then, at special showings; *Caligari*, of course, *Zorro*, *Intolerance*, a dozen others. And the last reels of *The Strong Man* are just as funny, the scene in *The Thief* where Doug conjures up the army from the dust is still pure enchantment.

Well—wondering out loud—was it radio, or television, or the smart-aleck "inside stuff" attitude adopted generally in a world where everybody was busy dispensing the "lowdown" on celebrities?

Was it the war, the postwar era, the new age of fear; had the Bomb done more than split the atom, had it also shattered the dreams?

"Such stuff as dreams are made of." Yes, Franklin was an old repertory ham, all right. He rolled out the quotation with sonorous relish, but I sensed the sincerity behind it.

"Odd that you've speculated along those lines," he mused. "I didn't think anyone else but ourselves had noticed the change." He noted my look. "Walter Harland and Tom Humphrey, some of the others, still get together and reminisce. You'll probably be talking to them, if you're planning a series of articles. They've aged pretty gracefully, you'll find."

I took the opening. "I hope you won't be offended if I report the same thing about you," I said. "Frankly, I can't get over seeing you like this. I admit I expected—"

"This?" Jeffrey Franklin rose and abruptly disappeared. In his place was a bent, hobbling oldster with withered, clawlike fingers scrabbling at a wobbly chin. Once again I remembered that he'd been an actor—remembered, too, that one of his tricks as a director was to play every role for the benefit of his actors before doing a take.

He straightened up, resumed his seat. "The years have been kind. Everything has gone well since *Revolution*. That was my only mistake, thinking I could go against their wishes. I haven't tried to change the plot since, and neither has Walter or Tom or Peggy, any of the others."

My ears stood up, my forepaw raised, and I came to the point. I smelled *story* here. "Plot?" I said. "Then there is something to all those rumors—they did try to force you out when sound came and the studio reorganized. I suppose they threatened the company with the blacklist and squeezed you out with a stock reshuffle?"

Jeffrey Franklin did a very odd thing. He looked up at the ceiling and I could have sworn he was *listening* for a moment before he answered. Once a ham, always a ham.

But his answer, when he gave it, was casual. "Sorry to disappoint you once again. I told you we weren't forced out, and that's the truth. Check with the others. They all had offers, plenty of offers. Most of them had legitimate stage experience, and they could have switched to the talkies without any trouble. But we decided it was time to quit while we were ahead of the game. As I say, *Revolution* flopped. And there were other examples; people who didn't have sense to quit when they should."

"You mean Gilbert, and Lew Cody and Charles Ray, people like that?"

"Perhaps. But I was thinking specifically of Roland Blade, Fay Terris, Matty Ryan."

Funny how the names took on long-forgotten meanings to me.

Roland Blade, whose name belonged up there with Navarro and LaRoque and Ricardo Cortez—yes, he'd done a talkie or two, and then he went over the cliff in his fancy car. Fay Terris was vintage stuff, a sort of American Negri. Come to think of it, she'd made a few sound films before the fire in her beach-house. Ryan I didn't recall very well. He'd been an independent producer and a rather big one; something like Thomas Ince. Let's see, whatever happened to him? Suddenly I remembered the headlines. He'd been one of the early aviation enthusiasts, like Mary Astor's first husband. He crashed, and they found his body cut almost in two—

Odd. Very odd. They all met violent deaths. And now I could recall a half-dozen more, all around that time. Some were mysterious suicides. One had been the victim of a still-unsolved murder. Others perished in freak fires, drowned, disappeared.

"Do you mean you were superstitious about going along with the new era and making talking pictures?" I asked.

Franklin smiled. "Once a reporter, always a reporter," he said. "Putting words in peoples' mouths. Please don't quote me to that effect, because I don't mean any such thing at all." He paused, and once again his eyes sought the ceiling before he continued.

"If anything, I mean that we were all at the same point when the change came to Hollywood. We'd all started around the turn of the 'twenties, made our names together, did our best work and reaped the rewards at the same time. The best times were past, for most of the silent stars, directors, producers. All that remained was the struggle to stay on top, the resultant strain, the recklessness which would inevitably invade our personal life-patterns and which resulted in tragedy for those who chose to stay on. They used to call it 'going Hollywood.' You remember the stories of Lloyd Hamilton's fancy parties, and Tom Mix with his sixteen-thousand-dollar car, and the things that happened to people like poor Wally Reid, Arbuckle, and the rest of the crowd.

"No, we just decided to quit, and that's all. I'm afraid it's not a very sensational lead for you."

I made one last try. "Didn't you say something about 'going against their wishes' and something about a 'plot'?"

Jeffrey Franklin rose. "You misunderstood me," he said. "I was speaking of our wishes, as a group, to leave films. And I've already told you there was no plot. Now, if you'll excuse me—I'm rather tired. But I've enjoyed this interview very much."

He was lying, and I knew it.

But there was nothing else to do but shake hands and head for the door. I smiled at him. And he looked at the ceiling . . .

3.

I walked into the little bookstore, still wondering if I had the right address. Nobody was out front, and only a single bulb burned over the table at the rear of the shop. A stocky, middle-aged, bespectacled man dropped his book on the table and looked up at me.

"Yes?"

"I'm looking for Walter Harland."

The man stood up. He was taller than I'd thought, and not nearly as old as he seemed at first glance. He took off his glasses and smiled. And there, of course, stood Walter Harland.

There was something quite dramatic in the very simplicity of the revelation. And something else, something vaguely frightening. He was too young. Franklin was too young. They looked the way they had back in '29 or '30.

I wrestled the thought, two falls out of three, while I introduced myself, explained my errand, and alluded to my visit with Jeffrey Franklin.

Walter Harland nodded. "I expected you," he said. "Mr. Franklin w— told me that you might visit me."

"It was kind of Mr. Franklin to w— tell you," I answered. He got it, and lowered his eyes.

"Don't say anything," I went on. "I can understand. This sort of thing isn't exactly my idea of good taste, either."

That got a smile out of him, and an invitation to sit down. I went through the same routine with him as I did with Franklin and got virtually the same answers. I began to wonder if Franklin hadn't given them all mimeographed copies of a script to memorize.

Yes, he had other offers when Franklin's production unit disbanded. No, he hadn't wanted to continue. Yes, he had plenty of money to live on; he'd bought this bookstore and was quite content. He'd discovered it was much more pleasant to read other people's plots than to act them out.

I had to make the effort, then. "What's all this about plots?" I asked. "There's a rumor going around that you're the victim of some kind of plot to force you into obscurity."

It would be appropriately dramatic, at this moment, to report that Walter Harland gasped and turned pale. But actually he merely choked on his cigarette smoke—and if he had any dermatological reaction at all, the light was much too dim to disclose it.

"Don't believe everything you hear," he said, when his brief choking-spell was over with. "This isn't a B-movie, you know. I assure you, we got out because it was time. True, we talked it over, but we talked sensibly. And we agreed it was time to quit."

"Because you were all at the height of your fame, and you had reaped the rewards and didn't want to go downhill," I finished for him. "Is that it?"

"Precisely." He was happy now. We were back on the script again. I wished I could leave him there, but a man has to eat. So I gave him my sweetest smile and let him have it right between the eyes.

"I've heard that song before," I said, "and I don't buy it. Not a note rings true. Listen, Mr. Harland—I don't mean this to be offensive, but merely as a statement of known fact. Back in the twenties, you had a reputation for being one of the biggest hams in the business. Oh, I'm not casting any reflections on your ability as an actor. You were good, and everybody knows it. It's right down there in the book.

"But you were a ham, like all the rest. You always played it big because you loved it that way. Signing autographs. Posing in those satin dressing-gowns, with the initials on the lapels, yet. Attending premieres in your Rolls, with the flappers kissing the tires. Dragging those wolfhounds into the Montmartre. That was your meat, wasn't it?"

He chuckled; a good, hearty actor's chuckle. "I suppose so. But a man gets older. He grows up."

"Listen, Peter Pan—actors never grow up in that sense of the word, and you know it! Nothing could make a matinee idol like you give up the glamour routine. Nothing except, perhaps, an awful scare of some kind. Come on now, what was it?"

I felt pretty proud of my D.A. routine, because it seemed to work. He sat there, breathing heavily for a long moment. Then he spoke.

"All right," he said softly. "There was a scare. An awful scare. Remember the films I played in? The fencing sequences, the fights, the acrobatics—Fairbanks stuff? That's what I was identified with. One day I went to the doctor for a routine checkup. He got excited, took cardiograms. You know the answer. My ticker was going bad. He warned me to take things easy if I wanted to be around for encores."

For a moment I was a little ashamed of myself. Then that word "warned" cropped up again. And I remembered that if I could play the D.A., Walter Harland could play the part of a man with a bad heart. And I realized that before he'd spoken, he'd looked up at the ceiling.

Maybe there was a fly up there, buzzing around. But something else kept buzzing in my brain.

I didn't say a word. I just shook my head.

He was already on his feet, ready to finish the script that Jeffrey Franklin had so carefully prepared. He held out his hand, then hesitated.

"You really want to know, don't you?" he said softly. "Not just to get an article, but because it means something to you."

I nodded.

"I'm afraid there's no way of explaining." He led me to the door, paused, put his hand on my shoulder. "Do you enjoy reading?" he asked.

"Yes."

"So do I. I've had a lot of time for it these past twenty years and more. I was particularly impressed with the writings of a man named Charles Fort. You know his work? Good. Well, Fort had an idea about cycles and events. Almost Spenglerian. He once said that when it's *steam-engine* time, people suddenly begin to *steam-engine*. Nothing much can be done to hasten that time. But, on the other hand, nothing much can be done to retard it. Maybe we all did the right thing because we recognized it was the right time."

I was back out on the street, looking up at the sky. And Walter Harland was back in his shop, looking at the ceiling. Or was it the ceiling?

4.

Let's save the rest for the kindergarten class. I found Peggy Dorr in Pasadena. Danny Keene had a boat at Balboa. Tom Humphrey—of all people!—operated a TV service repair shop not far from Farmer's Market.

And you know what else I found when I found them. Too-young faces, too-evasive answers, too-uniform a story. And that faraway look in their eyes.

It all added up to one big puzzle. Unfortunately, detective stories aren't my line. I was out after stories which I couldn't get. The whole assignment was turning out to be one grand and glorious fiasco.

Where was the drama in it, the old heart-throb, the pathos, the violin-music in the background? Everything stopped for them in 1930, and the whole story belonged in the era before then when they made— literally *made*—the movies.

And nobody cared about *that* any more.

Or—did they?

Riding back from the visit with Tom Humphrey, the notion hit me.

By Louis B. Mayer and all the saints, here was a story!

Not a lousy article, or a series of articles. *This* was a movie!

Look at how they flocked to the Jolson pictures, the life of Will Rogers, and all these phoney stage biography films. What about using the same gimmick on the life of Jeffrey Franklin? The whole silent-picture story, in glorious Technicolor, Warnercolor, Cinecolor, who cares?

Sure, Twentieth did *Hollywood Cavalcade*, but that was over twenty years ago. And besides, I had the kicker. Call it coincidence, fate, or just a happy accident for the benefit of yours truly, I had something that would really sell such a film. No more working with imitators and phoneys—with the aid of a little modern lighting and makeup, the film could actually be done with the original cast playing real-life roles!

Natural. Socko. Boffo. The whole *Variety* lexicon flashed through my mind, and then the plot started to take shape, and before I knew it I was sitting at the typewriter banging out a treatment.

It was a good treatment. I didn't have to take my word for it. I had Cy Charney's word for it. Sat in his office and braved the blasts fired by two complete cigars as he read through it—then had the satisfaction of seeing one of the biggest agents on the Strip going crazy over my idea.

"I can place this one tomorrow," he said. "It's completely copasetic. Of course you're not a name, but the idea is big enough. I think I can start the bidding at—lemme see now—thirty-forty

Gs. And maybe a writing assist for you on the real script. You free to take an assignment, boy?"

I damn' near broke my neck nodding.

"Keep in touch," said Charney. "Now get outta here and let me use my fine Eyetalian hand on this deal."

I got out of there, but things were happening so fast I couldn't quite believe my ears. Then again, I wasn't depending on my ears in this deal. I had Mr. Charney's fine Eyetalian hand.

And what a fine hand it was, too! He called me exactly twenty-six hours later. "All sewed," he said. "Freeman is crazy about it, and Jack wants it too. And I can get fifty from one of them if the other knows he's got competition. I'll have a contract in my office before the week is out. Can you line them up by that time?"

"Line who up?"

"The cast, boy! Old Franklin and Harland and the rest. I'm taking your say-so on this that they're still what you say they are instead of strictly for the glue-factory. Of course, they'll have to be tested and all, but I'm selling the story that they're still full of p. and v. Right? Now I'm asking you to line 'em up. Course, if you want me to come with you and put on the old pressure—"

"No, that won't be necessary," I cut in. "Let me handle it."

"Tell 'em not to worry about figures," Charney said. "I'll represent 'em—and they oughta know what that means in this town. And say, be sure you wangle a release out of old Franklin. It isn't exackly his life-story, but it's close enough so maybe you gotta cut him in on the story price. You work it out with him, huh?"

"Yes," I said. "I'll work it out with him."

But as I hung up, I wondered. I sat back and glanced up at the ceiling. There was no answer up there—not for me.

But then, I wasn't superstitious. Maybe that was the answer—actors were superstitious. Actors were superstitious, actors were always "on," actors were always hams.

Hams! I had it.

First thing I did, I sent a copy of the treatment, marked *PER-SONAL*, to everybody I'd interviewed. Sent it Special Delivery, with an accompanying confidential letter. Gave it the complete buildup, including what a wonderful opportunity this would be to recreate the real art of the motion picture as it existed in the old days. I also hinted (and hoped I could actually make good on it, too) that a portion of the film's profits might be donated to the welfare funds for the benefit of less fortunate old-timers. And—in each letter—I stressed what a tremendous part was waiting for the recipient.

I gave the deal just twenty-four hours to get rolling. Then I went around to Walter Harland's bookshop.

The first thing I noticed as I came in was that he didn't wear his glasses any more. And he had on a suit that had nothing in it to attract or impress the bibliophile. He'd sharpened up. And that was fine. "Well?" I said.

"Congratulations. It's tremendous. I had no idea what was in back of all this—your phoney interview approach fooled me completely."

He not only offered, he ushered me, to a chair. And pushed a package of Players my way. "Did me good to read it," he said. "I feel twenty years younger."

"You look it," I told him, truthfully. "And that's what a new generation of movie fans are going to say when they see you on the screen."

He beamed. "Danny and Tom called me last night. And Lucas—remember him? Used to do the heavies, with the long cigarette-holder, the sideburns and all? They're so excited—"

Something small stumbled into the bookshop; something old and withered and trembling like autumn's last leaf. It had a piping whiskey tenor, and it bleated, "Walt, I dowanna in'errupt you, but I just gotta talk t'you a minute."

"Sure, Tiny." Harland got up, walked over to counter. The little man bleated in his ear for a moment. Harland went to the cash-register, rang up a NO SALE, and palmed something in the rummy's hand. "Now, if you'll excuse me—"

"Yeah, Walt. Yeah. God bless you." And autumn's last leaf blew away.

"Sorry." Harland came up to me, smiling.

"You don't have to be sorry."

"Yes I do."

"Meaning?"

"I can't do it. We can't do it. Your picture."

"But—"

"Spare me the sales-talk. You know I'm dying to do it. So are the others. I wouldn't fool you. Why, it would be like starting life all over again. What I wouldn't give to see my name up there, show all these young punks how a real actor can project."

"Then why—"

He was on stage and it was his scene all the way. "Because I told you we agreed to quit, all of us. And we did. There were one or two exceptions, but they aren't around any more. You didn't know it, but you just caught a glimpse of somebody who tried the other way. He only did one job for Franklin, and it was a minor comedy role, so I guess he got off easy in consequence. But it's no go. We couldn't take the risk."

"What risk?" I argued. "It's bound to be a smash. You can't lose a thing, and look what you stand to gain."

He shook his head. "Remember what I said about *steam-engine* time? We're horse-and-buggy people. And we've got to stay where we belong." He smiled, because he was doing *Pagliacci* now. "Besides, here's one thing you can bet on. There's no picture without the old man, and he'll never go for it. Never."

I shrugged myself out of the store, fast. I had a reason. I was looking for the last leaf. I knew him now—Tiny Collins. Never a big-name comic, but an old reliable. On a par with Heinie Mann, Billy Bevan, Jack Duffy.

One look at him, and at the little act he'd put on with Harland in the store, and I could figure out where to find him. It was just four doors down the street.

He was up there at the end of the bar, all alone with a small shot and a large beer for company. He'd stopped trembling, now that he was back home again.

I uttered the magic formula. "Aren't you Tiny Collins? I'll buy."

Just so happens that I was able to dredge up the names of several of his pictures. Just so happens that I was able to dredge up several more shots and beers. Just so happens that I got him into the back booth and steered the conversational boat into my particular idea of a snug harbor.

Tiny was funny. Drinking sobered him up. He stopped slurring his sentences and became thoughtful. I didn't mention the picture at all, but I did set the scene for him. I hinted that I might do an article on him, and that was enough. We were pals. And you can ask a pal anything, can't you?

"Level with me, now," I said. "What's got into all your old friends? Why are they so publicity-shy, and why did they quit?"

"You're asking me? Question I been asking myself for twenty years—why they quit. Different with me. I got the old axe. But they didn't have to quit. Seems like they all got together at once and decided."

"I know, Tiny. And I was wondering why. It just doesn't make sense."

"Nothin' makes sense," he agreed. "They wanna quit, so they get offers. I dowanna quit and right like that—snap!—I can't get a job. Me, Tiny Collins, that's played with Turpin and Fields and whatzisname and—"

"I know, Tiny. I know. Here, let's have another." We did, and I waited for the gulping to subside before I continued. "But surely you have a theory."

"Course I have a theory. Lotsa theories. First one is, they're all dead."

"Dead?"

"Sure. They got together and formed one of those—whatcha call 'em?—suicide pacts. When they heard about Blade and Terris and Ryan and Todd and all the others bumping at the same time, they figured they hadda go too. So they made a agreement and killed themselfs." He meant to laugh, but midway it turned into a cough. I rode that one out, too.

"Only they're not dead, Tiny."

"What? Oh, sure. They're not dead. Only they look like they're dead. Didn't you notice? Now take me, frinstance. I'm same age as Tom Humphrey. But look at the difference. I'm all beat up and him—he looks just like he did in *The Black Tiger*. That was his last one, for First National 'r somebody. And all of them are alike. They look like they stopped when they stopped making pictures. Like they died and somebody embalmed 'em and wound 'em up."

I considered the theory a moment. I also considered that Tiny's shot-and-a-beer routine might have something to do with the difference in appearances.

"You have any other theories?" I asked.

Tiny looked at me. That is, he made a good effort. But he was weaving again. "Yes. Yes, I got a theory. You won't tell anybody?"

"Honor bright."

"Good enough. Because—well, I know it sounds screwy. But I think they got scared." He groped for the beer-glass.

"Scared," I prompted.

"Good and scared. The old man, Franklin, he done it. He filled 'em full of the old juice. I heard stories. I ain't the one to confirm or deny. Confirm or deny." He liked the phrase.

"What stories?"

"The old man. He went off his trolley. After *Revolution*. And the talkies comin' in. And everybody croakin'. He got scared bad it might happen to him. And he—he was like God to the others. What he said—says—goes. He says quit, they quit. Also, you know how screwy they can get out here. Way I personally dope it out, maybe the old man he got roped into one of those phoney cults. You heard about phoney cults?"

I assured him I had heard about phoney cults, all right.

"Suppose they got to him and sold him a billa goods on one of them religions-like? And the high potentate or whoever said it's not in the cards for you to make pictures no more. It's not in the stars—"

Something clicked. *Stars. The ceiling.*

"Thanks, Tiny." I rose.

"Hey, where you goin'?"

"I've got a date."

"But I was just gettin' ready to buy a round—"

"Some other time. Thanks. Thanks very much." And I meant it.

I got out of there and drove home. I drove slowly, because I had a lot to think about. *In vino veritas.* Tiny made sense to me, at last.

Pieces began to form and fit together. I remembered a lot I'd forgotten about Jeffrey Franklin. His acknowledged superstitions. The way he'd hold up a scene for days until he got just the right actor for a walk-through bit. The way he'd junk whole sequences, just like Stroheim, because something didn't look *right*. The way he handled his actors; never cursing them, but praying for them instead. *Praying* for them. And (I remembered now) he had this trick of looking up in the air as if seeking divine guidance. Now just suppose he had been sneaking off to astrologers—Lord knows, plenty of them did in the old days and were still doing it today—and one of them gave him the word that Cancer was in Uranus or wherever. And stopped, just like that.

Could be. And could be, I might find out who his personal star-gazer was and make a little deal. Or switch him onto another astrological or half-astrological quack. It was a cinch I had to do something, and fast.

I got home, let myself in, and prepared to go to work. The astrologers had listings in the phone-book. I'd call every single one if necessary and—

It wasn't necessary. *My* phone rang, instead. And the voice said:

"This is Jeffrey Franklin. I received your communication and I was wondering when I could see you."

"Why, tonight if you like, Mr. Franklin."

"Good. We have a lot to talk about. I'm going to do your picture."

5.

We sat in the suite, drinking scotch. The sun went down in the Pacific, courtesy M-G-M, and then Universal put the moon up in Technicolor.

Franklin did the talking. "So you see, it wasn't your story idea that convinced me, although I admit I was tempted. But when he called me up—the head of the studio, mind you!—and said his own car was on the way . . ."

I nodded, suddenly realizing that I'd underestimated Mr. Charney's fine Eyetalian hand.

". . . and you can't imagine how it felt, just being back on a lot once more! Of course, many things are different, but I'm quite sure I have a grasp of technique. I've kept up on all the technical data—would you believe it, I still read every issue of *The American Cinematographer*—and I see everything that's released. And he has faith in me. He knows what it means to have me back in the Industry, actually directing—"

"*Directing?*"

"Certainly!" Franklin's smile outshone the moon. "That's the biggest surprise of all. I'm to direct as well as act in my own story."

What a fine Eyetalian hand!

There was no mistaking what this meant to Franklin. He was drunk on his own adrenalin. "I never realized they still remembered me," he said. "Of course, there was this Academy dinner thing, a few years ago, but I thought that was merely a gesture. And then, today, sitting there in the Executive Office, with everybody on the lot—I mean just that, everybody of any importance—literally begging to get in and meet me! You can't begin to realize what it means, son. You get used to the idea that it's all over, you even think of yourself as a has-been." He sighed. "But I'm ready, now. For the first time in years, I'm being honest with myself when I say that I've always been ready. And I think, working together, all of us, that we can come up with a few tricks that will surprise the Industry."

Intoxication is contagious. I began to get a little high myself now. Fifty thousand less ten per cent is forty thousand, knock off half for taxes and it's still twenty thousand clear, plus an assist on the screenplay—Franklin would go to bat for me on that, I knew—and I'd be working on an A-budget special, and who knows where it might lead to? Three cheers for the *Grand Old-Timers!* Yes, and three cheers for—

The phone rang. Jeffrey Franklin walked over and picked it up in that very special way, the graceful actor's way. And his inflection, his modulation, was impeccable. "Yes, this is Jeffrey Franklin speaking."

I watched him do the scene, noted the sudden faltering, the sag. "No ... not really ... terrible ... when? ... of course, certainly, anything you think he needs ... Friday, afternoon, yes ... where will it be? ... yes ... tomorrow ... thanks."

The phone clicked. Franklin sat down. For a moment he almost looked his age. "Bad news," he said. "An old friend of mine was killed early this evening, in an accident. He was run over by a truck. The funeral will be Friday afternoon, and of course I'll attend. Our studio conference must be delayed until Monday." He shook his head. "It's hard to see them go, one by one," he mused. "You'll understand that, son, when you're my age."

"I'm sorry," I said. "Was it anyone I know?"

"I don't think so. Just somebody from the old days. He once did a bit in one of my productions. Tiny Collins."

This was my cue. I took it and kept my mouth shut. I kept it shut after I left Franklin, kept it shut all the next day. Of course there was a meeting with the gleeful Mr. Charney, during which he paced the floor and waved both of his fine Eyetalian hands in ecstasy over our good fortune. But I kept away from Harland and the others. They mustn't know that I'd talked to Tiny Collins. They mustn't know what I was beginning to suspect—because I didn't want to admit it, even to myself.

But Friday afternoon was the time set for the funeral, and I was there. And so was Danny Keene and Peggy Dorr and Tom Humphrey and Walter Harland and four other people whose names I never did learn. The local press and the *Reporter* had inserted routine squibs; but Tiny Collins, alive or dead, wasn't news. He wasn't even a *Grand Old-Timer*, or the studios would have sent flowers, charged off to the p-r fund.

I sat with Jeffrey Franklin as the hired reverend went through the stock routine with the assistance of the hired undertaker and the hired pallbearers. It was a poor performance. Two of the four strangers present were fat old ladies and they cried the way fat old ladies always cry—loudly and unconvincingly. The cheap chapel set looked as though it might be struck right in the middle of the scene, and the lighting was inferior—the kind rented by a quickie unit on a *per diem* basis.

And that was the kind of funeral accorded Tiny Collins who had played with Turpin and with Fields and with whatzisname, who had literally sunk to the gutter and was now making his final comeback, playing his one big scene as the star of the show. Too bad it was such a turkey. He wouldn't have approved.

The organist did routine things—why did that remind me so strongly of the old silents?—as we filed out. We had to finish the production at the cemetery.

It didn't take long. The sky was overcast, and the coming storm was so obvious that even the Chamber of Commerce would have scuttled for cover. The reverend mumbled his lines, performed his inevitable gestures, and then they lowered the body. It was a single take, and they muffed it—let it down too fast. But nobody seemed to mind. Everyone started walking back to the path. The little group broke up, everybody seeking his car and eyeing the clouds whirling in from the west.

I stuck close to Jeffrey Franklin. Both of us had been pretty quiet throughout. He strode along the path, puffing on his pipe, and as I followed I realized he wasn't joining the group at the cars.

We walked over a little knoll into another part of the cemetery. There were more trees here, and plenty of monuments. A turn in the path took us into the exclusive residential district—for every cemetery out here has its own miniature Beverly Hills.

He climbed another knoll. There was a stone bench on top; a stone bench facing an imposing monument which featured a D'Artagnan figure heroically poised atop a marble globe.

I looked twice at the figure, and recognition came to me before I read the name.

"Roland Blade!" I said.

"Yes." Jeffrey Franklin sat down on the stone bench facing the monument. He refilled his pipe as I joined him. The wind whistled through the treetops and I didn't like the tune.

This was the time to use the old psychology. I felt the need of a fine Eyetalian hand of my own—to grab Franklin by the scruff of his neck and raise his spirits. Not knowing exactly how to do it, or what to say, I blurted out what was on my mind.

"The funeral certainly wasn't much of a production, was it?"

He shrugged. "Why should it be? Tiny wasn't important enough to be worthy of a script. The whole scene was done off the cuff."

That was odd. He must have been thinking the same way I was—comparing the funeral to a motion picture. I remembered his comment on the *Restlawn* nurse, and his references to "type-casting." Peculiar.

"Look, son," said Franklin. "I'd better talk to you."

"Go right ahead. It won't rain for a while."

"Depends on the script."

"What script?"

Franklin emptied his pipe. "That's what I'm going to tell you. It isn't easy, but now that we're going ahead with the movie, you'll be a part of things, whether you like it or not. And the chances are, you won't like it. I don't."

I steadied myself (here it comes, boy, here's your astrology or whatever it is, and you'd better not argue or laugh in his face).

"Omar Khayyam must have known when he wrote those lines about a chess game. In Omar's time it might have been chess. Shakespeare put it down when he said, 'All the world's a stage.' And perhaps it *was* a stage when he lived. For us, it's motion picture production. *Steam-engine* time. *Movie* time. And it amuses them to write a script, cast it, produce and direct."

He paused, just long enough for me to say, "*Them?*"

"Them. They. It. One or many. Call the forces what you will—gods, demons, Fates, or cosmic intelligences. All I know is that *they* exist, have always existed, will always exist. And it amuses them to select certain mortals to enact roles in the little dramas they devise."

I forgot my good resolutions and burst out. "Are you trying to tell me that the whole world is being run as a movie-plot, with some superhuman forces directing everyone's actions?"

He shook his head. "Not everyone's. Just a few, a select few. The superior ones, and those brought into contact with them by the necessity of the plot. Omar must have known, Shakespeare must have known, for they were superior. The majority of mankind goes along, 'shooting off the cuff' and conducting affairs in the usual shoddy, shabby manner. Even their crimes, their love-affairs, their deaths are undramatic and unconvincing. Their lines are pedestrian and uninspired, and they never *create*.

"Don't you see it now? That's the whole criterion—if you're creative, you have some affinity with *them*. *They* notice you and write you into the script. You spoke of me, and some of the others, as being dream-makers. We are. We were, rather, in the old days, because it was a part of the plot."

The wind was roaring in from the ocean, but it didn't bother me any longer. I had other things to worry about, now. Franklin was batty, and—

"I wish I could get you to understand," he said. "Because it's really quite important, you know. Once you accept the fact, you'll learn how to adjust. You won't make the mistake of going against the Producer or the Director or the Writer. You won't run the risk of being edited or cut out of the film. Because you're an actor now, like it or not. And you can't fight the script. If you do, the Director will catch you. And he'll have the Cutter slice your scenes. That's what happened to Blade, and a lot of the others."

You can't reason with a loony, but I tried. "Look, Mr. Franklin—you just aren't getting through to me. You sound more like Tiny Collins the other night, when he—"

It slipped out, just like that. (Was it *supposed* to, *was* it in the script?)

"You knew Tiny Collins?"

"Well, I talked to him." And I told him what had happened. He listened, shaking his head. He glanced up at the sky, at the scudding clouds. Was he waiting for another cue before he spoke?

"Then perhaps Tiny's accident wasn't an—accident. He got back in the script again."

"Please, Mr. Franklin. I wish you wouldn't talk that way. This idea that all the important people in the world are part of some cosmic movie just doesn't make sense."

"What does make sense?" he shot back. "World wars, atom-bombs, plagues, famines? Perhaps it isn't a movie for everyone, just for moviemakers. Maybe *they* play War up there for generals and statesmen. And *others* might run a Business for executives. If you ever get to know any military leaders or high politicians or industrial tycoons, you might ask them. If it's true, they'll know. They'll find out—when they try to drop the script, run their own show."

A punctuation of distant thunder.

"Omar knew. He wrote what he was supposed to write—perhaps that's why *they* do it, *they* might feed on creative energy in some way we'll never comprehend—and then he stopped. Never wrote another line but retired to obscurity. Because *they* tired of the scene and set a new one. *Rubaiyat-time* was over. And Shakespeare stopped writing, too. Think about it for a while; think of the names, the big names, who flourished for a given period and then dropped out of the picture forever. They were still at the height of their powers, too."

I tried to use logic. "But think of all the others who have kept going," I said. "The thousands who didn't quit."

"Some of them weren't big enough to be directed," Franklin answered. "Some of them undoubtedly knew, but were defiant. Napoleon's script ended at Elba, but he was greater than the Producer. He came back. Well, you don't make come-backs in this world. They end in disaster. *Napoleon-time* was over. He held out for exactly one hundred days."

The sky was dark. Franklin lit his pipe and a thousand tiny red eyes winked out in the wind. "But I'm not talking theory, son. I'm talking reality. I'm talking about myself, and my company, and a dozen others who must have learned the secret in the days when we made the silent dreams. The script was right for us to succeed, then, and our success was sudden and spectacular. That was *silent-time*. But *talkie-time* came, and there was a new script, calling for new players. We had our choice; get out or be cut out. The wise ones retired. The Cutter got the rest. Now do you see?"

I saw. "Maybe you're right. But—why are you telling me this?"

Franklin smiled. It was a ghost-smile in ghost-light, but I sensed it. "Because in the last few days I've found out that I'm more than an actor. I'm a man. And a man must lead his own life. I thought, at one time, that I could take my bow and sit in the audience for the rest of the show. And for more than twenty years, I did.

"Then you came along, with your script. Your script, not *theirs*. And I want to do it. I want to direct it. I'm a director, too."

"Good." And it *was* good, I thought. "Then we'll do the picture."

He patted my shoulder. "Of course we will, son. But it wouldn't be fair to go ahead without warning you. There's the Cutters to consider. If the Director spots us ad-libbing and raises his finger—"

So help me, the old ham lifted his own finger and pointed dramatically at the statue of Roland Blade. And the thunder came booming in, right on cue.

For a moment, there, he almost had me sold. I thought of

Blade, of Fay Terris, Matty Ryan and all the others who defied the coming of sound, who died before their time, died in sudden and inexplicable violence. Died before their time? No! *Cut off* before their time. Or, *cut off after* their time.

I wondered if *they* were watching us now, listening in on the scene, appreciating the gestures. I wondered if *they* had just sent out a signal to turn on the rain-making machine.

The downpour came. I rose hastily from the bench and started off down the path. I looked back, expecting Jeffrey Franklin to join me.

"In a minute," he said. "I'm just—thinking—"

"Now, look," I called. "You promised."

Jeffrey Franklin straightened up. He stood there in the rain, legs apart, feet firmly planted, chin jutting forth aggressively.

"You have my word," he called. "I promised you, I promised myself, and I promise *them*. From now on, I direct and act my own life. I'll make the picture."

I was a hundred feet away, the night was dark, and the rain a deluge; but even so, I caught his face. The chin was tilting up, now. Jeffrey Franklin was staring at the sky again.

Then it happened.

It was lightning, of course; a single, sharp bolt that chopped down Jeffrey Franklin and the picture, my hopes, everything. As the papers said later, and as I desperately told myself over and over again, even as I ran towards the dismembered corpse, it was only a freak accident.

But I couldn't hide from myself, as I ran, the final revelation or realization. Oh, it was a lightning-bolt, all right—but to me, in the single instant that I saw it, it was more like the sharp blade of a gigantic scissors.

The Sorcerer's Apprentice

I wish you would turn off the lights. They hurt my eyes. You don't need the lights because I'll tell you anything you want to know. I'll tell you all about it, everything. But turn off the lights.

And please, don't stare at me. How can a man think, with all of you crowding around and asking questions, questions, questions—

All right, I'll be calm. I'll be very calm. I didn't mean to shout. It is not like me to lose my temper. I am not like that, really. You know I'd never hurt anyone.

What happened was an accident. It was only because I lost the Power.

But you don't know about the Power, do you? You don't know about Sadini and his gift.

No, I'm not making anything up. That is the truth, gentlemen. I can prove it if you'll listen. I'll tell you what happened from the very beginning.

If only you'll turn off the lights—

My name is Hugo. No, just Hugo. That's all they ever called me at the Home. I lived at the Home ever since I can remember, and the Sisters were very kind to me. The other children were bad, they would not play with me at all, because of my back and my squint, you know, but the Sisters were kind. They didn't call me "Crazy Hugo" and make fun of me because I couldn't recite. They didn't get me in the corner and hit me and make me cry.

No, I'm all right. You'll see. I was telling you about the Home, but it's not important. It all started after I ran away.

You see, I was getting too old, the Sisters told me. They wanted me to go with the Doctor to another place, a County place. But Fred—he was one of the boys who didn't hit me—he told me that I mustn't go with the Doctor. He said the County place was bad and the Doctor was bad. They had rooms with bars on the windows in this place, and the Doctor would tie me to a table and cut out my brain. He wanted to operate on my brain, Fred said, and then I would die.

So I could see that the Sisters really thought I was crazy too, and the Doctor was coming for me the very next day. That's why I ran away, sneaking out of my room and over the wall that night.

But you're not interested in what happened after that, are you? I mean, about when I was living under the bridge and selling newspapers and in winter it was so cold—

Sadini? Yes, but that's part of it; the winter and the cold, I mean. Because it was the cold that made me faint in that alley behind the theatre, and that's how Sadini found me.

I remember the snow in the alley and how it came up and hit me in the face, the icy, icy snow just smothering me in cold, and I sank down into it forever.

Then, when I woke up, I was in this warm place inside the theatre, in the dressing-room, and there was an angel looking at me.

I thought she was an angel, anyway. Her hair was long, like golden harp strings, and I reached up to feel it and she smiled.

"Feeling better?" she asked. "Here, drink this."

She gave me something nice and warm to drink. I was lying on a couch and she held my head while I drank.

"How did I get here?" I asked. "Am I dead?"

"I thought you were when Victor carried you in. But you'll be all right now, I guess."

"Victor?"

"Victor Sadini. Don't tell me you haven't heard of the Great Sadini?"

I shook my head.

"He's a magician. He's on now. Good heavens, that reminds me, I'll have to change!" She took the cup away and stood up. "You just rest until I get back."

I smiled at her. It was very hard to talk, because everything was going round and round.

"Who are you?" I whispered.

"Isobel."

"Isobel," I said. It was a pretty name, I whispered it over and over again until I went to sleep.

I don't know how long it was until I woke up again—I mean, until I woke up and felt all right. In between times I would be sort of half-awake, and sometimes I could see and hear for a little while.

Once I saw a tall man with black hair and a mustache bending over me. He was dressed all in black, too, and he had black eyes. I thought maybe it was the Devil coming to carry me down to Hell. The Sisters used to tell us about the Devil. I was so frightened I just fainted again.

Another time I could hear voices talking, and I opened my eyes again and saw the man in black and Isobel sitting over on the side of the room. I guess they didn't know I was awake, because they were talking about me.

"How much longer do you think I'm going to put up with this, Vic?" she was saying. "I'm sick and tired of playing nursemaid to a lousy tramp. What's the big idea? You don't know him from Adam, anyway."

"But we can't just throw him out in the snow to die, can we?" The man in black was walking up and down, pulling on the ends of his mustache. "Be reasonable, darling, The poor kid's been starving to death, can't you tell? No identification, nothing; he's in trouble and needs help."

"Nuts to that noise! Call the wagon—there's charity hospitals, aren't there? If you expect me to spend all my time between shows cooped up with a mangy—"

I couldn't understand what she meant, what she was saying. She was so beautiful, you see. I knew she must be kind, and it was all a mistake, maybe I was too sick to hear right.

Then I fell asleep again, and when I woke up I felt better, different, and I knew it was a mistake. Because she was there, and she smiled at me again.

"How are you?" she asked. "Ready to eat something now?"

I could only stare at her and smile. She was wearing a long green cloak all covered with silver stars, and now I knew she must be an angel for sure.

Then the Devil came in.

"He's conscious, Vic," said Isobel.

The Devil looked at me and grinned.

"Hi, pal! Glad to have you with us. For a day or so there, I didn't think we'd have the pleasure of your company much longer."

I just stared at him.

"What's the matter, my makeup frighten you? That's right, you don't even know who I am, do you? My name's Victor Sadini. The Great Sadini—magic act, you know."

Isobel was smiling at me too, so I guessed it was all right. I nodded. "My name is Hugo," I whispered. "You saved my life, didn't you?"

"Skip it. Leave the talking till later. Right now, you've got to eat something and get some more rest. You've been camping here on the sofa for three days now, chum. Better get some strength, because the act closes here Wednesday and we jump to Toledo."

On Wednesday the act closed, and we jumped to Toledo. Only we didn't really jump, we took a train. Oh yes, I went along. Because I was Sadini's new assistant.

This was before I knew he was a servant of the Devil. I just thought he was a kind man who had saved my life. He sat there in the dressing-room and explained everything to me; how he grew the mustache and combed his hair that way and wore black just because that's the way stage magicians are supposed to look.

He did tricks for me; wonderful tricks with cards and coins and handkerchiefs that he pulled out of my ears and colored water he poured from my pockets. He could make things vanish, too, and I was afraid of him until he told me it was all a trick.

On the last day he let me get up and stand behind the stage while he went out in front of the people and did what he called his "act" and then I saw wonderful things.

He made Isobel stretch out on a table and then he waved a wand and she floated up in the air with nothing to hold her. Then he lowered her down and she didn't fall, just smiled while all the people clapped. Then she would hand him things to do tricks with, and he would point his magic wand at them and make them vanish, or explode, or change. He made a big tree grow out of a little plant right before my eyes. And then he put Isobel into a box and some men wheeled out a huge steel blade, with teeth in it, and he said he was going to saw her in half. He tied her down, too.

I almost ran out on the stage then, to stop him, but she wasn't really afraid, and the men who pulled the curtains behind the scenes were laughing too, and so I guessed it must be another trick.

But when he turned on the electric current and began to saw into the box I stood there with the sweat popping out all over me because I could see him cutting into her. Only she smiled, even when he sawed right through her. She smiled, and she wasn't dead at all!

Then he covered her up and took the saw away and waved his magic wand and she jumped up, all in one piece again. It was the most wonderful thing I'd ever heard of, and I guess it was seeing the show that made me decide I'd have to go with him.

So after that I talked to him, about how he'd saved my life and who I was, and not having any place to go, and how I'd work for him for nothing, do anything, if only I could come along. I didn't tell him I wanted to go just so I could see Isobel, because I guessed he wouldn't like that. And I didn't think she'd like it either. She was his wife, I knew that now.

It didn't make much sense, what I told him, but he seemed to understand.

"Maybe you can make yourself useful at that," he said. "We have to have someone to look after the props, and it would save time for me. Besides, you could set them up and pack them again."

"Ixnay," said Isobel. "Utsnay." I didn't understand her, but Sadini did. Maybe it was magic talk.

"Hugo's going to be all right," he said. "I need somebody, Isobel. Somebody I can really depend on—if you know what I mean."

"Listen, you cheap ham—"

"Take it easy, Isobel." She was scowling, but when he looked at her she just sort of wilted and tried to smile.

"All right, Vic. Whatever you say. But remember, it's your headache, not mine."

"Right." Sadini came over to me. "You can come along," he said. "From now on you're my assistant."

That's how it was.

That's how it was for a long, long time. We went to Toledo, and to Detroit and Indianapolis and Chicago and Milwaukee and St. Paul—oh, a lot of places. But they were all alike to me. We would ride on a train and then Sadini and Isobel would go to a hotel and I would stay behind and watch them unload the baggage car. I would get the trunks filled with props (that's what Sadini called the things he used in his act) and hand a slip of paper to a truck driver. We would go to the theatre then, and the truck driver took the props into the alley where I'd haul them up to the dressing-room and backstage. Then I unloaded props and that's how it went.

I slept in the theatre, in the dressing room most of the time, and I'd eat with Sadini and Isobel. Not often with Isobel, though. She liked to sleep late at the hotel, and I guess she was ashamed of me at first. I didn't blame her, the way I looked, with my clothes and my eyes and back.

Of course Sadini bought me new clothes after a while. He was good to me, Sadini was. He talked a lot about his tricks and his act, and he even talked about Isobel. I didn't understand how such a nice man could say such things about her.

Even though she didn't seem to like me, and kept away from Sadini too, I knew she was an angel. She was beautiful the way the angels were in the books the Sisters showed me. Of course Isobel wouldn't be interested in ugly people like myself or Sadini, with his black eyes and his black moustache. I don't know why she ever married him in the first place when she could find handsome men like George Wallace.

She saw George Wallace all the time, because he had another act in the same show we travelled with. He was tall, and he had blonde hair and blue eyes, and he was a singer and dancer in the show. Isobel used to stand in the wings (that's the part on the side of the stage) when he was singing, and look at him. Sometimes they would talk together and laugh, and once when Isobel said she was going to the hotel because she had a headache, I saw her and George Wallace walk into his dressing room.

Maybe I shouldn't have told Sadini about that, but it just came out before I could stop it. He got very angry, and he asked me questions, and then he told me to keep my mouth shut and my eyes open.

It was wrong for me to say yes, I know that now; but all I could think of then was that Sadini had been kind to me. So I watched Isobel and Frank Wallace, and one day when Sadini was downtown between shows, I saw them again in Wallace's dressing room. It was on the balcony, and I tiptoed up to the door and looked through the keyhole. Nobody else was around, and nobody could see me blushing.

Because Isobel was kissing George Wallace and he was saying, "Come on, darling—let's not stall any longer. When the show closes, it's you and me. We'll blow out of here together, head for the coast and—"

"Quit talking like a schmoe!" Isobel sounded mad. "I'm nuts about you, Georgie-boy, but I know a good deal when I see it. Vic's a headliner; he'll be pulling in his grand a week when you're doing a single for smokers. Fun's fun, but there's no percentage in such a deal for me."

"Vic!" George Wallace made a face. "What's that phoney got, anyway? A couple of trunks full of props and a mustache. Anybody can do a magic act—I could myself, if I had the stake for the gimmicks. Why hell, you know all his routines. You and I could build our own act, baby. How's that for an angle? The Great Wallace and Company—"

"Georgie!"

She said it so fast and she moved so fast, I didn't have time to get away. Isobel walked right over to the door and yanked it open, and there I was.

"What the—"

George Wallace came up behind her and when he saw me he started to reach out, but she slapped his hands down.

"Can it!" she said. "I'll handle this." Then she smiled at me, and I knew she wasn't angry. "Come on downstairs, Hugo," she said. "Let's you and I have a little talk."

I'll never forget that little talk.

We sat there in the dressing room, just Isobel and me, all alone. And she held my hand—she had such soft, sweet hands—and looked into my eyes, and talked with her low voice that was like singing and stars and sunshine.

"So you found out," she said. "And that means I'll have to tell you the rest. I—I didn't want you to know, Hugo. Not ever. But now I'm afraid there's no other way."

I nodded. I didn't trust myself to look at her, so I just stared at the dressing table. Sadini's wand was lying there—his long black wand with the golden tip. It glittered and shone and dazzled my eyes.

"Yes, it's true, Hugo. George Wallace and I are in love. He wants me to go away."

"B-but Sadini is such a nice man," I told her. "Even if he does look that way."

"How do you mean?"

"Well, when I first saw him, I thought he was the Devil, but now—"

She sort of caught her breath. "You thought he looked like the Devil, Hugo?"

I laughed. "Yes. You know, the Sisters, they said I wasn't very bright. And they wanted to operate on my head because I couldn't understand things. But I'm all right. You know that. I just thought Sadini might be the Devil until he told me everything was a trick. It wasn't really a magic wand and he didn't really saw you in half—"

"And you believed him!"

I looked at her now. She was sitting up straight, and her eyes were shining. "Oh, Hugo, if I'd only known! You see, I was the same way, once. When I first met him, I trusted him. And now I'm his slave. That's why I can't run away, because I'm his slave. Just as he is the slave of—the Devil."

My eyes must have bugged out, because she kept looking at me funny as she went on.

"You didn't know that, did you? You believed him when he said he just did tricks, and that he sawed me in half on the stage for an illusion, using mirrors."

"But he does use mirrors," I said. "Don't I pack them and unpack them and set them up just so?"

"That's only to fool the stagehands," she said. "If they knew he was really a sorcerer they'd lock him up. Didn't the Sisters tell you about the Devil and selling your soul?"

"Yes, I have heard stories, but I thought—"

"You believe me, don't you Hugo?" She took my hand again

and looked right at me. "When he takes me out on the stage and raises me from the ground, that's sorcery. One word and I would fall to my death. When he saws me in half, it's real. That's why I can't run away, that's why I'm his slave."

"Then it must have been the Devil who gave him the magic wand that does the tricks."

She nodded, watching me.

I looked at the wand. It was glittering away, and her hair glittered, and her eyes glittered.

"Why can't I steal the wand?" I asked.

She shook her head. "It wouldn't help. Not as long as he's alive."

"Not as long as he's alive," I repeated.

"But if he were to—oh, Hugo, you must help me! There's only one way, and it wouldn't be a sin, not when he's sold his soul to the Devil. Oh, Hugo, you must help me, you will help me—"

She kissed me.

She *kissed* me. Yes, she put her arms around my back, and her golden hair wound round and round me, and her lips were soft and her eyes were like glory, and she told me what to do, how to do it, and it wouldn't be a sin, he was sold to the Devil, no one would ever know.

So I said yes, I would do it.

She told me how.

And she made me promise never to tell anyone, no matter what happened, even if things went wrong and they asked questions of me.

I promised.

And then I waited. I waited for Sadini to come back that night. I waited until after the show, when everyone went home. Isobel left, and she told Sadini to stay behind and help me pack because I was sick, and he said he would. It all worked just as she promised it would.

We started packing, and there was nobody left in the theatre but the doorman, and he was way downstairs in the room next to the alley. I went out into the hall while Sadini was packing, and saw how dark and still it was. Then I came into the dressing-room again and watched Sadini putting away his props.

He hadn't touched the wand, though. It glittered and glittered, and I wanted to pick it up and feel the magic of the Power the Devil had given him.

But there was no time for that, now. Because I had to walk up behind Sadini as he bent over the trunk. I had to take the piece of iron pipe out of my pocket and raise it over his head and bring it down once, twice, three times.

There was an awful cracking sound, and then a thump, when he fell to the floor.

Now all I had to do was lift him into the trunk and—

There was another sound.

Somebody knocked on the door.

Somebody rattled the doorknob as I dragged Sadini's body over to the corner and tried to find a place to hide it. But it was no use. The knocking came again and I heard a voice calling, "Hugo—open up! I know you're there!"

So I opened the door, holding the pipe behind my back. George Wallace came in.

I guess he was drunk. Anyway, he didn't seem to notice Sadini lying on the floor at first. He just looked at me and waved his arms.

"Hugo, I gotta talk t'you." He was drunk all right, I could smell the liquor now. "She told me," he whispered. "She told me what was up. Tried to get me drunk, but I'm wise to her. I sneaked away. Gotta talk t'you before you do 'nything foolish.

"She told me. Gonna frame you, that's what. You kill Sadini, she'll tell the cops, deny everything. You're supposed t'be—well, kinda soft in the head. 'N when you spill that hooey about the Devil they'll figure you're crazy for sure, lock you up. Then she wanted us to run away, take the act. I hadda come back here, warn you before—"

Then he saw Sadini. He just sort of froze up, standing there stiff as a board with his mouth open. That made it easy for me to come up behind him and hit him with the pipe; hit him and hit him and hit him.

Because I knew he lied, he was lying about her, he couldn't have her, he couldn't run away, I wouldn't permit it. I knew what he really wanted—he wanted the wand of Power, the Devil's wand. And it was mine.

I walked over and took it up in my hands, felt the Power surging along my arm as I looked at the glittering tip. I was still holding it in my hand when she came in.

She must have followed him, but she was too late now. She could tell, when she saw him lying there on the floor with the back of his head laughing up like a big red mouth.

She was frozen for a moment too, but then before I could say anything, Isobel slid to the floor. She just fainted.

I stood there, holding the wand of Power, looking down at her and feeling sorry. Sorry for Sadini, burning in Hell. Sorry for George Wallace because he had come here. Sorry for her, because all the plans had gone wrong.

Then I looked at the wand, and I got this wonderful idea. Sadini was dead, and George was dead, but she still had me. She wasn't afraid of me—she had even kissed me.

And I had the wand. That was the secret of the magic. Now, while she was still asleep, I could find out if it was true. And then when she woke up, what a surprise for her! I would tell her, "You were right, Isobel. It does work. And from now on, you and I will do the act. I have the wand and you need never be afraid again. Because I can do it. I already did it when you were asleep."

There was nothing to interfere. I carried her out to the stage. I carried the props, too. I even turned on the spotlight, because I knew where it was. It felt funny, standing there all alone in the empty theatre, bowing into the blackness.

But I was wearing Sadini's cloak, and I stood there for a moment with Isobel lying before me. With the magic wand in my hand I felt like a new person—like Hugo the Great.

And I was Hugo the Great.

That night, in the empty theatre, I was Hugo the Great. I knew just what to do, how to do it. There were no stagehands so I didn't need to bother with the mirrors, and I had to strap her and turn on the electric current myself. The blade didn't seem to turn so fast, either, when I put it right up against the board box covering her, but I made it work.

It buzzed away and buzzed away, and then she opened her eyes and screamed, but I had her strapped down, and besides there was nothing to be afraid of. I showed her the magic wand, but she just screamed and screamed until the buzzing drowned out her voice and the blade came through.

The blade was red. Dripping red.

It made me sick to look at it, so I closed my eyes and waved the magic wand of Power very quickly.

Then I looked down.

Everything was—the same.

I waved the wand again.

Still nothing happened.

Something had gone wrong. That's when I knew something had gone wrong.

Then I was screaming, and the doorman finally heard and ran in, and then you came and took me away.

So, you see, it was just an accident. The wand didn't work. Maybe the Devil took the power away when Sadini died. I don't know. All I know is that I'm very tired.

Will you turn off the lights now, please?

I want to go to sleep . . .

I Kiss Your Shadow—

Joe Elliot sat down in my favorite chair, helped himself to a drink of my best whiskey, and lighted one of my special cigarettes.

I didn't object.

But when he said, "I saw your sister last night," I was ready to protest. After all, a man can only take so much.

So I opened my mouth and then realized there was nothing to say. What *could* I say to a statement like that? I'd heard it from his lips a hundred times before, during their engagement, and it sounded perfectly natural then.

It would sound perfectly natural now, except for one thing— my sister had been dead for three weeks.

Joe Elliot smiled, not too successfully. "I suppose it sounds crazy," he said. "But it's the truth. I saw Donna last night. Or, at least, her shadow."

He still wasn't giving me the opportunity for a sensible answer; the only sensible thing I could do was remain silent and listen.

"She came into the bedroom and leaned over me. I've had trouble getting to sleep nights, ever since the accident, but I guess you know that. Anyway, I was lying there looking up at the ceiling and trying to decide if I should get up and pull down the shade, because the moonlight was so bright. Then I turned on my side and got ready to swing my legs out of bed, and there she was. Just standing there, bending over me and holding her arms out."

Elliot leaned forward. "Sure, I know what you're thinking. The moonlight was deflected by something in the room and made a shadow, and I made the rest of it myself. Or I really was asleep and didn't know it. But I know what I saw. It was Donna, all right—I'd recognize her anywhere, just from the silhouette."

I found my voice, or a reasonable facsimile. "What did she do?" I asked.

"*Do?* She didn't do anything. Just stood there, holding her arms out as if she were waiting for something."

"What was she waiting for?"

Elliot stared at the floor. "This is really the hard part," he murmured. "It sounds so—well, the hell with how it sounds. When Donna and I were engaged, she had this trick of hers. We'd be talking, or perhaps getting ready to do the dishes when I ate over at her place, some ordinary thing like that. And then, all at once she'd hold out her arms. I got so I recognized the gesture. It meant she wanted to be kissed. So I'd kiss her. And—go ahead, laugh!—that's what I did last night. I got up out of bed and kissed her shadow."

I didn't laugh. I didn't do anything. I just sat there and waited for him to continue. When he showed no signs of saying anything further, I had to fill the gap. "You kissed her. And then what happened?"

"Why, nothing. She just went away."

"Disappeared?"

"No. She went away. The shadow released me and then turned around and walked through the door."

"The shadow *released* you," I said. "Does this mean you—?"

He nodded. I'm not a nod-interpreter, but it was obvious that there was no defiance in his movement; only a sort of resignation. "That's right. When I kissed her she put her arms around me. I—I saw it. And I *felt* it. I felt her kiss, too. Funny sensation, kissing a shadow. Real, and yet not all there." He glanced down at the glass in his hand. "Like a watered drink."

There was something wrong with his comparison, but then there was something wrong with the whole story. I suppose the main trouble lay in mere chronology—he'd come to me with it just about fifty years too late.

Fifty years ago, it might not have sounded quite so odd. Not in the days when people still believed in ghosts, by and large; the days when even so eminent and hardheaded a psychologist as William James was active in the Society for Psychical Research. There was a certain receptivity then to the sentimental approach—undying love, capable of reaching beyond the grave, and all that sort of thing. But to hear it *now* was wrong.

The only thing that kept me from coming right out and saying so was the realization that there was another aspect to the business even wronger than the rest. Joe Elliot himself. *He* was the professional skeptic, the confirmed scoffer.

Of course, maybe the shock of Donna's death—

"Don't say it," he sighed. "I know how cockeyed and corny it all sounds, and I know what you're thinking. I won't argue with you. The accident did hit me pretty hard, you understand that. And I admit I was in some kind of shock-state when they pulled me out of the car down there in the ravine. But I snapped out of it before the funeral. You know that, too. And if you don't believe it, just check with Doc Foster."

My turn to nod.

"I was all right at the funeral and after," he continued. "You've seen me almost every day since then. Have you noticed anything—offbeat?"

"No."

"So it wasn't just imagination. It couldn't be."

"Then what's your answer?"

He stood up. "I have no answer. I just wanted to tell you what happened. Because it's one of those things where you must tell someone, and you're the logical person. I can trust you not to go around repeating it. Besides, you're her brother, and there's a chance that she might—come to you."

Joe Elliot moved to the door.

"Leaving so soon?" I asked.

"Tired," he said. "I didn't sleep very much last night, afterwards."

"Look," I said. "How about a sedative? I've got some stuff here that—"

"Thanks, but I'd rather not." He opened the door. "I'll call you in a day or so. We can have lunch together."

"You're sure you're—"

"Yes, I'm all right." He smiled and went out.

I frowned and stayed in. I was still frowning as I got ready for bed. Something was definitely wrong with Elliot's story and that meant something was definitely wrong with Elliot. I wished I knew the answer.

"There's a chance that she might—come to you."

I crawled between the sheets and noted that the moonlight was bright on my ceiling tonight, too. But I didn't look at the moonlight very long. I closed my eyes and contemplated the chance. It seemed to be a very slim one, as chances go.

My sister Donna was dead and in her grave. I hadn't seen her die, but I was the first one summoned right after the accident, as soon as the police arrived on the scene. I saw them lift her out of the crumpled car, and she was dead, no doubt about it. I didn't like to think about seeing her. I didn't like to think about seeing Joe Elliot, either, shaking in shock; unconscious of my presence, unconscious of the gash in his forehead, unconscious even of the fact that Donna was dead. He'd kept talking to her while they carried her to the ambulance, trying to make her understand that it was an accident, there was oil-slick on the road, the car had skidded. But Donna never heard him because she was already dead. She had died when her head went through the windshield.

That's what they thought at the inquest, too. Verdict of accidental death. And surely the morticians who embalmed her had no doubts, nor did the minister who preached the sermon over her casket, the workmen who lowered her body into the grave out there at Forest Hills. Donna was dead.

And now, three weeks later, Joe Elliot came to me and said, "I saw your sister. Or at least, her shadow." Hardheaded Joe, a rewrite man on the desk and cynical as they come, kissing a shadow. He had said she stood there with her arms extended and he recognized her.

Well, I hadn't seen fit to mention it, but I recognized that particular gesture from his description. Because it so happens I'd seen it myself, long before Joe Elliot came into the picture. Way back when Donna was engaged to Frankie Hankins, she used to pull the same trick with him. I wondered if Frankie had heard the news yet, over there in Japan. He'd enlisted and that broke the affair up.

Come to remember, there was another time Donna used the open-arms technique. With Gil Turner. Of course, that hadn't lasted, it was obvious from the start: Turner was just a namby-pamby. Surprised everybody to see a wishy-washy character like him pull up stakes and leave town in such a hurry.

It must have surprised Donna, too, but not for long. Because just about that time I introduced her to Joe Elliot and the heat was on.

There was no question about this being the big thing for both of them. They were engaged inside of a month, and planning to be married before the summer was out. Donna just took over, lock, stock and barrel.

Of course I'd always known my sister was a determined woman (let's face it, she made a habit of getting her own way, and she was a hellcat if you crossed her) but it was interesting to watch how she worked on Joe Elliot. Talk about Pygmalion—here was one case where Galatea reversed the play. Before anyone knew it, Joe Elliot was out of his sloppy sports-jacket and into gray tweeds, out of smelly cigars and into briar pipes, out of cuppa-cawfee-'n-a-hamburger and into Donna's comfortable little apartment for regular evening meals.

Oh, she made a lot of changes in that boy! Got so that he was shaving twice a day, and he trotted around the corner to the bank with his paycheck instead of over to Smitty's Tap.

I had to give Donna credit. She knew what she wanted, and she knew just how to get it. Maybe she was ruthless, but she was feminine-ruthless. She remade Joe Elliot, but she also made him like it. He certainly didn't seem to object. I got so used to the new Elliot that I virtually forgot about the old one—the old one who used to sit in Smitty's and swear a mighty oath that the girl didn't breathe who could ensnare him into unholy dreadlock.

By the time the wedding drew near, Donna was already openly talking about their plans for buying a house—"You can't raise a family in an apartment"—and Elliot would listen and actually grin.

"And another thing," he used to say, shaking his finger at Smitty in solemn warning, "I may be a poor downtrodden wage-slave, but you'll never catch me being a house-slave. Or turning into that typical figure of fun—the American Father. Dear Old Dad, the butt of every family radio and TV show in the country! Not for me. I believe in the old saying: children should be seen and not had."

But this was *before* Donna. Before, I suppose, he found out how nice it is to have a woman around who lights your pipe, and straightens your tie, and fixes the fried potatoes at just the right time so they won't get soggy when the steak is served. Before he found out what it is to have somebody who holds out her arms and doesn't say anything, except with her eyes.

This much I was sure of: Donna wasn't playing any trick. She loved the guy. She died loving him, the night they were driving back from my party. That part was real.

Everything was real, up to now. Now, and Joe Elliot's story of the shadow.

I looked up at the shimmering ceiling. Somehow, here in the dark, with its mingling of moonlight, I could almost begin to believe.

Maybe we're not quite as sophisticated as we like to think we are; ghosts happen to be unfashionable, and the concept of love conquering the grave went out with *Outward Bound*. But set a sophisticate down in the pitch-black bowels of a haunted house, bar the exit, and leave him there for the night. Maybe his hair won't turn white by morning; still, there'll be some reaction. Intellectually, we reject. Emotionally, we're not so sure. Not when the chips are down and the lights are low.

Well, the lights were low and I kept waiting for Donna to come. I waited and waited, and finally I guess I just fell asleep.

I told Joe Elliot about it at lunch two days later. "She never showed," I said.

He cocked his head at me. "Of course not," he answered. "She couldn't. She was at my place."

I finally managed to speak. "Again?"

"Two nights ago, and last night."

"Same thing?"

"Same thing." He hesitated. "Only—she stayed longer."

"How much longer?"

More than hesitation now; a lasting silence. Until he brushed his napkin from his lap, stooped down to pick it up, and barely whispered, "All night."

I didn't ask the next question. I didn't have to. One look at his face was enough.

"She's real," Elliot said. "Donna. The shadow. You remember

what I said the first time? About the watered whiskey?" He leaned forward. "It's not like that now. Maybe they get stronger once they break through. Do you think that's it? They learn the way, and then they get stronger."

He was close enough so that I could smell his breath, and he hadn't been drinking—any more than he'd been drinking the night of the accident. I'd testified to that, and it helped seal the verdict.

No, Elliot wasn't drunk. I wished to heaven he was, so I wouldn't have to say what I was going to say. But I had to.

"Why don't you take a run up to see Doc Foster?" I asked him.

Joe Elliot spread his palms on the table. "I knew you'd say that," he grinned. "So I already called him this morning, for an appointment."

I managed to withhold the sigh of relief, but it was there, and I could feel it. For a minute I'd been afraid of an argument—not because I dreaded arguments, but because of what it would imply about Elliot. I was glad to see he hadn't gone completely overboard.

"You needn't worry," he assured me. "I know what Doc will tell me. Sedatives, relaxation, and if that doesn't work, see a head-shrinker. And if he does, I'll follow orders."

"Promise?"

"Sure." He gave me the grin again, but this time it was a little twisted. "Want to know something funny? I'm beginning to be a bit scared of that sister of yours—even if she is only a shadow."

I put a large *No Comment* sign on my face and we went out together in silence. We separated in the street—I went back to the office and Elliot went over to Doc Foster's.

I didn't learn about his visit for several days. Because when I got back to the office they had a surprise for me.

The same newspaper employing Joe Elliot on the rewrite desk sees fit to retain me in the capacity of roving correspondent. And the M.E. was waiting for me with a suggestion that I rove in the direction of Indo-China. As of two days from now, with all watches synchronized.

I got busy. So busy that I never managed to call Joe Elliot. So busy that if he called me, I wasn't around to get the message.

He finally caught me at the airport, actually, just before I took off for the west coast and the first leg of the flight.

"Sorry I couldn't be on hand," he said. *"Bon voyage* and all that."

"You sound pretty happy."

"Why not?"

"Doc's sedatives do the trick?"

He chuckled. "Not exactly. When I told him, he didn't even bother with the first part of the routine. Sent me packing right away to the you-know-who. Name of Partridge. Heard of him?"

I had. "Good man," I said.

"The best." He paused. "Well, I mustn't keep you—"

"You're all right?" My voice was insistent.

"Sure. I'm fine. I sailed for the works. Some of the things the guy told me make sense. I guess I'm more tangled up than I thought—oh, not just what I told you about, but there are other angles. Anyway, I'm going in to him twice a week for I don't know how long. And it's not as phoney as I thought it might be, either. None of this couch business. He really gets results." Another pause. "I mean, I've been there just twice, and she's gone."

"The shadow, you mean?"

"The guilt-fantasy." He chuckled again. "See, I'm picking up the lingo already. Time you come back, I'll be ready to hang out my shingle. Well, lots of luck, kid. And keep in touch."

"Will do," I said. And hung up, listening to them announce my flight. And took the flight, and made my transfer in Frisco, and went to Manila, and went from there to Singapore, and from there to hell.

It was hot as hell in hell, and although I managed to get enough dispatches back to satisfy my M.E., I had no opportunity to keep in touch.

You know what happened in Indo-China, and when they opened a branch hell in Formosa, my M.E. sent me over there, and when hell got too hot for even a roving correspondent I was based in Manila and then Japan. I'm not trying to make a production out of it; just explaining why it turned out that I was gone for eight months instead of eight weeks.

When I got back they gave me a leave, and some information.

Not much, but just enough to send me scurrying around to Joe Elliot's apartment the first opportunity I got.

I didn't waste any time on hello-how-are-you. "What's this I hear about you leaving the paper?" I began.

He shrugged. "I didn't leave. I got canned."

"Why?"

"Hitting the sauce."

He looked it, too. The sports-jacket was back, and it was dirty. He wasn't bothering to shave once a day, either, let alone twice. He was thin, and twitchy.

"Let's have it," I said. "What happened to you?"

"Nothing."

"Quit stalling. What does Partridge say?"

He gave me a grin, and to say it was twisted doesn't even begin to describe it. They could have made a cast and used it to cut pretzels with.

"Partridge," he echoed. "Sit down. Have a drink."

"All right, but keep talking. I asked you a question. What does Partridge say?"

He poured for me. I was a guest; I got a glass. He gulped out of the bottle. Then he put it down. "Partridge doesn't say anything any more," he told me. "Partridge is dead."

"No."

"Yes."

"When did this happen?"

"Month or so back."

"Why didn't you go to another hea—psychiatrist?"

"What? And have him jump out of the window, too?"

"What's all this about jumping out of a window?"

He picked up the bottle. "That's what I'd like to know." *Gulp.* "Personally, I'm not even sure he jumped. Maybe he was pushed."

"Are you trying to tell me—?"

"No. I'm not trying to tell you anything. Any more than I'd try to tell Doc Foster or the boys down at the office. You can't tell anyone a story like that. Just got to keep it to yourself. Yourself and the little old bottle." *Gulp.*

"But you said—I mean, you sounded as if everything was going so well."

"That's right. And it went fine. Up to a point."

"What point?"

"The point where I found out why she wasn't coming back any more." He stared out of the window, and then he went a million miles away and only his voice remained. I could hear what he said, plainly enough. Too plainly.

"She wasn't coming back to me because she was going to him. Night after night after night. Not with her arms out—not the way she'd come to me, in love. She went to him out of hate. Because she knew he was trying to drive her away. Don't you see, when he worked on me it was like—like exorcism. You know what exorcism is, don't you? Casting out demons. Ghosts. A succubus."

"Joe, you've got to stop this. Get hold of yourself."

He laughed. "All I can get hold of is this." And reached for the bottle, as he spoke. "You're asking me to stop this? But I didn't start it. I didn't make it up. Partridge told me himself. Finally he broke down and he *had* to tell me. Do you get the picture now?— *he* came to *me* for help. And I couldn't help him. I was getting well, there's a laugh for you, I was getting over *my* delusions. I talked to him the way you're trying to talk to me, real Dutch uncle stuff.

"And I went out of his office, and the next morning I read where he jumped. Only he didn't jump—she must have pushed him—he was afraid of her, she kept getting stronger and stronger, just as I thought she would. They found him spattered all over the sidewalk—"

This time I reached for the bottle. "So you quit your job and started drinking, just because a psychiatrist cracked up and committed suicide," I said. "Because one poor overworked guy went to pieces, you had to do likewise. I thought you were smarter than that, Joe."

"So did I." He took the bottle away from me. "You heard what I told you. I thought I was completely well. Even when he died, I still wasn't sure about some things. Until that night, when she came back."

I watched him drink and waited.

"Sure. She came back. And she's been coming back, every night, since then. I can't fight it off, I can't fight her off, she keeps clinging and clinging to me. But why try to explain? You don't believe me anyway. I saw the look on your face when I mentioned the part about a succubus."

"Please," I said. "I want to hear the rest. I've read about those things, you know. A succubus takes the form of a woman and comes to men at night—"

He was nodding and then he cut in. "So that explains it, don't you see? What she was whispering to me. I guess I didn't tell you, but she talks now. She talks to me, she tells me things. She says she's glad, and it won't be long now, then she'll have everything she wanted—"

His voice trailed off, and I stood up just in time to catch him as he slumped. He was out cold; his body was limp and light in my arms. Too light. He must have lost a lot of weight. I guess Joe Elliot had lost a lot of things.

I suppose I could have tried to bring him around, but I didn't make the effort. It seemed kinder just to carry him over to the bed, take off his things and let him rest. I found pajamas in one of the bureau drawers, got them on him—it was like dressing a rag doll instead of a man—and covered him up. Then I left him. He'd sleep now, sleep without shadows.

And while he slept, I'd figure out something. There had to be an answer. Because Donna was my sister and I'd loved her, and because Joe Elliot was my friend, there had to be an answer.

If Partridge were only alive. If I could just talk to him and find out what he'd really learned about this delusion! He must have learned something, in eight months. Even if Elliot deliberately tried to hold back, in eight months a man like Partridge would learn—

The thought hit me then; a stinging blow. I tried to duck. But it hit harder and this time there was a numbing reaction.

"No," I told myself. "No."

I kept telling myself no, but I was telling the cab-driver to take me down to the office again. I told myself no, but I told the M.E. I wanted all the stuff in the house on Partridge's suicide.

Then I was reading it, and then I was over at the Coroner's office, checking the report of the inquest.

I didn't ask any fancy questions, and I didn't do any fancy detective work. That's out of my line. I won't pretend to have done anything more except to jump at a wild conclusion. That's all the records showed—Partridge had jumped to a wild conclusion.

But knowing what I did, I was more inclined to agree with Joe Elliot. Partridge hadn't jumped, he'd been pushed.

There wasn't a single solitary thing I could hang onto as tangible evidence; nothing to build a case around. But I checked and rechecked, and I fitted the pieces together and then everything shattered apart when I recognized the picture.

I left the Coroner's office and went over to Smitty's Tap and drank a very late supper, not talking to anyone. I didn't know who to talk to now—surely not the Coroner, or the D.A., or the cops. They couldn't help, because I had no evidence. Besides, I owed Joe Elliot a chance.

There was still the shadow of a doubt. A *shadow* named Donna, who'd come back. Maybe she'd be coming back tonight, but I wasn't going to wait.

After a while it was quite late, but I was on my way, back to Elliot's apartment. Chances were that he was still sleeping, and I hoped so in a way. Then again, I knew I had to see him now.

I went up the stairs slowly, one voice saying *let him sleep* and the other voice saying *knock*, and two of them fighting together, *let him sleep—knock—let him sleep—knock—*

It turned out that neither voice won, because when I got to the door, Joe Elliot opened it and looked out.

He was awake all right, and maybe he'd been back to the bottle again and maybe he hadn't: he looked as if he'd swallowed strychnine. And his voice was the voice of a man with a burned throat.

"Come in," he said. "I was just going out."

"In your pajamas?"

"I had an errand—"

"It can wait," I told him.

"Yes, it can wait." He led me inside, closed the door. "Sit down," he murmured. "I'm glad you're here."

I sat down, but I kept a grip on the arms of the chair, ready to move in a hurry if necessary. And I waited very carefully until he sat down, too, before I spoke.

"Maybe you won't be so glad when I speak my piece," I said.

"Go ahead. It doesn't matter what you say now."

"Yes it does, Joe. I want you to listen carefully. This is important."

"Nothing's important."

"We'll see. After I left you this afternoon, I did a little investigating. I went to the Coroner's office, among other things. And I agree with you now. Partridge *was* pushed out of the window."

For the first time his face showed interest. "Then I was right, wasn't I?" he began. "She did push him, you found some evidence—"

I shook my head. "I didn't find any evidence. Not any *new* evidence. I just began to check the facts and see if they fitted in with a theory of my own. They did." I spoke very slowly, very deliberately. "I checked on one particular phase of the report, Joe. The account you gave of your own movements after leaving Partridge's office the day he jumped. The whole story about not taking the elevator down because it was crowded and you were in a hurry to get to the office. And the part about not going to the office after all because you remembered you'd forgotten your hat and went back upstairs to get it. And how you came in just as they were looking out the window where Partridge had jumped.

"I read it all, Joe. I read your account of the last meeting with Partridge, how upset he seemed. Only I was a *special* reader."

He was more than interested now; he was alert.

"They tried pretty hard to break down your story, didn't they, Joe? Only they couldn't, because there was no evidence to the contrary, and what you said made sense. About how Partridge was fidgeting and nervous and kept looking out the window. About how jumpy he'd been the past few weeks. Good word, that *jumpy*. Good enough for the Coroner's Jury, anyway. But not good enough for me.

"Because you didn't mention anything about the shadow in your story to the Jury. You told something entirely different."

He hit the arm of his chair hard. "Of course I did, man! I couldn't tell them what I told you, they'd think I was crazy."

"But you *were* crazy, Joe. Crazy enough so that your story to me makes sense. Partridge didn't jump, he was pushed—and you pushed him."

Joe Elliot made a noise in his chest. Something came out of his mouth that sounded like, "Why?"

"I wish I knew the answer to that. The real answer. All I can do is guess. And my guess is that there wasn't anything to this story of yours about Partridge being afraid of a shadow. My guess is that *you* were the one who was afraid—because in session after session, Partridge kept getting nearer and nearer to something you didn't want him to find. Something you tried to hide, but couldn't. Something he, as a trained analyst, found anyway. Or was on the very verge of finding. When you realized that, you panicked—and destroyed him."

"Rave on," he said.

"All right, I will. Joe, you're not crazy. You never were. I think this is all an act. You wouldn't murder a man except for a very important reason. Whatever Partridge found out, or was about to find out, was something vitally necessary for you to conceal."

"Such as?"

"Such as the fact that you killed my sister."

The words hit the wall and bounced. The words hit his face and twisted it up into the gargoyle grin, the spasmodic twitch.

"All right. So you know."

"Then it's true," I said.

"Of course it's true. But what you don't know is *why*. You wouldn't know, and you're her own brother. How could I expect anyone else to understand if you never saw it? What Donna was *really* like, I mean. The way she tried to fasten her claws into me, pulling me down, trying to possess me, never letting go for an instant. Sure I loved her, she knew how to make a man love her, she had a thousand tricks to drive you mad with wanting her, holding out her arms was just the beginning. But that wasn't enough, to possess me that way. She had to have *everything*, she wanted every minute, every movement, every thought. She was making me over and trying to turn me into all the things I always hated. I could see it, I knew what lay ahead, a life of slavery to *her* house and *her* kids and *her* future."

He stopped because he had to, and I said, "Why didn't you get out, then? Break the engagement?"

"I tried. Don't you think I tried? But she wouldn't let go. Not her, not Donna. Even then she was a succubus. She had her claws in me and she wanted to drain me. I can't help it; there was something about her, and when she came into my arms I couldn't break free because then I didn't want to any more.

"But when I was alone again, I wanted to. You never heard about this part, but just before your party, I tried to sneak out of town. She caught me. There was a scene—or there would have been, except that Donna never made scenes. She made love. Do you understand?"

I nodded.

"And after that I was sick. Not physically sick, but worse than that. Because I knew it would always be this way; me trying to get free and she clawing me back. There'd always be a succubus. Unless I got rid of her."

Another pause, another breath, and then he rushed on. "It wasn't difficult. I knew the spot on the road where the rail hung over the edge of the ravine. I had a wrench in the car. You remember we left late, and the road was deserted. When we got to the ravine I suggested we park and look at the moon. Donna liked that kind of suggestion. So then I—I hit her. And sent the car over. And went down myself, and finished cracking the windshield and gave myself a gash in the forehead and crawled into the car. I didn't have to do much pretending about the shock. Only it was a shock of relief, because I knew now she was really dead."

I put my hands in my lap. "And that's what Partridge was on the verge of finding out, isn't it?" I asked. "All this business about the shadow was just what he told you it was—a guilt-fantasy. You felt compelled to spring it on me first because of the guilt-feeling, and you didn't want to tell Partridge anything about the possible cause of the delusion. Only he kept probing until he was too close for safety. Your safety, and his. So you killed again."

"No."

"Why bother to deny it? You've already confessed to one murder, so—"

"Killing Donna wasn't murder," he said. "It was self-defense. And that's the end of it. I didn't kill Partridge, no matter what you think. *She* did.

"I told you how she went to him night after night, torturing him, breaking him down, trying to get him to the point where he was ready to jump.

"And when he told me, that day in his office, I couldn't stand it. So I got ready to explain, I was going to tell him the truth about the shadow and what I'd done.

"I remember he was bending over me, asking me about the accident, and then he straightened up and looked surprised and I saw that *she* was there. A shadow, but not a shadow on the wall. A shadow in the room, right behind us, tugging at his arm. And he tried to scream but there was this blackness over his mouth, her hand, and she was pulling him over to the window, and his feet made little scuffing noises sliding along the carpet, and he tried to grab the window-frame but the shadow is strong and the shadow laughed so you could hear it above the scream when he went down and down and down—"

He snapped out of it suddenly. "Too bad you weren't here earlier tonight. You'd have believed me then, because you would have seen her. She came a while before you arrived and woke me. Said she wanted me to go out there, because there was a surprise. Something to show me. At first I didn't know what she was hinting at, but I know now. You see, I counted back, but you'd only laugh. I could take you along to look, too, but you'd laugh and—"

"I'm not laughing, Joe," I said.

"Well, you'd better not. She wouldn't like that. She wouldn't like to have anyone get in her way. And she's so strong now, stronger than anyone. She's already proved that. I'm going to do what she says. Now that she has a real claim on me, nothing can stop her."

I stood up. "But she can be stopped. There's a way, you know."

"You mean you believe in exorcism now?"

"Joe," I said, "you're partially exorcised already. By confessing to me you've rid yourself of a portion of her power. You might have banished her forever if you'd succeeded in telling Partridge the truth, because he represented authority to you. That's the answer, Joe. You've got to tell this to an authority. Then there won't be any more guilt-feelings or guilt-fantasy, either. You'll remember what actually happened to Partridge, and once they understand the situation you can put in a plea. I'll help you all I can. There's a pretty smart lawyer downtown who—"

Now Elliot stood up. "I get it," he murmured. "You're humoring me because I'm a psycho and that's what you want them all to think. Maybe you're afraid she'll be coming after you, too. Well, don't worry. She won't, unless you try to stand in her way. I'm the one she really wants, and I'm going to her. I want to see—"

"Listen, Joe," I began, but he wasn't listening.

He reached out suddenly and his hand swept across the table-top, gripped the half-empty bottle, raised it, and smashed it down until it shattered. Then he took a quick step forward, swinging the glittering weapon.

The whole operation from start to finish was almost instantaneous, and it silenced me.

He stood there, holding the jagged length of glass that splintered down from the broken bottle-top.

"Sorry to cut you off," he said. "Now you'd better go. Before I really cut you off."

I took one step forward. The gargoyle grin returned to his face, and I took two steps backward.

"I'm the one she wants," he said. "You can't stop me. And no sense going to the cops. They can't stop me, either. She won't let them."

I should have jumped him then, even though he was a maniac with a broken bottle in his hand for a weapon. I often wonder what would have happened if I *had* jumped him.

But I didn't.

I turned and ran, ran out of the apartment and down the stairs and through the hall and into the street, and I kept telling myself it wasn't just because I was afraid. I had to find help, this was a job for the police.

There was a call-box two blocks down and around the corner, and I used it. I suppose it didn't take more than five minutes between the time I left the apartment and the time I got back to meet the squad car as it pulled up.

That was enough, however. Joe Elliot had disappeared. They sent out a prowl car, and they put it on the police broadcast band, and you'd think a pajama-clad man would be easy to spot on a deserted city street.

But it wasn't until I broke down and told them where I thought

Joe Elliot was headed for that we got any action—and then it was because we piled into the squad car and drove all the way out to Forest Hills.

He couldn't have made the trip out there in that time on foot. He must have stolen a car, although they never found one or heard a report of a missing vehicle.

But he was there, of course, lying across her grave. And he'd been digging long enough to claw down a good six inches through the thick turf and solid soil.

That's when the stroke must have hit him. They never did agree as to the exact cause. The point is, he was dead.

And that left me to answer the questions.

I tried.

I tried to answer questions, and at the same time to leave out all the crazy stuff, the unfashionable stuff about ghosts and shadows and a succubus that kept getting stronger and stronger. *They* brought up the idea of a love reaching past the grave; it was their own idea, only of course they thought *he* was trying to reach *her*.

I tried to keep the murder part out of it too—because there was no sense opening that up now.

But they were the ones who finally got around to it, and they opened it up. The case, I mean. And then the grave.

If it had been just the case, I could have managed to hold on, I think. Hold on to my story, and to my belief, too.

But when they opened the grave, it was too much.

They dug down the rest of the way through the thick turf and solid soil; dug down to what hadn't been disturbed for ten long months.

And they found her, all right, although there were no marks or anything to prove murder. No proof at all.

And there was no explanation for what else they found, either. The tiny body of a newborn infant in Donna's intact coffin— lying there just as dead as Donna was.

Or just as alive.

I can't make up my mind which is which any more. And of course the police keep asking me questions for which there are no answers. None that they'd believe.

I can't tell them Donna wanted Joe so badly even death

couldn't deny her. I can't tell them she came to him at the last and summoned him proudly, that he went out to Forest Hills to see their child.

Because there is no such thing as a succubus. And a shadow does not speak, or move, or hold out its arms.

Or *does* it?

I don't know. I just lay in bed at night, now, when the bottle is empty, and look up at the ceiling. Waiting. Maybe I'll see a shadow.

Or *shadows*.

Mr. Steinway

The first time I saw Leo, I thought he was dead.

His hair was so black and his skin was so white—I'd never seen hands so pale and thin. They lay crossed on his chest, concealing the rhythm of his breathing. There was something almost repellent about him; he was thin and still and there was such a *nothingness* in his face. It was like a death-mask that had been made a little too late, after the last trace of the living personality had forever fled. I stared down at Leo, shuddered a little, and started to move away.

Then he opened his eyes, and I fell in love with him.

He sat up, swung his legs over the side of the enormous sofa, grinned at me, and rose. At least I suppose he did these things. All I really noticed was the deep brown of his pupils and the warm, rich hunger that poured from them into me, the hunger that poured and found a feeding-place somewhere in my heart.

I know what it sounds like. But I'm not a schoolgirl, and I don't keep a diary, and it's years since I've had a mad, mad crush. I'd been quite assured of my own emotional maturity for some time.

But he opened his eyes, and I fell in love at first sight.

Harry was making the introductions, now.

". . . Dorothy Endicott. She heard you play in Detroit last week and she wanted to meet you. Dorothy, this is Leo Winston."

He was quite tall, and he managed a little bow, or rather an inclination of his head, without once moving his gaze. I don't know *what* he said. "Charmed" or "delighted" or "pleased to meet you"—it didn't matter. He was *looking* at me.

I did all the wrong things. I blushed. I giggled. I said something about how much I admired his playing, and then I repeated myself and tripped over the words.

But I did *one* right thing. I looked back. All the while Harry was explaining how we'd just happened to stop up and we didn't mean to disturb him but the door was open so we walked right in. And he wanted to remind Leo about placing the piano for tomorrow night's concert, and the ticket-sales were going good according to the latest report this noon. And now he had to run along and arrange for the puffs for tomorrow's papers, so—

"There's no reason for you to hurry off, is there, Miss Endicott?"

There was, I agreed, no reason at all. So Harry left, like the good little Samaritan he was, and I stayed and talked to Leo Winston.

I don't know what we talked about. It's only in stories that people seem able to remember long conversations *verbatim*. (Or is it long *verbatim* conversations? It's only in stories that people have perfect control of grammar, too).

But I learned that his name was once Leo Weinstein . . . that he was thirty-one years old . . . unmarried . . . he liked Siamese kittens . . . he broke his leg once, skiing up at Saranac . . . he liked Manhattans made with dry vermouth, too.

It was over the second of these, after I told him all about myself (and nothing, unless he could read my eyes) that he asked me if I wanted to meet Mr. Steinway.

Of course I said yes, and we went into the other room, the one behind the sliding doors. There sat Mr. Steinway, all black and polished to perfection, grinning a welcome with his eighty-eight teeth.

"Would you like to hear Mr. Steinway play something for you?" asked Leo.

I nodded, feeling a warmth far beyond the power of two Manhattans to inspire—a warmth born of the way he said it. I hadn't felt that way since I was thirteen and in love with Bill Prentice and he asked if I'd like to see him do a Full Gaynor off the high board.

So Leo sat down on the bench and he patted Mr. Steinway on the leg the way I sometimes pat Angkor, my Siamese kitten. And they played for me. They played the *Appassionata* and the *berceuse* from *The Firebird* and something very odd by Prokofieff and then several things by the two Scotts—Cyril, and Raymond. I suppose Leo wanted to show his versatility, or perhaps that was Mr. Steinway's idea. Anyway, I liked it all, and I said so, emphatically.

"I'm glad you appreciate Mr. Steinway," Leo said. "He's very sensitive, I'll have you know, like everyone in my family. And he's been with me a long time—almost eleven years. He was a surprise from my mother, when I made my debut at Carnegie."

Leo stood up. He was very close to me, because I'd been sitting on the piano bench beside him ever since the *berceuse*, and that made it easier for me to see his eyes as he closed the black lip over Mr. Steinway's teeth and said, "Time for a little rest, before they come and get you."

"What's the matter?" I asked. "Is Mr. Steinway ill?"

"Not at all—I thought he sounded in the best of spirits." Leo grinned (how could I ever have imagined him dead, with his incandescent vitality?) and faced me. "He's going over to the concert hall this evening—he has a date to play with me tomorrow night. Which reminds me, will you be there?"

The only answer for that one was "Silly boy!" but I restrained it. Restraint did not come easy with me when I was with Leo. Not when he looked at me like that. With his eyes holding such hunger, and the long slim fingers caressing the panelling as they had caressed the keys, as they could so easily caress—

I trust I'm making myself clear?

Certainly I was transparent enough the following evening. After the concert we went out, just the four of us; Harry and his wife, Leo and I. And then just Leo and I, in the candlelight of the apartment, in the big room that looked so bare and empty without Mr. Steinway squatting there where he belonged. We watched the stars over Central Park and then we watched the reflections in each other's pupils, and what we said and what we did are not meant for sharing.

The next day, after we read the notices, we went for a walk in the Park. Leo had to wait until they'd moved Mr. Steinway back into the apartment, and it was lovely in the Park, as always. As it must have been for millions who, somewhere in their memories, hold an instant when they walked in Central Park in May and owned it all—the trees, the sunshine, the distant laughter rising and falling as transiently as the heartbeat quickened by a moment of ecstasy.

But—"I think they're on the way over," Leo said, glancing at his watch and rising from the bench. "I really ought to be there when they move him in. Mr. Steinway's big, but he's quite delicate, actually."

I took his hand. "Come on, then," I said.

He frowned. I'd never seen him frown before, and it seemed out of character to me. "Maybe you'd better not, Dorothy. I mean, it's a slow job up those stairs, and then I'll have to practice. Don't forget, I'm booked for Boston next Friday, and that means four hours a day for the next week—Mr. Steinway and I must get our program in shape. We're doing the Ravel Concerto, the Left-Hand one, with the Symphony, and Mr. Steinway isn't fond of Ravel. Besides, he'll be leaving on Wednesday morning, so there really isn't too much time."

"But you aren't taking the piano with you on tour, are you?"

"Certainly. Where I go, Mr. Steinway goes. I've never used another instrument since Mother gave him to me. I wouldn't feel right about it, and I'm sure it would break Mr. Steinway's heart."

Mr. Steinway's heart.

I had a rival, it seems. And I laughed about it, we both laughed about it, and he went away to his work and I went back to my apartment to sleep, perchance to dream . . .

I tried phoning him about five. No answer. I waited a half-hour, and then I grabbed the nearest rosy pink cloud and floated over to his apartment.

As usual—as was customary with Leo, whose mother had literally kept "open house" out on the Cape—the door was unlocked. And I naturally took advantage of the situation to tiptoe in and surprise Leo. I pictured him playing, practicing, absorbed in his work. But Mr. Steinway was silent, and the sliding doors to the other room were closed. I got my surprise in the ante-room.

Leo was dead again.

He lay there on the huge couch, his pallor almost phosphorescent in the gathering twilight. And his eyes were closed and his ears were closed and his very heart seemed closed until I bent down and blended the warmth of my lips with his own.

"Dorothy!"

"Sleeping Beauty, in reverse!" I exclaimed, triumphantly, rumpling his hair. "What's the matter, darling? Tired after your rehearsal? I don't blame you, considering—"

It was still light enough for me to recognize his frown.

"Did I—startle you?" It was a B-movie line, but this was, to me, a B-movie situation. The brilliant young concert pianist, torn between love and a career, interrupted in his pursuit of art by the sweet young thing. He frowns, rises, takes her by the shoulders as the camera pans in close and says—

"Dorothy, there's something you and I must talk about."

I was right. Here it comes, I told myself. The lecture about how art comes first, love and work don't mix—and after last night, too! I suppose I pouted. I make a very pretty pout, on occasion. But I waited, prepared to hear him out.

And he said, "Dorothy, what do you know about Solar Science?"

"I've never heard of it."

"That's not surprising. It's not a popular system; nothing in parapsychology has gained general acceptance. But it works, you know. It works. Perhaps I'd better explain from the beginning, so you'll understand."

So he explained from the beginning, and I did my best to understand. He must have talked for over an hour, but what I got out of it boils down to just a little.

It was his mother, really, who got interested in Solar Science. Apparently the basis of the concept was similar to Yoga or some of these new mental health systems. She'd been experimenting for about a year before her death—and during the past four years, since her passing, Leo had worked on it alone. The trance was part of the system. Briefly, as near as I could make out, it consisted of concentration—"but effortless effort of concentration, that's important"—on one's inner self, in order to establish "complete self-awareness." According to Solar Science one can become perfectly and utterly aware of one's entire being, and "communicate" with the organs of the body, the cells, the very atomic and molecular structure. Because everything, down to the very molecules, possesses a vibration-frequency and is therefore alive. And the personality, as an integrated unit, achieves full harmony only when complete communication is established.

Leo practiced four hours a day with Mr. Steinway. And he devoted at least two hours a day to Solar Science and "self-awareness". It had done wonders for him, done wonders for his playing. For relaxation, for renewal, for serenity, it was the ultimate answer. And it led to an *extension* of awareness. But he'd talk about that some other time. What did I think?

What *did* I think?

I honestly didn't know. Like everyone else, I'd heard a lot, and listened to very little, about telepathy and extra-sensory perception and teleportation and such things. And I'd always associated these matters with the comic-strip idea of scientists and psychologists and outright charlatans and gullible old women given to wearing long ropes of wooden beads which they twisted nervously during seances.

It was something different to hear Leo talk about it, to feel the intensity of his conviction, to hear him say—with a belief that burned—that this meditation was all that had preserved his sanity in the years after his mother died.

So I told him I understood, and I'd never interfere with his scheme of living, and all I wanted was to be with him and be *for* him whenever and wherever there was a place for me in his life. And, at the time, I believed it.

I believed it even though I could only see him for an hour or so, each evening, before his Boston concert. I got a few TV leads during the week—Harry arranged some auditions, but the client postponed his decision until the first of the month—and that helped to pass the time.

Then I flew up to Boston for the concert, and Leo was magnificent, and we came back together with nary a thought or a word about Solar Science or anything except the two of us.

But on Sunday morning, we were three again. Mr. Steinway arrived.

I dashed over to my own apartment and came running back after lunch. Central Park shimmered in the sunlight, and I admit I shared something of its radiance.

Until I was in the apartment, and heard Mr. Steinway rumbling and growling and purring and screeching and cachinnating, and I hurried in to Leo and the piano stopped.

He frowned. It seemed I was developing quite a talent for making an unexpected entrance.

"I didn't expect you so soon," he said. "I was just practicing something new."

"So I heard. What's the rest of it?"

"Never mind, now. Did you want to go out this afternoon?" He said it just as if he didn't see the new shoes, the suit, the hat I'd bought from Mr. John just to surprise him.

"No. Honestly, darling, I didn't mean to interrupt. Go on with your playing."

Leo shook his head. He stared down at Mr. Steinway.

"Does it bother you to have me around when you practice?"

Leo didn't look up.

"I'll go away."

"Please," he said. "It isn't me. But I'm afraid that Mr. Steinway doesn't—respond to you properly."

That tore it. *That* ripped it to shreds. "Now wait a minute," I said, coolly (if white-hot rage is cool). "Are we doing a scene from *Harvey*, now? Is this some more of your Solar Science, and am I to infer that Mr. Steinway is alive? I admit I'm not very bright, not overly perceptive, and I couldn't be expected to share your sensitive reactions. So I've never noticed that Mr. Steinway had an existence of his own. As a matter of fact, to me, it's just another piano. And its legs don't begin to compare with my own."

"Dorothy, please—"

"Dorothy doesn't please! Dorothy isn't going to say one more word in the presence of your—your—incubus, or whatever it is! So *Mr.* Steinway doesn't *respond* to me properly, is that it? Well, you tell *Mr.* Steinway for me that he can go plumb to——"

Somehow he got me out of the apartment, into the sunlight, into the park, into his arms. And it was peaceful there, and his voice was soft, and far away the birds made a song that hurt me in my throat.

"... so you weren't far wrong at that, darling," Leo told me. "I know it's hard to believe for anyone who hasn't studied Solar Science or ultrakinetic phenomena. But Mr. Steinway *is* alive in a way. I can communicate with him, and he can communicate with me."

"You *talk* to it? It *talks* to you?"

His laughter was reassuring, and I desperately wanted to be reassured, now. "Of course not. I'm talking about vibrationary communication. Look at it this way, darling. I don't want to sound like a lecturer—but this is science, not imagination.

"Did you ever stop to think what makes a piano? It's a highly complicated arrangement of substances and materials—thousands of tiny, carefully calculated operations go into the construction of a truly fine instrument. In a way, the result is comparable to the creation of an artificial being; a musical robot. To begin with, there's a dozen different kinds of wood, of various ages and conditions. There're special finishes, and felt, gut, animal matter, varnish, metal, ivory—a combination of elements infinitely complex. And each has its own vibrationary rate, which in turn forms part of the greater vibrationary rate of the whole. These vibrations can be sensed, contacted and understood."

I listened, because I wanted to find sense and sanity and serenity somewhere in it all. I wanted to believe, because this was Leo talking.

"Now, one thing more, and that's the crux of the matter. When vibration occurs, as it does in all being, electronic structure is disturbed. There's an action sequence—and a record of that action is made on the cellular structure.

"Now if you record many messages on a single piece of tape at different speeds, you'd have to play them back at these speeds in order to understand the message as a whole. Inability to do so would keep you from knowing or comprehending these messages. That's what ordinarily bars our communication with non-human life forms and gives us the impression that they have neither thought nor sentience.

"Since we humans use the development of the human brain as criterion, we aren't aware of the intelligence of other life-forms. We don't know how intelligent they are because we, most of us, don't realize that rocks and trees and everything in the material universe can 'think' or 'record' or 'communicate' at its own level.

"That's what Solar Science has taught me—and it has given me the method of entering into communication with such forms. Naturally, it isn't simple. But from self-awareness I have slowly proceeded into a more general awareness of vibrationary rates. It's only logical that Mr. Steinway, so much a part of my life and a part of me, would be a logical subject for an experiment in communication. I've made that experiment and succeeded, at least partially. I can share communication with Mr. Steinway; and it's not all one-way, I assure you. You remember what the Bible said about 'sermons in stones'—it's literally true."

Of course he said more than that, and less, and in different words. But I got the idea. I got the idea only too well. Leo wasn't altogether rational.

"It's really a functional entity, too, darling," he was saying. "Mr. Steinway has a personality all his own. And it's a growing one, thanks to my ability to communicate with him in turn. When I practice, Mr. Steinway practices. When I play, Mr. Steinway plays. In a sense, Mr. Steinway does the actual playing and I'm really only the mechanism that starts the operation. It may sound incredible to you, Dorothy, but I'm not fooling when I say there are things Mr. Steinway refuses to play. There are concert halls he doesn't like, certain tuning practices he refuses to respond to or adjust to. He's a temperamental artist, believe me, but he's a great one! And I respect his individuality and his talent.

"Give me a chance, darling—a chance to communicate with him until he understands you and your place in our lives. I can override his jealousy; after all, isn't it natural that he'd be jealous? Let me attune our vibrations, until he senses the reality of your presence as I sense it. Please, try not to think of me as crazy. It's not hallucination. Believe me."

I stood up. "All right, Leo. I believe you. But the rest is up to you. I shan't be seeing you again until—until you've made some arrangements."

My high heels clip-clip-clipped up the path. He didn't try to follow me. A cloud covered the sun, wrapped it in a ragged cloth, torn and dirty. Torn and dirty—

I went to Harry, of course. After all, he was Leo's agent and he'd know. But he *didn't* know. I found that out at once, and I cut myself off before I said too much. As far as Harry was concerned, Leo was perfectly normal.

"Except, of course, you may be thinking of that business with his mother. The old lady's death hit him pretty hard: you know what show business moms are like. She ran the whole shooting-match for years, and when she kicked off like that, he kind of went haywire for a while. But he's all right now. A good man, Leo. A comer. Thinking of a European flier next season—they think Solomon is such hot stuff. Wait until they hear Leo."

That's what I got out of Harry, and it wasn't much. Or *was* it?

It was enough to set me thinking, as I walked home—thinking about little Leo Weinstein, the boy prodigy, and his adoring mother. She watched over him, shielded him, saw to it that he practiced and rehearsed, regulated the details of his life so he came to depend upon her utterly. And then, when he made his debut like a good boy, she gave him Mr. Steinway.

Leo had cracked up, a bit, when she died. I could imagine that very easily. He had cracked up until he turned to his mother's gift for support. Mr. Steinway had taken over. Mr. Steinway was more than a piano, but not in the way Leo said. In reality, Mr. Steinway had become a surrogate for the mother. An extension of the Oedipus-situation, wasn't that what they called it?

Everything was falling into a pattern, now. Leo, lying on the couch and looking as though he were dead—returning, in fantasy, to the womb. Leo "communicating" with the vibrations of inanimate objects—trying to maintain contact with his mother beyond the grave.

That was it, that must be it, and I knew no way of fighting the situation. Silver cord from the mother or silver chord from the piano—it formed a Gordian knot either way, and I was weaponless.

I arrived at my apartment and my decision simultaneously. Leo was out of my life. Except—

He was waiting for me in the hall.

Oh, it's easy to be logical, and reason matters out coldly, and decide on a sensible course of action. Until somebody holds you in his arms, and you have the feeling that you *belong* there and he promises you that things will be different from now on, he understands, he can't live without you. He said all the tried and true things, the trite and true things, the right and true things. And all that had gone before faded away with the daylight, and the stars came out and spread their splendour . . .

I must be very exact now. It's important that I be exact. I want to tell just how it was the next afternoon when I walked around to his apartment.

The door was open and I came in, and it was like coming home. Until I saw that the sliding doors to the other room were closed, until I started towards them, until I heard the music. Leo—and Mr. Steinway—were playing again.

I called it "music", but it wasn't *that*, any more than the sudden anguished scream thrust from a human throat is normal communication. All I can say is that the piano was playing and the sound came to me as vibrations, and for the first time I understood something of what Leo had meant.

For I heard, and understood that I heard, the shrill trumpeting of elephants, the deep groaning of boughs in the night wind, the crash of toppling timber, the slow rumble of ore filling a furnace, the hideous hissing of molten metal, the screech of steel, the agonized whine of sandpaper, the tormented thrum of twisted strings. The voices that were not voices spoke, the inanimate was animate, and Mr. Steinway was alive.

Until I slid the doors open, and the sound suddenly ceased, and I saw Mr. Steinway sitting there alone.

Yes, he was alone, and I saw it as surely as I saw Leo slumped in the chair on the far side of the room, with the look of death on his face.

He couldn't have stopped in time and run across the room to that chair—any more than he could have composed that atonal *allegro* Mr. Steinway played.

Then I shook Leo, and he came alive again, and I was crying in his arms and telling him what I'd heard, and hearing him say, "It's happened, you can see that now, can't you? Mr. Steinway exists—he communicates directly—he's an integrated personality. Communication is a two-way affair, after all. And he can tap my energy, take what he needs from me to function. When I let go, he takes over. Don't you see?"

I saw. And I tried to keep the fear from my eyes, tried to banish it from my voice, when I spoke to him. "Come into the other room, Leo. Now. Hurry, and don't ask questions."

I didn't want questions, because I didn't want to tell him that I was afraid to talk in Mr. Steinway's presence. Because Mr. Steinway could hear, and he was jealous.

I didn't want Mr. Steinway to hear when I told Leo, "You've

got to get rid of it. I don't care if it's alive or if we're both crazy. The important thing is to get rid of it, now. Get away from it. Together."

He nodded, but I didn't want nods.

"Listen to me, Leo! This is the only time I'll ask it, and your only chance to answer. Will you come away with me now, today? I mean it—pack a suitcase. Meet me at my apartment in half an hour. I'll phone Harry, tell him something, anything. We haven't time for anything more. I know we haven't time."

Leo looked at me, and his face started to go dead, and I took a deep breath, waiting for the sound to start again from the room beyond—but his eyes met mine, and then the color came back to his face and he smiled at me, *with* me, and he said, "I'll see you in twenty minutes. With suitcase."

I went down the stairs swiftly, and I know I had perfect control. I had perfect control out on the street, too, until I heard the vibrations of my own high heels. And the sound of tires on the pavement, and the singing of the telephone wires in the wind, and the *snick* of traffic-lights, and the creaking of an awning, and then came the sense of the sounds *under* the sounds and I heard the voice of the city. There's agony in asphalt and a slow melancholy in concrete, and wood is tortured when it splinters, and the vibrations of a piece of cloth twisted into clothing weaves terror from a threnody of thread. And all around me I felt the waves, the endless waves, beating in and pulsing over, pouring out their life.

Nothing looked different, and everything was changed. For the world was *alive*. For the first time, everything in the world came alive, and I sensed the struggle to survive. And the steps in my hallway were alive, and the banister was a long brown serpent, and it hurt the key to be twisted in the lock, and the bed sagged and the springs complained when I put down the suitcase and crushed my protesting clothes into its confines. And the mirror was a silver shimmer of torment, and the lipstick was being bruised by my lips, and I could never, never eat food again.

But I did what I had to do, and I glanced at my watch and tried to hear only the ticking, not the cries of coils and the moan of metal; tried to see only the time and not the hands that turned in ceaseless supplication.

Twenty minutes.

Only, now, forty minutes had passed. And I hadn't even phoned Harry yet (the black mouthpiece, the bakelite corroding, the wires nailed to the crosses of telephone poles) and I couldn't phone because Leo wasn't here.

To go down again into the street was more than flesh could bear, but the need was stronger than the needs of flesh. And I went out into the seething symphony where all sound was vibration and all vibration was life, and I came to Leo's apartment and everything was dark.

Everything was dark except Mr. Steinway's teeth, gleaming like the tusks of elephants in forests of ebony and teak. Leo couldn't have moved Mr. Steinway from the inner room to the outer room. And he hated Chopin. He wouldn't sit there in the dark playing the *Funeral March* . . .

Mr. Steinway's teeth were spotted with little drops and they gleamed, too. And Mr. Steinway's heavy legs were wet. They brushed against me, because Mr. Steinway was rolling and rumbling towards me across the room, and he was playing and playing and telling me to look, look, look at the floor where I could see Leo dead, *really* dead, and all the power was Mr. Steinway's now, the power to play, the power to live, the power to kill. . .

Yes, it's true. I scraped the box and liberated the sulphur and released the flame and started the fire and let its roaring drown out the vibrations, drown out the voice of Mr. Steinway as he screamed and gnashed his eighty-eight teeth. I set the fire. I admit it. I killed Mr. Steinway. I admit it.

But I *didn't* kill Leo.

Why don't you ask *them? They're* burned, but *they* know. Ask the sofa. Ask the rug. Ask the pictures on the wall. *They* saw it happen. *They* know I'm not guilty.

You can do it. All you need is the ability to communicate with the vibrations. Just as I'm doing it now. See? I can hear everything they're saying, right in this room. I can understand the cot, and the walls, and the doors, and the bars.

I don't have anything more to say. If you don't believe me, if you won't help me, then go away. Let me just sit here and listen. Listen to the bars . . .

The Proper Spirit

Mr. Ronald Cavendish wheeled the laden tea-cart into the dining room. Depositing the *entree* and side-dishes on the table, he turned and surveyed himself in the mirror.

What he saw did not displease him. He was, he reflected—and so did the mirror—a gentleman of the old school. A cynic might have dismissed him as type-casting for a stage butler, but Mr. Cavendish took little heed of cynics.

The fashionable address of his old brownstone house, the solidity of the mahogany and sterling amongst its contents, the tangibility of his banked assets; all were sufficient answers to cynics. Yes, and that included cynical relatives, too.

Mr. Cavendish made a face at the mirror. It was not a nice grimace and he wished his relatives could see it. Well, they'd be seeing it soon enough, over the dinner-table.

Here it was, six o'clock, and everything was arranged. Everything was quite ready for them.

Ready. Mr. Cavendish crossed hastily to the parlor. He'd almost forgotten something. The big Sarouk had been rolled back, and now he knelt on the bare floor and rubbed out the blue chalk-marks with his handkerchief. It would never do to let them see the pentagram. And he'd better light incense, to get that faint odor out of the room. Someone could just possibly recognize it.

"There." Mr. Cavendish stood up, flexing his knee joints. After all, he was pushing sixty—or was sixty pushing him, eh? Might be a good idea to check on the affair of that fellow, what's-his-name, Doctor Faust. Perhaps there was a similar deal available to him without, of course, the element of risk. Maybe tonight, after the family dinner, he could hold a little session and inquire of—

Ping!

Mr. Cavendish shot his cuffs and marched to answer the doorbell. He had just time to assume his "dear old Uncle Ronald" expression, and then they burst past him into the parlor.

Fat, simpering Clara, wizened little Edwin, sideburned Harry, and hennaed Dell. Last one in is a dirty dog—that would be Jasper, of course. He wheezed and he waddled and he joined the inane medley of "Hello, Uncle Ronald," and "My, you're looking fit," and "Just like old times, the family all together under one roof again."

Seats. Cigarettes. Tiny glasses of brandy. Ronald Cavendish saw to all the amenities, and even managed a smile when Edward lifted his glass and murmured, "To your good health."

Then, "Shall we go in to dinner?" he proposed. "I have everything waiting."

At the mention of dinner, Jasper was already on his feet. A greedy type. But then they were all greedy, Mr. Cavendish reflected, wistfully.

Take Clara. "My, what a lovely silver service." That was Clara. Her gimlet eyes peering from folds of fat needed only a jeweler's loop to complete the picture as she took inventory down to the last penny.

Edwin, her husband, sniffed the brandy. "Napoleon or Armangac, Uncle Ronald?" he asked. As if Mr. Cavendish would serve Napoleon to them, and before dinner, too! Edwin didn't know, but he lusted to learn. It wasn't money he wanted, but luxury.

Then there was Harry. "Squab under glass, by golly! You must have been playing the winners, eh, Unc?" Thus Harry, at sight of the breast of guinea-hen. Harry with his racing-form and his— ugh!—"Unc". Harry was greedy for luck.

And Dell. Mr. Cavendish contemplated her kohled, cold eyes and the figure alternately swelled and svelte. He knew what *she* was greedy for. Right now she probably found it easily available during those afternoons when Harry was out at the track; in ten years she'd need money for gigolos, or whatever they called them nowadays.

Nowadays. That's what Jasper was talking about. Mr. Cavendish forced himself to pay attention.

"Nowadays you seldom sit down to a meal like this." *Chomp-chomp.* "Don't know how you do it, Ronald, with Grace gone these seven years." *Chomp-chomp*. "Rattling around in a big old barn like this, without servants or anyone to look after you. Wish you'd"—*chomp-chomp*—"move down to the Club with me."

Yes, that was Jasper. Move down to the Club and let him take over. Lock, stock and barrel. He'd handle the sale of the house and the investments like a big, benevolent brother-in-law. Mr. Cavendish, who always prided himself on giving the devil his due, had to admire Jasper's utter impartiality—*he* was greedy about *everything*.

So thinking, he addressed himself to a glass of warm milk and partook of French toast from a small casserole set beside his plate.

"Whassamatter, Unc, this chow too rich for you?" This from Harry, along with a gratuitous dirty look from wife Dell which he ignored.

"Touch of ulcers," Mr. Cavendish said. "Doctor's orders."

"Doctor?" Clara brightened. "Have you been seeing Doctor Barton again? What did he say? Nothing serious, I hope. You know, lots of times they say it's ulcers, but it turns out to be stomach can—"

"*Errumph!*" Edwin knew how to turn her off, and he thought he was doing it just in time. "I'm sure Uncle Ronald takes good care of himself, dear. Seven years a widower, and you'd never know it from this table."

"Thank you," said Mr. Cavendish. "Might I help you to another guinea-hen? There's plenty here for all."

"I'm ready," Jasper said. "And some of that sauce. Never tasted better. For an old bachelor, you do yourself proud. Of course, the chef at the Club—"

"How come you never re-married?" Dell asked. "The women would be after a man like you in droves. I mean, you're still sort of well-preserved like, and with all that moola—"

It was Harry's turn to issue an unlaundered glance. But Mr. Cavendish was not offended.

"You know the reason," he said. "I still have Grace with me whenever I want her."

Well, here it was. Mr. Cavendish braced himself for the onslaught.

Jasper was the first to waddle over the barricade, armored in false geniality. "Really, Ronald," he said. "We're a bit disturbed, all of us. This morbid fancy of yours—that Grace is always with you—it's not sound."

"Neither are your assumptions," Mr. Cavendish answered, helping Jasper to his third portion, with more of the savory sauce. "My belief is neither morbid nor a fancy. Ever since the dawn of history, enlightened men have known it's possible for the departed to return when properly summoned. If you'd investigate the annals of psychic research, you'd understand that communication with the spirits is quite commonplace."

Clara offered a fatlipped pout. "You see?" she addressed the others. "It's just like I said, not Uncle Ronald's fault at all. He's merely repeating what that crazy medium told him—the one he went to after Grace died. She's the one who filled him with all this nonsense."

Edwin was *errumph*ing violently.

Mr. Cavendish smiled and served coffee. "It's true I went to a medium after Grace's passing. You all know that, and I shall not distress you by alluding to the hullabaloo you stirred up when you heard of it. But you needn't have worried. After a few visits I made a most gratifying discovery. I learned that a medium was unnecessary—I, myself, am a psychic sensitive. Since then I have conducted my own investigations. I dare say I've managed to go further than most practicing mediums today."

"Ghosts!" Dell shuddered. "I hate to talk about 'em. Not that I believe in that stuff, understand."

"If you did, you'd not be subject to either fear or hatred," Mr. Cavendish assured her. "Actually, except for certain limitations, they're just like one of us. Take Grace, for example. The last time I saw her she seemed as real as you are."

"Be reasonable, Ronald," said Jasper. "You don't mean to tell us you spend all your time talking to the imaginary spirit of your dead wife?"

Ronald Cavendish finished the last of his French toast, took a sip of milk, and then lit the candles on the table.

Tapers put forth blossoms to flower against the shadows.

"I've told you no such thing," he declared. "True, at first I spent a good deal of time with Grace here. But—I blush to admit it—I tired of that. Of *her*, rather. Why, I asked myself, should I confine my companionship to Grace when there are so many other fascinating personalities available? After all, our marriage ended with her passing; where she is now, there's neither marriage nor giving in marriage. So for your information, I haven't summoned Grace for over four years."

"You mean you've given up all this medium malarkey?" Harry asked.

"Quite the contrary. It's just that there's such an infinite number of other contacts available to me." Mr. Cavendish smiled in the shadows. "I wish I could make you understand. Why, it's like having the combined libraries of all the world right here at your fingertips. It's like owning the greatest museum, the largest record collection. You've seen my pianoforte in the parlor, for example. Oftentimes during dinner I regale myself with the music of Handel and Haydn—played by the composers themselves."

"Nuttier'n a fruitcake!" Dell murmured, but Mr. Cavendish didn't hear her.

"Think of being able to summon the greatest shades in history," he continued. "To be able to converse with Shakespeare, Julius Caesar, Napoleon, while listening to Chopin at the piano."

"You mean them dead longhairs come here and knock out tunes?" Harry was fascinated in spite of himself. "Say, about those spirits, now. Is it true they can see the future? I mean, like say if there's gonna be a horse in the sixth at Belmont tomorra, you think maybe somebody like Michael Angelo or whatever could give you a tip?"

Mr. Cavendish smiled. "Perhaps," he said. "Although I've never cared for racing."

"Enough of this!" Even in the shadows, Jasper's face loomed in mottled purple. "I'm getting dizzy myself, and no wonder. Ronald, you're talking like a madman. And in such a case, we have no choice but to treat you as one."

"Calling up the ghost of Napoleon!" Clara scoffed. "I'll say he's crazy, all right. Grace's ghost isn't good enough for him any more, he says. Suppose he wants us to believe he spends his evenings with Cleopatra."

"A very much overrated female, I assure you," said Mr. Cavendish, softly. "Of course, I may be doing the lady an injustice, owing to the language barrier. Although my opinion is not based upon our lingual activities alone."

"You been playing around with the famous babes of history?" Dell grew suddenly animated. "That sounds kinda interesting, you know? I mean, I always wondered about some of them. Take this here Madame Pompadour, and Anne Boleyn."

Mr. Cavendish shuddered slightly. "I'd rather not talk about *her*," he said. "When I summoned that particular young woman, I'd forgotten she had been decapitated. She appeared with her head tucked underneath her arm."

Jasper punctuated his remarks with a resounding belch, then turned to Ronald Cavendish with the humoring smile generally reserved for those in their first or second childhood.

"Ronald, you've got to listen to us now. After all, we're your *family*. We've tried to be patient. Very patient." And he registered his interpretation of patience; his head cocked for all the world like a fat vulture perched on a limb above its victim.

"We've tolerated your eccentricities," Jasper continued. "But outsiders won't take so charitable a view. What will other people say when they hear such things?"

"Nothing," replied Mr. Cavendish. "Unless you tell them."

"I'm afraid the time has come when someone has to be told," Jasper answered. "After all, you're—*burp!*—responsible for a sizeable fortune. If the banks and your brokers ever got wind of your ideas, they'd go wild."

Jasper had never been a brilliant speaker, Mr. Cavendish reflected, but this time he was apparently surpassing his most boring previous efforts. It appeared as though he had already put Edwin and Clara to dozing, and Harry slouched in his chair in a listless fashion. But for some reason, Mr. Cavendish himself was fascinated by what he heard.

"What are you driving at?" he demanded, suddenly.

"Well, it's not me, understand—it's all of us. We got together beforehand and talked things over. We agreed the best solution would be for you to step out of the active investment end. You aren't getting any younger, and perhaps the strain contributes to your—*burp!*—eccentricities. Time for you to sit back and take things easy. What I suggest is that you turn over your power-of-attorney to someone. Me, for instance. I can handle the estate for you without any trouble. You just sit back and enjoy yourself. This is serious, Ronald. I'm making you a fair offer. Surrender your power-of-attorney and go on living as you like. Call up all the spooks you want; we won't mind. If not—"

Jasper belched again, portentously. "If not, we'd have no choice. We'd be forced to call in an alienist. You know what that means. Why, on the basis of what we've heard here tonight alone, you'd be certified in jig-time. Right, folks?"

He glanced down the table and noted that a slumber-party was in progress. "Too hot in here," he complained. "Can't you open a window or something?"

"Presently," Mr. Cavendish told him.

Jasper fumbled at his vest. "Sauce too rich for my blood," he murmured. "Got to watch that—doctor told me—" He slumped forward in a doze. Before drifting off he managed a weak wheeze. "What's the answer?"

Mr. Cavendish stood up. He leaned forward and spoke quite loudly, as if to waken his guests and make sure they heard every word.

"My answer," he said, "is no. No power-of-attorney, no alienist, no asylum. Do you hear that, my dear family? This is a farewell dinner. For tonight, having liquidated all my assets, I am flying to Thibet, to pursue my studies in the occult sciences.

"Yes," he continued, "this is a farewell. A long farewell. But I perceive you have already departed."

Indeed, they had. Slumped and seated in the shadows, there was no longer a semblance of sleep. Sightlessly staring at the skeletal remnants of the guinea-hens, the family was quite dead.

Mr. Cavendish surveyed them, shuddered slightly, and prayed that no medium would ever be unfortunate enough to evoke them.

Then he moved around the table, glanced at his watch, and noted that he had less than an hour to reach the airport. He opened the sideboard door and extracted a bulging valise.

There. He was ready now. He stepped back to the table and bent over the tapers. "Out, brief candle," he said.

Mr. Cavendish was in the dark, but he was not afraid. Some of his best friends were in the dark. He'd met some very nice people under those circumstances. Madame Pompadour, Dell had said. Ha! He could have told her about Guinevere, and Montespan, and Helen of Troy. There was life in the old dog yet, and he had quite a way with the ladies.

Ladies. That reminded him of something. He couldn't leave without showing the proper spirit.

Mr. Cavendish chuckled. "Proper spirit" indeed! Why, he owed the entire success of tonight's party to the proper spirit.

It was time to express his gratitude for the guinea-hen, with its most unusual savory sauce. Perhaps the kitchen was still occupied—at any rate, he'd make the gesture. Pure genius, his summoning a culinary expert for the last meal.

Mr. Cavendish tiptoed quietly to the kitchen door, opened it just a trifle, and whispered into the darkness.

"Thank you, Lucrezia," said Mr. Cavendish.

Catnip

Ronnie Shires stood before the mirror and slicked back his hair. He straightened his new sweater and stuck out his chest. Sharp! Had to watch the way he looked, with graduation only a few weeks away and that election for class president coming up. If he could get to be president then, next year in high school he'd be a real wheel. Go out for second team or something. But he had to watch the angles—

"Ronnie! Better hurry or you'll be late!"

Ma came out of the kitchen, carrying his lunch. Ronnie wiped the grin off his face. She walked up behind him and put her arms around his waist.

"Hon, I only wish your father were here to see you—"

Ronnie wriggled free. "Yeah, sure. Say, Ma."

"Yes?"

"How's about some loot, huh? I got to get some things today."

"Well, I suppose. But try to make it last, son. This graduation costs a lot of money, seems to me."

"I'll pay you back some day." He watched her as she fumbled in her apron pocket and produced a wadded-up dollar bill.

"Thanks. See you." He picked up his lunch and ran outside. He walked along, smiling and whistling, knowing Ma was watching him from the window. She was always watching him, and it was a real drag.

Then he turned the corner, halted under a tree, and fished out a cigarette. He lit it and sauntered slowly across the street, puffing deeply. Out of the corner of his eye he watched the Ogden house just ahead.

Sure enough, the front screen door banged and Marvin Ogden came down the steps. Marvin was fifteen, one year older than Ronnie, but smaller and skinnier. He wore glasses and stuttered when he got excited, but he was valedictorian of the graduating class.

Ronnie came up behind him, walking fast.

"Hello, Snot-face!"

Marvin wheeled. He avoided Ronnie's glare, but smiled weakly at the pavement.

"I said hello, Snot-face! What's the matter, don't you know your own name, jerk?"

"Hello—Ronnie."

"How's old Snot-face today?"

"Aw, gee, Ronnie. Why do you have to talk like that? I never did anything to you, did I?"

Ronnie spit in the direction of Marvin's shoes. "I'd like to see you just try doing something to me, you four-eyed little——"

Marvin began to walk away, but Ronnie kept pace.

"Slow down, jag. I wanna talk to you."

"Wh-what is it, Ronnie? I don't want to be late."

"Shut your yap."

"But—"

"Listen, you. What was the big idea in History exam yesterday when you pulled your paper away?"

"You know, Ronnie. You aren't supposed to copy somebody else's answers."

"You trying to tell me what to do, square?"

"N-no. I mean, I only want to keep you out of trouble. What if Miss Sanders found out, and you want to be elected class president? Why, if anybody knew—"

Ronnie put his hand on Marvin's shoulder. He smiled. "You wouldn't ever tell her about it, would you, Snot-face?" he murmured.

"Of course not! Cross my heart!"

Ronnie continued to smile. He dug his fingers into Marvin's shoulder. With his other hand he swept Marvin's books to the ground. As Marvin bent forward to pick them up, he kicked Marvin as hard as he could, bringing his knee up fast. Marvin sprawled on the sidewalk. He began to cry. Ronnie watched him as he attempted to rise.

"This is just a sample of what you got coming if you squeal," he said. He stepped on the fingers of Marvin's left hand. "Creep!"

Marvin's snivelling faded from his ears as he turned the corner at the end of the block. Mary June was waiting for him under the trees. He came up behind her and slapped her, hard.

"Hello, you!" he said.

Mary June jumped about a foot, her curls bouncing on her shoulders. Then she turned and saw who it was.

"Oh, Ronnie! You oughtn't to—"

"Shut up. I'm in a hurry. Can't be late the day before election. You lining up the chicks?"

"Sure, Ronnie. You know, I promised. I had Ellen and Vicky over at the house last night and they said they'd vote for you for sure. All the girls are gonna vote for you."

"Well, they better." Ronnie threw his cigarette butt against a rosebush in the Eisners' yard.

"Ronnie—you be careful—want to start a fire?"

"Quit bossing me." He scowled.

"I'm not trying to boss you, Ronnie. Only—"

"Aw, you make me sick!" He quickened his pace, and the girl bit her lip as she endeavored to keep step with him. "Ronnie, wait for me!"

"Wait for me!" he mocked her. "What's the matter, you afraid you'll get lost or something?"

"No. *You* know. I don't like to pass that old Mrs. Mingle's place. She always stares at me and makes faces."

"She's nuts!"

"I'm scared of her, Ronnie. Aren't you?"

"Me scared of that old bat? She can go take a flying leap!"

"Don't talk so loud, she'll hear you."

"Who cares?"

Ronnie marched boldly past the tree-shadowed cottage behind the rusted iron fence. He stared insolently at the girl, who made herself small against his shoulder, eyes averted from the ramshackle edifice. He deliberately slackened his pace as they passed the cottage, with its boarded-up windows, screened-in porch and general air of withdrawal from the world.

Mrs. Mingle herself was not in evidence today. Usually she could be seen in the weed-infested garden at the side of the cottage; a tiny, dried-up old woman, bending over her vines and plants, mumbling incessantly to herself or to the raddled black tomcat which served as her constant companion.

"Old prune-face ain't around!" Ronnie observed, loudly. "Must be off someplace on her broomstick."

"Ronnie—please!"

"Who cares?" Ronnie pulled Mary June's curls. "You dames are scared of everything, ain't you?"

"*Aren't*, Ronnie."

"Don't tell *me* how to talk!" Ronnie's gaze shifted again to the silent house, huddled in the shadows. A segment of shadow at the side of the cottage seemed to be moving. A black blur detached itself from the end of the porch. Ronnie recognized Mrs. Mingle's cat. It minced down the path towards the gate.

Quickly, Ronnie stooped and found a rock. He grasped it, rose, aimed, and hurled the missile in one continuous movement.

The cat hissed, then squawled in pain as the rock grazed its ribs.

"Oh, Ronnie!"

"Come on, let's run before she sees us!"

They flew down the street. The school bell drowned out the cat-yowl.

"Here we go," said Ronnie. "You do my homework for me? Good. Give it here once."

He snatched the papers from Mary June's hand and sprinted ahead. The girl stood watching him, smiling her admiration. From behind the fence the cat watched, too, and licked its jaws.

2.

It happened that afternoon, after school. Ronnie and Joe Gordan and Seymour Higgins were futzing around with a baseball and he was talking about the outfit Ma promised to buy him this summer if the dressmaking business picked up. Only he made it sound as if he was getting the outfit for sure, and that they could all use the mask and mitt. It didn't hurt to build it up a little, with election tomorrow. He had to stand in good with the whole gang.

He knew if he hung around the school yard much longer, Mary June would come out and want him to walk her home. He was sick of her. Oh, she was all right for homework and such stuff, but these guys would just laugh at him if he went off with a dame.

So he said how about going down the street to in front of the pool hall and maybe hang around to see if somebody would shoot a game? He'd pay. Besides, they could smoke.

Ronnie knew that these guys didn't smoke, but it sounded cool and that's what he wanted. They all followed him down the street, pounding their cleats on the sidewalk. It made a lot of noise, because everything was so quiet.

All Ronnie could hear was the cat. They were passing Mrs. Mingle's and there was this cat, rolling around in the garden on its back and on its stomach, playing with some kind of ball. It purred and meowed and whined.

"Look!" yelled Joe Gordan. "Dizzy cat's havin' a fit 'r something, huh?"

"Lice," said Ronnie. "Damned mangy old thing's fulla lice and fleas and stuff. I socked it a good one this morning."

"Ya did?"

"Sure. With a rock. This big, too." He made a watermelon with his hands.

"Weren't you afraid of old lady Mingle?"

"Afraid? Why, that dried-up old——"

"Catnip," said Seymour Higgins. "That's what he's got. Ball of catnip. Old Mingle buys it for him. My old man says she buys everything for that cat; special food and sardines. Treats it like a baby. Ever see them walk down the street together?"

"Catnip, huh?" Joe peered through the fence. "Wonder why they like it so much. Gets 'em wild, doesn't it? Cat's'll do anything for catnip."

The cat squealed, sniffing and clawing at the ball. Ronnie scowled at it. "I hate cats. Somebody oughta drowned that damn thing."

"Better not let Mrs. Mingle hear you talk like that," Seymour cautioned. "She'll put the evil eye on you."

"Bull!"

"Well, she grows them herbs and stuff and my old lady says—"

"Bull!"

"All right. But I wouldn't go monkeying around her or her old cat, either."

"I'll show you."

Before he knew it, Ronnie was opening the gate. He advanced towards the black tomcat as the boys gaped.

The cat crouched over the catnip, eyes flattened against a velveteen skull. Ronnie hesitated a moment, gauging the glitter of claws, the glare of agate eyes. But the gang was watching—

"Scat!" he shouted. He advanced, waving his arms. The cat sidled backwards. Ronnie feinted with his hand and scooped up the catnip ball.

"See? I got it, you guys. I got—"

"Put that down!"

He didn't see the door open. He didn't see her walk down the steps. But suddenly she was there. Leaning on her cane, wearing a black dress that fitted tightly over her tiny frame, she seemed hardly any bigger than the cat which crouched at her side. Her hair was grey and wrinkled and dead, her face was grey and wrinkled and dead, but her eyes—

They were agate eyes, like the cat's. They glowed. And when she talked, she spit the way the cat did.

"Put that down, young man!"

Ronnie began to shake. It was only a chill, everybody gets chills now and then, and could he help it if he shook so hard the catnip just fell out of his hand?

He wasn't scared. He had to show the gang he wasn't scared of this skinny little dried-up old woman. It was hard to breathe, he was shaking so, but he managed. He filled his lungs and opened his mouth.

"You—you old witch!" he yelled.

The agate eyes widened. They were bigger than she was. All he could see were the eyes. Witch eyes. Now that he said it, he knew it was true. Witch. She was a witch.

"You insolent puppy. I've a good mind to cut out your lying tongue!"

Geez, she wasn't kidding!

Now she was coming closer, and the cat was inching up on

him, and then she raised the cane in the air, she was going to hit him, the witch was after him, oh Ma, no, don't, oh—

Ronnie ran.

3.

Could he help it? Geez, the guys ran too. They'd run before he did, even. He had to run, the old bat was crazy, anybody could see that. Besides, if he'd stayed she'd of tried to hit him and maybe he'd let her have it. He was only trying to keep out of trouble. That was all.

Ronnie told it to himself over and over at supper time. But that didn't do any good, telling it to himself. It was the guys he had to tell it to, and fast. He had to explain it before election tomorrow—

"Ronnie. What's the matter? You sick?"

"No, Ma."

"Then why don't you answer a person? I declare, you haven't said ten words since you came in the house. And you aren't eating your supper."

"Not hungry."

"Something bothering you, son?"

"No. Leave me alone."

"It's that election tomorrow, isn't it?"

"Leave me alone." Ronnie rose. "I'm goin' out."

"Ronnie!"

"I got to see Joe. Important."

"Back by nine, remember."

"Yeah. Sure."

He went outside. The night was cool. Windy for this time of year. Ronnie shivered a little as he turned the corner. Maybe a cigarette—

He lit a match and a shower of sparks spiralled to the sky. Ronnie began to walk, puffing nervously. He had to see Joe and the others and explain. Yeah, right now, too. If they told anybody else—

It was dark. The light on the corner was out, and Ogdens weren't home. That made it darker, because Mrs. Mingle never showed a light in her cottage.

Mrs. Mingle. Her cottage was up ahead. He'd better cross the street.

What was the matter with him? Was he getting chicken-guts? Afraid of that damned old woman, that old witch! He puffed, gulped, expanded his chest. Just let her try anything. Just let her be hiding under the trees waiting to grab out at him with her big claws and hiss—what was he talking about, anyway? That was the cat. Nuts to her cat, and her too. He'd show them!

Ronnie walked past the dark shadow where Mrs. Mingle dwelt. He whistled defiance, and emphasized it by shooting his cigarette butt across the fence. Sparks flew and were swallowed by the mouth of the night.

Ronnie paused and peered over the fence. Everything was black and still. There was nothing to be afraid of. Everything was black—

Everything except that flicker. It came from up the path, under the porch. He could see the porch now because there was a light. Not a steady light; a wavering light. Like a fire. A fire—where his cigarette had landed! The cottage was beginning to burn!

Ronnie gulped and clung to the fence. Yes, it was on fire all right. Mrs. Mingle would come out and the firemen would come and they'd find the butt and see him and then—

He fled down the street. The wind cat howled behind him, the wind that fanned the flames that burned the cottage—

Ma was in bed. He managed to slow down and walk softly as he slipped into the house, up the stairs. He undressed in the dark and sought the white womb between the bedsheets. When he got the covers over his head he had another chill. Lying there, trembling, not daring to look out of the window and see the glare from the other side of the block, Ronnie's teeth chattered. He knew he was going to pass out in a minute.

Then he heard the screaming from far away. Fire-engines. Somebody had called them. He needn't worry now. Why should the sound frighten him? It was only a siren, it wasn't Mrs. Mingle screaming, it couldn't be. She was all right. He was all right. Nobody knew . . .

Ronnie fell asleep with the wind and the siren wailing in his ears. His slumber was deep and only once was there an interruption. That was along towards morning, when he thought he heard a noise at the window. It was a scraping sound. The wind, of course. And it must have been the wind, too, that sobbed and whined and whimpered beneath the windowsill at dawn. It was only Ronnie's imagination, Ronnie's conscience, that transformed the sound into the wailing of a cat . . .

4.

"Ronnie!"

It wasn't the wind, it wasn't a cat. Ma was calling him.

"Ronnie! Oh, Ronnie!"

He opened his eyes, shielding them from the sunshafts.

"I declare, you might answer a person." He heard her grumbling to herself downstairs. Then she called again.

"Ronnie!"

"I'm coming, Ma."

He got out of bed, went to the bathroom, and dressed. She was waiting for him in the kitchen.

"Land sakes, you sure slept sound last night. Didn't you hear the fire-engines?"

Ronnie dropped a slice of toast. "What engines?"

Ma's voice rose. "Don't you know? Why boy, it was just awful—Mrs. Mingle's cottage burned down."

"Yeah?" He had trouble picking up the toast again.

"The poor old lady—just think of it—trapped in there—"

He had to shut her up. He couldn't stand what was coming next. But what could he say, how could he stop her?

"Burned alive. The whole place was on fire when they got there. The Ogdens saw it when they came home and Mr. Ogden called the firemen, but it was too late. When I think of that old lady it just makes me—"

Without a word, Ronnie rose from the table and left the room. He didn't wait for his lunch. He didn't bother to examine himself in the mirror. He went outside, before he cried, or screamed, or hauled off and hit Ma in the puss.

The puss—

It was waiting for him on the front walk. The black bundle with the agate eyes. The cat.

Mrs. Mingle's cat, waiting for him to come out.

Ronnie took a deep breath before he opened the gate. The cat didn't make a sound, didn't stir. It just hunched up on the sidewalk and stared at him.

He watched it for a moment, then cast about for a stick. There was a hunk of lath near the porch. He picked it up and swung it. Then he opened the gate.

"Scat!" he said.

The cat retreated. Ronnie walked away. The cat moved after him. Ronnie wheeled, brandishing the stick.

"Scram before I let you have it!"

The cat stood still.

Ronnie stared at it. Why hadn't the damn thing burned up in the fire? And what was it doing here?

He gripped the lath. It felt good between his fingers, splinters and all. Just let that mangy tom start anything—

He walked along, not looking back. What was the matter with him? Suppose the cat did follow him. It couldn't hurt him any. Neither could old Mingle. She was dead. The dirty witch. Talking about cutting his tongue out. Well, she got what was coming to her, all right. Too bad her scroungy cat was still around. If it didn't watch out, he'd fix it, too. He should worry now.

Nobody was going to find out about that cigarette. Mrs. Mingle was dead. He ought to be glad, everything was all right, sure, he felt great.

The shadow followed him down the street.

"Get out of here!"

Ronnie turned and heaved the lath at the cat. It hissed. Ronnie heard the wind hiss, heard his cigarette butt hiss, heard Mrs. Mingle hiss.

He began to run. The cat ran after him.

"Hey, Ronnie!"

Marvin Ogden was calling him. He couldn't stop now, not even to hit the punk. He ran on. The cat kept pace.

Then he was winded and he slowed down. It was just in time, too. Up ahead was a crowd of kids, standing on the sidewalk in front of a heap of charred, smoking boards.

They were looking at Mingle's cottage—

Ronnie closed his eyes and darted back up the street. The cat followed.

He had to get rid of it before he went to school. What if people saw him with her cat? Maybe they'd start to talk. He had to get rid of it—

Ronnie ran clear down to Sinclair Street. The cat was right behind him. On the corner he picked up a stone and let fly. The cat dodged. Then it sat down on the sidewalk and looked at him. Just looked.

Ronnie couldn't take his eyes off the cat. It stared so. Mrs. Mingle had stared, too. But she was dead. And this was only a cat. A cat he had to get away from, fast.

The streetcar came down Sinclair Street. Ronnie found a dime in his pocket and boarded the car. The cat didn't move. He stood on the platform as the car pulled away and looked back at the cat. It just sat there.

Ronnie rode around the loop, then transferred to the Hollis Avenue bus. It brought him over to the school, ten minutes late. He got off and started to hurry across the street.

A shadow crossed the entrance to the building.

Ronnie saw the cat. It squatted there, waiting.

He ran.

That's all Ronnie remembered of the rest of the morning. He ran. He ran, and the cat followed. He couldn't go to school, he couldn't be there for the election, he couldn't get rid of the cat. He ran.

Up and down the streets, back and forth, all over the whole neighborhood; stopping and dodging and throwing stones and swearing and panting and sweating. But always the running, and always the cat right behind him. Once it started to chase him and before he knew it he was heading straight for the place where the burned smell filled the air, straight for the ruins of Mrs. Mingle's cottage. The cat wanted him to go there, wanted him to see—

Ronnie began to cry. He sobbed and panted all the way home. The cat didn't make a sound. It followed him. All right, let it. He'd fix it. He'd tell Ma. Ma would get rid of it for him. Ma.

"Ma!"

He yelled as he ran up the steps.

No answer. She was out. Marketing.

And the cat crept up the steps behind him.

Ronnie slammed the door, locked it. Ma had her key. He was safe now. Safe at home. Safe in bed—he wanted to go to bed and pull the covers over his head, wait for Ma to come and make everything all right.

There was a scratching at the door.

"Ma!" His scream echoed through the empty house.

He ran upstairs. The scratching died away.

And then he heard the footsteps on the porch, the slow footsteps; he heard the rattling and turning of the doorknob. It was old lady Mingle, coming from the grave. It was the witch, coming to get him. It was—

"Ma!"

"Ronnie, what's the matter? What you doing home from school?"

He heard her. It was all right. Just in time, Ronnie closed his mouth. He couldn't tell her about the cat. He mustn't ever tell her. Then everything would come out. He had to be careful what he said.

"I got sick to my stomach," he said. "Miss Sanders said I should come home and lay down."

Then Ma was up the stairs, helping him undress, asking should she get the doctor, fussing over him and putting him to bed. And he could cry and she didn't know it wasn't from a gut-ache. What she didn't know wouldn't hurt her. It was all right.

Yes, it was all right now, and he was in bed. Ma brought him some soup for lunch. He wanted to ask her about the cat, but he didn't dare. Besides, he couldn't hear it scratching. Must have run away when Ma came home.

Ronnie lay in bed and dozed as the afternoon shadows ran in long black ribbons across the bedroom floor. He smiled to himself. What a sucker he was! Afraid of a cat. Maybe there wasn't even a cat—all in his mind. Dope!

"Ronnie—you all right?" Ma called up from the foot of the stairs.

"Yes, Ma. I feel lots better."

Sure, he felt better. He could get up now and eat supper if he wanted. In just a minute he'd put his clothes on and go downstairs. He started to push the sheets off. It was dark in the room, now. Just about supper-time—

Then Ronnie heard it. A scratching. A scurrying. From the hall? No. It couldn't be in the hall. Then where?

The window. It was open. And the scratching came from the ledge outside. He had to close it, fast. Ronnie jumped out of bed, barking his shin against a chair as he groped through the dusk. Then he was at the window, slamming it down, tight.

He heard the scratching.

And it came from *inside the room!*

Ronnie hurled himself upon the bed, clawing the covers up to his chin. His eyes bulged against the darkness.

Where was it?

He saw nothing but shadows. Which shadow moved?

Where was it?

Why didn't it yowl so he could locate it? Why didn't it make a noise? Yes, and why was it here? Why did it follow him? What was it trying to do to him?

Ronnie didn't know. All he knew was that he lay in bed, waiting, thinking of Mrs. Mingle and her cat and how she was a witch and died because he'd killed her. Or had he killed her? He was all mixed up, he couldn't remember, he didn't even know what was real and what wasn't real any more. He couldn't tell which shadow would move next.

And then he could.

The round shadow was moving. The round black ball was inching across the floor from beneath the window. It was the cat, all right, because shadows don't have claws that scrape. Shadows don't leap through the air and perch on the bedpost, grinning at you with yellow eyes and yellow teeth—grinning the way Mrs. Mingle grinned.

The cat was big. Its eyes were big. Its teeth were big, too.

Ronnie opened his mouth to scream.

Then the shadow was sailing through the air, springing at his face, at his open mouth. The claws fastened in his cheeks, forcing his jaws apart, and the head dipped down—

Far away, under the pain, someone was calling.

"Ronnie! Oh, Ronnie! What's the matter with you?"

Everything was fire and he lashed out and suddenly the shadow went away and he was sitting bolt upright in bed. His mouth worked but no sound came out. Nothing came out except that gushing red wetness. "Ronnie! Why don't you answer me?"

A guttural sound came from deep within Ronnie's throat, but no words. There would never be any words.

"Ronnie—what's the matter? Has the cat got your tongue—?"

The Cheaters

I. *Joe Henshaw*

The way I got those spectacles, I bought a blind lot off the City for twenty bucks.

Maggie hollered fit to raise the dead when I told her.

"What you wanna load up on some more junk for? The store's full of it now. Get yourself a lot of raggedy old clothes and some busted furniture, that's what you'll get. Why, that dump's over two hunnert years old! Ain't nobody been inside it since Prohibition, it's padlocked tight shut. And you have to throw away twenty bucks for whatever you find for salvage."

And so on and so on, about what a bum I was and why had she ever married me and who wanted to be stuck away for life in the junk and second-hand business.

Well I just walked out on her and let her keep right on jawing to Jake. He'd listen to her—listen for hours, sitting in back of the shop drinking coffee when he should have been working.

But I knew what I was doing. Delehanty at City Hall tipped me off about this old house and told me to get in my bid, he'd take care of it.

The dump was near the wharf and it must have been class once, even though they made a speak out of it back in Prohibition days and slapped a padlock on it ever since. Delehanty told me that upstairs, where nobody ever went while it was a rummy hangout, there was all kinds of old furniture from way back. So maybe Maggie was right about it being junk and maybe she was wrong. You never can tell. Way I figured, there might be some real antique pieces up there. You got to take a chance once in a while, so I slapped in my bid and got the lot. City gave me three days to move the stuff out before they started razing and Delehanty slipped me a key.

I walked out on Maggie and took the truck down there. Usual

thing, I have Jake drive and help me load, but this time I wanted to case the joint myself. If there really was something valuable in there—well, Jake would want a cut. So I let him stay back there and listen to Maggie. Maybe I am a dried-up old jerk like she tells it. And maybe I'm also a pretty smart guy. Just because Jake liked to dress up Saturdays and go down to the Bright Spot—

Anyway, I'm not talking about that, I'm talking about these glasses, these here cheaters I found.

That's all I found, too. All I could use. Downstairs was just rubbish and slats; they must have ripped out the bar when the Feds raided it. I kind of counted on finding bar stools and maybe some scrap metal, but no dice.

Upstairs was even worse. Eight big rooms, all dust and broken sticks of furniture. Busted beds, chairs with the springs sprung, nothing I could use. Old rags in some of the closets, and rotted shoes; it looked as if the people who lived here cleared out in a hurry a long time ago. Delehanty tipped me off this was supposed to be a haunted house, but in my line that's strictly a gag. I salvaged maybe two hundred haunted houses in my time—every old dump is supposed to be haunted. But I never run into anything in these places except maybe some cockroaches.

Then I came to this end room with the locked door. This looked a little better; all the other doors was open, but this one was locked tight. I had to use a crowbar on it. Got kind of excited, because you never can tell what a locked door means. Worked and sweated and finally pried it open.

Dust hit me in the face, and an awful stink. I switched on the flashlight and saw a big room with mounds of dirt all over the floor and bookshelves lining the walls. There must of been a thousand books in that room, no kidding, a regular library like.

I waded through the dust and pulled out a couple of the nearest books. The bindings were some kind of leather—that is, they used to be. Now the things just sort of crumbled in my hands, and so did the pages. All yellow and musty, which was why the stink was so bad in here.

I began to swear. I'm no *schmoe*, I know there's dough in old books. But not unless they're in good condition. And this stuff was rotten.

Then I saw this here desk in the corner and so help me, right on top of it was a human skull. A human skull, all yellow and grinning up at me under the light, and for a minute I almost went for that haunted house routine.

Then I noticed how the top was bored out for one of them old-fashion goose-quill pens. The guy who collected all these books used the skull for an inkwell. Screwy, hey?

But the desk was what really interested me because it was antique all right. Solid mahogany and all kinds of fancy scrollwork on it; little goofy faces carved in the wood. There was a drawer, too, and it wasn't locked. I got excited, figuring you never can tell what you find in such places, so I didn't waste much time pulling it open.

Only it was empty. I was so mad I let out a couple of words and kicked the side of the desk.

That's how I found them. The cheaters, that is. Because I hit one of the little goofy faces and a sort of panel swung open on the left side and there was this other drawer.

I reached in and pulled out the spectacles.

Just a pair of glasses, is all, but real funny ones. Little square-shaped lenses with big ear-pieces—books, I guess they call them. And a silver bridge over the middle.

I didn't get it. Sure, there was silver in the frames but not more than a couple of bucks worth. So why hide the cheaters away in a secret drawer?

I held the glasses up and wiped the dust off the lenses, which was yellow glass instead of the regular clear kind, but not very thick. I noticed little designs in the temples, like engraving. And right across the bridge for the nose was a word carved into the silver. I remember that word because I never saw it before.

"*Veritas*" was the word, in funny square letters. Could that be Greek? Maybe the old guy was Greek—the guy who had the locked library and the skull for an inkwell and the glasses in the secret drawer, I mean.

I had to squint at the lettering to see it in the gloom there because my eyes weren't so hot—and that gave me an idea.

Get to be my age, sometimes you're kind of shortsighted. I always figured on going to the eye-doctor but kept putting it off. So looking at the cheaters I said to myself, why not?

I put them on.

At first my eyes hurt a little. Not hurt, exactly, but something else like hurting inside of me. Like I was being all pulled and twisted. The whole room went far away for a minute and then it came up close and I blinked fast.

After that it was all right and I could see pretty good. Everything was sharp and clear.

So I left the cheaters on and went downstairs, figuring to come back tomorrow with Jake and the truck. At least we could haul the desk and maybe sell the bed-frames for scrap. No sense in me lifting, when I had Jake for the heavy stuff.

I went on home, then.

I come in the shop and sure enough there was Jake and Maggie sitting in back having coffee.

Maggie kind of grinned at me. Then she said, "How did you make out, Joe, you lousy old baboon? I'm glad we're going to kill you."

No, she didn't *say* all that. She just said, "How did you make out, Joe?"

But she was *thinking* the rest.

I know because I *saw* it.

Don't ask me to explain. I *saw it*. Not words, or anything. And I didn't *hear*. I saw. I knew by looking at her what she was thinking and planning.

"Find a lot of stuff?" Jake asked, and I *saw*, "I hope you did because it's all mine as soon as we bump you and we're gonna bump you for sure tonight."

"What you look so funny for, Joe, you sick or something?" Maggie asked. And she said, to herself, "Who cares, he's gonna be a lot sicker soon, all right, does he suspect anything, no of course not, the old goat never got wise to us for a whole year now, just wait until Jake and I own this place together and his insurance too, it's all set."

"What you need, you need a little drink," Jake said to me, and to himself he was saying, "That's the way, get him drunk, and when he gets upstairs I'll push him down and if that don't finish him I'll clobber him with a board, it leaves the same kind of marks. Everybody knows he drinks, it'll look like an accident."

I made myself smile.

"Where'd you get the cheaters?" Maggie asked, saying also, "God what a homely mug on him, I get sick just looking at that face but it won't be long now."

"Picked them up over at the house," I said.

Jake got out a fifth and some water-glasses. "Drink up," he said.

I sat there trying to figure it out. Why could I read their minds? I didn't know, but I could see what they were up to. I could *see* it.

Could it be—the cheaters?

Yes, the cheaters. *They* were the cheaters, carrying on behind my back. Waiting now until I got drunk enough so they could kill me. Pretending to drink a lot while they got me loaded.

But I couldn't get drunk, not as long as I was *seeing* them. The thoughts going through their heads made everything turn to ice, and I was cold sober. I knew just what to do. I made them drink with me.

That helped, only their thoughts got worse. I listened to them talk but all the time I saw their thoughts.

"We'll kill him, just a little while now, why doesn't he hurry up and pass out, got to keep him from suspecting. God how I hate that puss of his. I want to see it smashed open, wait until he's out of the way and I have Maggie all to myself, he's going to die, die, die—"

I listened and I knew just what to do. After dark I said I'd put the truck in the garage for the night and they stayed behind, thinking about how to get me upstairs now, how to keep people from suspecting them.

Me, I didn't worry about people suspecting. I put the truck away and I came back into the kitchen carrying the crowbar. I locked the door and they saw me with the crowbar, standing there.

"Hey, Joe—" said Jake.

"Joe, what's wrong?" said Maggie.

I didn't say a word.

There wasn't any time to talk, because I was smashing Jake's face with the crowbar, smashing his nose and eyes and jaw, and then I was hammering Maggie over the head and the thoughts came out but not in words, just in screams now, and then there weren't even any screams left to see.

So I sat down and took off the cheaters to polish them. I was still scrubbing at the red stains when the squad car came and the fuzz took me in.

They wouldn't let me keep the glasses and I never did see them again. It didn't matter much, anyway. I could have worn them at the trial, but who cares what the jury thought? And at the end I would have had to take them off anyway.

When they put the black hood over my head . . .

2. *Miriam Spencer Olcott*

I distinctly remember it was on Thursday afternoon, because that's when Olive has her bridge club over, and of course she simply *must* have Miss Tooker help with the serving.

Olive is much too diplomatic to lock me in my room even when Miss Tooker isn't there, and I always wondered why I seemed to get so sleepy on Thursdays, just when I might have a chance to slip out without anyone noticing. Finally I realized she must be putting something into my tea at luncheon—more of Dr. Cramer's work, no doubt.

Well, I'm not a complete fool by any means, no matter what they think, and this Thursday I simply poured the tea down the you-know-what. So Olive was none the wiser, and when I lay down on the bed and closed my eyes she went away satisfied. I waited until her guests arrived, then tiptoed down the stairs.

Olive and her friends were in the parlor with the door closed. I had to rest a moment at the foot of the stairs because of my heart, you know, and for an instant I had the most peculiar temptation to open the parlor door and stick my tongue out at the guests.

But that wouldn't have been very ladylike. After all Olive and her husband Percy had come to live with me when Herbert died and they got Miss Tooker to help care for me after I had my first heart attack. I mustn't be rude to them.

Besides, I knew Olive would never permit me to go out alone any more. So it would be wiser if I didn't disturb her.

I managed to leave without being seen, and took a bus at the corner. There were several people on the bus and they kept staring at me—people are so rude nowadays! I know my clothing is not in the latest style, but there is no call for vulgar curiosity. I wear highbutton shoes for the support they afford my ankles, and if I choose to be sensible regarding draughts, that is my affair. My coat is fur and very expensive; it needs relining and possibly some mending, that is true, but for all strangers know I might be quite impoverished. They need not be so rude. Even my bag attracts their attention; my fine reticule which Herbert brought back for me from abroad, in '37!

I didn't like the way they stared at my bag. It was almost as if they knew. But how could they know, or even suspect?

I sniffed and sat back, trying to decide whether to walk north or south when I got off the bus.

If I walked north, I'd need my bag.

If I walked south, like the last time—

No, I couldn't do that. The last time was frightful. I remember being in that awful place, and then the men laughing, and I had been singing, I believe, was still singing when Percy and Olive came for me in the taxicab. How they found me I'll never know; perhaps the tavernkeeper telephoned to them. They got me home and I had one of my attacks and Dr. Cramer told them never to even mention it to me again. So there were no discussions. I hate discussions.

But I knew this time I must walk north. When I left the bus I began to get that tingly feeling all over. It frightened me but it felt—nice.

It felt even nicer when I went into Warram's and began to look at the cameos. The clerk was a man. I told him what I wanted and he went to look. He brought back a wide selection. I told him about my trip to Baden-Baden with Herbert and what we had seen in the jewelry stores there. He was very patient and understanding. I thanked him politely for his trouble and walked out, tingling. There was a brooch, a really lovely thing, in my reticule.

At Slade's I got a scarf. The clerk was an impertinent young snip and so I felt I really must buy a corsage to distract her attention. They were vulgar things, and cost sixty-nine cents. Not nearly worth it. But the scarf in my bag was of imported silk.

It was very exciting. I walked in and out of the shops and the bag began to fill. Then I started going into those second-hand stores near the City Hall. One never knows. My reticule was almost full, but I could still make purchases, too.

In Henshaw's I saw this lovely escritoire, obviously solid mahogany and beautifully carved. I smiled at the proprietor.

"I noticed that escritoire in your window, Mr. Henshaw," I began, but he shook his head.

"It's sold, lady. Beside, my name's Burgin. Henshaw's dead—didn't you read about it in the papers? Hanged him. I bought the place out—"

I held up my hand and sniffed. "Please, spare me. But I'll glance around a bit, if I may."

"Sure, lady."

I had seen the table with the ceramics and now I approached it, but he never let his eyes stray from me. I was tingling again and very nervous. There was one piece I simply adored. I had the bag open and it only needed an instant—

He was right behind me, watching my hand move.

"How much is this?" I asked, very quickly, picking up an object at random from one of the trays on the table.

"Two bits!" he snapped.

I fumbled in my pocket and gave him a quarter, then marched out of the store and slammed the door. It was only when I reached the street that I stopped to examine the object in my hand.

It was a pair of spectacles. How in the world had I ever managed to snatch eyeglasses from that tray? Still, they were rather unusual—quite heavy, with tarnished silver frames. I held them up to the light and in the sunset I noticed a word etched across the bridge.

"*Veritas.*" Latin. *Truth*. Strange.

At the same moment I noticed the clock on the City Hall. It was past five. This would never do. I should be found out and there might be a distressing scene—

I hailed a taxicab, and as I rode I remembered that Olive and Percy were dining out tonight, and Dr. Cramer was to come over and examine me. Surely by this time they would have ascertained my absence. How could I ever explain?

Fumbling in my pocket for the fare, my hands encountered the spectacles again. And that, of course, was the solution. I placed them firmly on the bridge of my nose and adjusted the bows just as we turned into the driveway. For a moment the tingling increased and I felt I might have another attack, but then I could see clearly again and the tingling drained away.

I paid the driver and walked into the house quickly, before he had time to comment on the absence of a "tip."

Olive and Percy were waiting for me at the door. I could see them so clearly, so very clearly; Olive so tall and thin, and Percy so short and fat. Both of them had pale skins, like leeches.

Why not? They *were* leeches. Moving into my house when Herbert died, using my property, living on my income. Getting Miss Tooker to come and keep her eye on me, encouraging Dr. Cramer to make an invalid out of me. Ever since Herbert died they had been waiting for *me* to die.

"Here's the old —— now."

I won't *repeat* the word.

For a moment I was shocked beyond all belief, to think that Percy would stand there smiling and *say* such a thing to my face! Then I realized he wasn't saying it. He was *thinking* it. Somehow, I was reading his mind.

He said, "Mother, darling, where on earth have you been?"

"Yes," said Olive. "We worried so. Why you might have been run over." Her tone was the familiar one of daughterly affection. And behind it, the thought came. "Why *wasn't* she run over, the old ——"

That word again!

I began to tremble.

"Where were you?" Olive murmured. Thinking, "Did you go off on another bat, you doddering old fool? Or were you making trouble for us, stealing from the shops again? The times Percy has had to go down and make good on merchandise—"

I caught the thought and blinked behind the spectacles. I hadn't suspected *that*. Did they *know*, in the stores, what I did? And did they permit it as long as Percy paid for what I had taken? But then I wasn't profiting at all! They were all against me. I saw it for the first time—could it be the spectacles?

"If you must know," I said, very rapidly, "I went downtown to be fitted for a pair of glasses."

And before they had time to reply, I brushed past them and went up to my room.

I was really quite upset. Not only by their thoughts but because I could tell what they were thinking. It couldn't be the spectacles. It couldn't be. Such things aren't really possible. It was only that I was so very tired and so very old—

I took off the glasses and lay down on the bed and suddenly I was crying. Perhaps I fell asleep, for when I awoke it was quite dark and Miss Tooker was coming into the room, carrying a tray. On the tray was a teapot and some biscuits. Dr. Cramer had put me on a strict diet; he knew I loved to eat and wouldn't permit it.

"Go away," I said.

Miss Tooker smiled weakly. "Mr. and Mrs. Dean have left for their dinner engagement. But I thought you might be hungry—"

"Go away," I repeated. "When Dr. Cramer comes, send him up. But you keep out of here."

Her smile faded and she started for the door. For a moment I had the queerest urge to put on the spectacles and *really* see her. But that was all an illusion, wasn't it? I watched her depart, then sat up and reached for my bag. I began to go through my souvenirs of the afternoon and was quite engrossed by the time Dr. Cramer appeared.

He knocked first, giving me time to hide the reticule and its contents, and then entered quietly. "What's all this I hear about you, young lady?" he chuckled. He always called me "young lady." It was our private joke.

"I hear you took a little trip this afternoon," he continued, sitting down next to the bed. "Mrs. Dean mentioned something about spectacles—"

I shrugged. He leaned closer. "And you haven't eaten your dinner. You were crying." He sounded so sympathetic. A wonderful personality, Dr. Cramer. One couldn't help but respond.

"I just wasn't hungry. You see, Olive and Percy just don't understand. I do so enjoy getting out into the fresh air and I hate to trouble them. I can explain about the glasses."

He smiled and winked. "First, some tea. I'd better heat it up again, eh?"

Dr. Cramer set the teapot on the little electric hotplate over on the endtable. He worked quickly, efficiently, humming under his breath. It was a pleasure to watch him, a pleasure to have him visit me. We would sit down now and have a cup of tea together and I would tell him everything. He would understand. It would be all right.

I sat up. The glasses clicked on the bed beside me. I slipped them on.

Dr. Cramer turned and winked at me again. When he winked I felt the glasses pulling on my own eyes and closed them for a moment. Then I opened them again and I knew.

I knew Dr. Cramer was here to kill me.

He smiled at me and poured two cups of tea. I watched him stoop over the cup on the left side of the tray and slip the powder into the hot tea.

He brought the tray over to the bed and I said, "A napkin, please." He went back, got the napkin, sat down beside me and handed me the cup from the left side of the tray.

We drank.

My hand didn't tremble, even though he watched me. I emptied my cup. He emptied his.

He winked once more. "Well, young lady—feeling better?"

I winked right back at him. "Much better. And you?"

"First rate. Now we can talk, eh? You were going to tell me something?"

"Yes," I said. "I was going to tell you something. I was going to tell you that I know all about it. Percy and Olive had the plan and they put you up to this. They will inherit and give you one-third. The time for action was indefinite, but when I came home distraught tonight they thought it a good idea if you acted at once. Miss Tooker knew I might have an attack, anyway, and she would be convenient as a witness. Not that witnesses would be needed. You would certify as to the cause of death. My heart, you know."

Dr. Cramer was perspiring. The tea had been quite hot. He raised his hand. "Mrs. Olcott, please—"

"Don't bother to speak. You see, I can read your mind. You

don't believe that, do you? You're wondering why, knowing these things, I permitted you to poison me."

His eyes bulged and he turned red as a beet.

"Yes," I whispered. "You wonder why I allowed it. And the answer is—I didn't."

He tugged at his collar and half-rose from his chair. "You— didn't?" he croaked.

"No." I smiled sweetly. "When you brought me the napkin I switched our teacups."

I do not know what poison he employed, but it was quite efficacious. Of course his excitement helped speed the process along. He managed to stand erect, but only for an instant, and then sank back into his chair.

His voice failed almost immediately. His head began to wobble. He frothed and retched and made little sounds. Then he began to bite his lips.

I wanted to read his thoughts, but there were no coherent thoughts any more, only images. Words of prayer and blasphemy commingled, and then the overpowering mastery of pain blotted out everything. It made me tingle all over.

At the end he had convulsions and tried to claw out his own throat. I stood over him and laughed. Not a very ladylike thing to do, I admit, but there was justification. Besides, it made me tingle.

Afterwards I went downstairs. Miss Tooker was sleeping and there was no one to stop me. I deserved a little celebration. So I raided the refrigerator and took up a tray loaded with turkey and dressing and truffles and kumquats—oh, they feasted well downstairs, my loving daughter and son-in-law!

I brought the brandy decanter, too.

It was enough to make me quite giddy, climbing the stairs with that load, but once I was back in my room I felt better.

I filled my teacup with brandy and toasted the figure sprawled in the chair before me. I inquired politely did he want a snack, would he care for some brandy, it was delicious and how was his heart behaving these days?

The brandy was strong. I finished all the food, every last bit of it, and drank again. The tingling was mixed with warmth. I felt like singing, shouting. I did both.

The teacup broke. I drank out of the decanter. No one to see me. I reached out and closed his eyes. Bulging eyes. My own eyes ached. I took off the spectacles. Shouldn't have worn them. But if I hadn't, I'd be dead. Now he was dead. I was alive, and tingling.

More brandy. Heartburn. Too much food. Brandy burned too. I lay back on the bed. Everything went round and round, burning. I could see him sprawled there with his mouth open, laughing at me.

Why did he laugh? He was dead. I was the one who should laugh. He had poison. I had brandy. "Liquor is poison to you, Mrs. Olcott."

Who said that? Dr. Cramer said that, the last time. But I wasn't poisoned. So why did it hurt when I laughed?

Why did it hurt my chest so and why did the room go around when I tried to sit up and fell face downwards on the floor why did I tear at the rug until my fingers bent backwards and snapped one by one like pretzel sticks but I couldn't feel them because the pain in my chest was so much stronger than anything, stronger than life itself—

Because it was death.

I died at 10:18 p.m.

3. Percy Dean

After the whole affair was hushed up, Olive and I went away for a while. We could afford to travel now and I made arrangements to have the whole place remodeled while we were gone.

When we returned Olive and I could really hold our heads up in the community. No more snubs, no more covert insults, no more gossip about, "Mrs. Olcott's son-in-law . . . *parvenu* . . . not altogether the sort of person who belongs."

We had the means now to take our rightful place in society at last. To entertain. That was the first step. The costume party was really Olive's idea, although I was the one who tied it in with our "housewarming."

It was important to invite the right people. Thorgeson, Harker, Pfluger, Hattie Rooker, the Misses Christie. I checked the list with Olive most carefully before we sent invitations.

"If we have Hattie Rooker we must invite Sebastian Grimm," she reminded me. "The writer, you know. He's visiting at her home for the summer."

We planned it all carefully, so carefully in fact that we almost forgot to select our own costumes. At the last moment Olive mentioned the fact. I asked her what she intended to wear.

"Something Spanish, with a mantilla. Then I can wear the earrings." She peered at me quizzically. "But you're going to be a problem. Frankly, Percy, you're too tubby for the usual things. Unless you choose to dress as a clown."

I almost spoke harshly to her, but it was true. I regarded my portliness in the mirror; my receding hairline, my double chin. She peered over my shoulder.

"Just the thing!" she exclaimed. "You shall be Benjamin Franklin."

Benjamin Franklin. I had to admit it wasn't a bad idea. After all, Franklin was a symbol of dignity, stability and wisdom—I am inclined to discount those absurd rumors about his mistresses—and that was the very effect I was seeking. I depended upon this evening to impress my guests. It might be an important first step.

The upshot of the matter was that I went to the costumer, told him my needs, and returned that evening with a Colonial costume, including a partial wig.

Olive was ecstatic over the results. I dressed hastily after dinner and she inspected me at the last moment. "Quite a striking likeness," she said. "But didn't Franklin always wear spectacles?"

"So he did. Unfortunately, it's too late now to procure a pair. I trust the guests will forgive the oversight."

They did.

I spent a most enjoyable evening. Everyone arrived, the liquor was good and plentiful, our catering service excellent, and the costumes added the proper note of frivolity. Although a total abstainer myself, I saw to it that old man Harker, Judge Pfluger, Thorgeson and the others imbibed freely, and their cordiality increased as the evening progressed.

It was particularly important to gain Thorgeson's friendship. Through him I could gain membership in the Gentry Club, and sooner or later I'd worm my way into Room 1200—the fabulous "poker room" where the really big deals were made; millions of dollars in contracts assigned casually as the powers-that-be dealt their cards.

The writer, Sebastian Grimm, put the next idea into my head. "Party's going nicely," he drawled. "Almost think it would be safe to leave the ladies to their own devices for an hour or so, now that the dancing has started. You haven't a poker table available, have you, Dean?"

"There's a room upstairs," I ventured. "Away from the crowd and the noise. If you gentlemen are interested—"

They were. We ascended the stairs.

I hate poker. I dislike all games of chance. But this was too perfect an opportunity to miss. Wouldn't it be natural for my guests to suggest another meeting in the future? Perhaps Thorgeson would mention the Gentry Club games, and I could remind him I was not a member. "That's easily remedied, Dean," he would boom. "Tell you what I'll do—"

Oh, it was an inspiration, and no mistake! I secured cards and chips and we gathered around the big table in the upstairs study—Thorgeson, Dr. Cassit, Judge Pfluger, Harker, Grimm and myself. I would have excluded Grimm if possible; the tall, thin sardonic writer was a disturbing element, and his presence was of no value to me. But it had been his suggestion and I couldn't very well shake him off.

Olive tapped on the door before we started our play.

"Oh here you are," she said. "I see you're in good company. Would anyone care to have a buffet luncheon sent up?"

There was an awkward silence. I felt annoyance.

"Very well, then, I shan't disturb you. Oh, Percy—I found something for you just now. In—in Mother's room." She came up behind me and slipped something over my nose and ears. "Spectacles," she giggled. "You remember, we couldn't find a pair for you? But these were in Mother's bureau drawer."

She stood back and surveyed me. "Now, that does it. He really looks like Benjamin Franklin, don't you think?"

I didn't want the spectacles. They hurt my eyes. But I was too embarrassed to reprove her; merely grateful when she slipped out of the room again. The men were already intent on the distribution of chips. Thorgeson was banking. I pulled out my wallet and placed a hundred dollar bill on the table. I received ten white chips.

Obviously, they played for "blood". Very well. I smiled and placed five hundred dollars more before me. "Now for some reds." Thorgeson gave me twenty red chips.

"That's better," I commented. And it was, for I meant to lose tonight. A thousand dollars or so invested properly here would almost guarantee my acceptance by this group, if I lost graciously, like a gentleman. That was my strategy for the evening.

But it didn't work.

I have heard of clairvoyance, of telepathy, of ESP, and these phenomena I have always discounted. Yet *something* was at work tonight. For as I squinted through my spectacles at the cards, I could read the hands of the other players. Not their hands, but their *minds*.

"Pair of eights under . . . raise, I'll get another . . . two queens . . . wonder if he's going for a straight? . . . better stay in . . . never make an inside . . . raise again, bluff them out."

It came to me in a steady stream. I knew when to drop, when to stay, when to raise, when to call.

Of course I meant to lose. But when a man *knows* what to do he's a fool to abandon his advantage. That's logic, isn't it? Sound business. These men respected shrewdness, good judgement. How could I help myself?

I do not wish to dwell upon the actual incidents of the game. Sufficient to say that I won almost every hand. This psychic sense never deserted me, and I must have been over nine thousand dollars ahead when Harker cheated.

I had paid no heed to any extraneous thought or circumstance; merely concentrated on the game and the bets. And then, "I'll keep the ace until the next hand," Harker thought. I could feel it, feel the strength and the desperate avariciousness behind it. Old Harker, worth close to a million dollars, cheating over the poker table.

It stunned me. Before I could make up my mind how to react, the next hand was in play—had been played—and I was sitting there calling with a full house, queens over fours, getting ready to rake in a three thousand dollar pot.

Harker's monkey-face creased into a grin. "Not so fast, my friend. I have"—he licked his thin lips eagerly—"four aces."

I coughed. "Sorry, Mr. Harker. But has it come to your attention that this is a seven-card stud game and you also have—eight cards?"

Everybody gasped. Gasped, then fell silent.

"An oversight, no doubt. But if you will be good enough to raise your left arm from the table—there, underneath your sleeve—"

The silence deepened. Yet suddenly it was filled with a clamor; not a clamor of words but of *thoughts*.

"The cur ... accusing Harker, of all people ... probably planted the card there himself ... cheating ... no gentleman ... nasty little fat-faced fool ... never should have come ... barred from decent society ... vulgar ... probably drove the old lady to her grave ..."

My head hurt.

I thought if I could talk the hurting would go away. So I told them what I knew and what I felt about them, and they only stared. So I thought if I shouted it might relieve the pressure in my head, and I shouted and ordered them out of my house and named them for what they were, but they gaped at me as if I were mad. And they kept on *thinking*.

Harker was the worst. He thought things about me which no man could endure. No man could endure such thoughts, even if his head weren't splitting and he didn't know it was all lost, they all hated him, they were mocking and sneering inside.

So I knocked over the table and I took him by the collar, and then they were all on me at once, but I had his wizened throat between my fingers and I wouldn't let go until I squeezed out all the hurting, all of it, and my glasses fell off and everything seemed to go dim. I looked up just in time to see Thorgeson aiming the water carafe at my head.

I tried to move to one side, but it was too late. The carafe came down and everything went away.

Forever.

4. *Sebastian Grimm*

This will be very brief.

When I picked up those peculiar yellow-lensed spectacles from the floor—slipping them into my pocket unobserved, in the confusion attendant upon calling the doctor and the police—I was motivated by mere curiosity.

That curiosity grew when, at the inquest, Olive Dean spoke of her mother and how she had brought a pair of glasses home with her on the night of her tragic death.

Certain aspects of that poker game had piqued my fancy, and the statements at the inquest further intrigued me.

The legend, *"Veritas"*, inscribed upon the bridge of the spectacles, was also interesting.

I shall not bore you with my researches. Amateur detection is a monotonous, albeit sometimes a rewarding procedure. It is sufficient to say that my private inquiry led me to a second-hand store and eventually to a partially-razed house near the docks. Research with the local historical society enabled me to ascertain that the spectacles had once been the property of Dirk Van Prinn; legends of his reputed interest in sorcery are common knowledge amongst antiquarians who delve into the early history of the community. I need not bother to underscore the obvious.

At any rate, my rather careful investigations bore fruit. I was able, taking certain liberties based upon circumstantial evidence, to "reconstruct" the thoughts and actions of the various persons who had inadvertently worn the spectacles since the time of their discovery in the secret drawer of old Van Prinn's escritoire. These thoughts and actions have formed the basis of this narrative, in which I have assumed the characters of Mr. Joseph Henshaw, Mrs. Miriam Spencer Olcott, and Mr. Percy Dean—all deceased.

Unfortunately, a final chapter remains to be written. I had no idea of this necessity when I started; had I suspected, I would have desisted immediately. But now I know, as Dirk Van Prinn must have known when he hid the spectacles away in that drawer, that there is danger in wisdom; that knowledge of the thoughts of others leads only to disillusion and destruction.

I mused upon the triteness of this moral, and not for anything in the world would I have emulated poor Joe Henshaw, or Mrs. Olcott, or Percy Dean, and put on the spectacles to gaze at other men and other minds.

But pride goeth before a fall, and as I wrote of the tragic fate of these poor fools whose search for wisdom ended in disaster, I could not help but reflect upon the actual purpose for which these singular spectacles had somehow been created by a long-dead savant and seer.

"*Veritas.*" The truth.

The truth about others brought evil consequences. But suppose the spectacles were meant to be employed to discover the truth about one's self?

"*Know thyself.*" Could it be that this was the secret purpose of the spectacles—to enable the wearer to look *inward?*

Surely there could be no harm in that. Not in the hands of an intelligent man.

I have always fancied that I "knew" myself in the ordinary sense of the word; was perhaps more aware, through constant introspection, of my inner nature. Thus I *fancied*, but I had to *know*.

And that is why I put them on, just now. Put them on and stared at myself in the hall mirror. Stared, and saw, and knew.

There are things about subliminal intelligence, about the so-called "subconscious," which psychiatry and psychology cannot encompass. I know these things now, and a great deal more. I know that the actual agony undergone by the victims who read the minds of others is as nothing compared to that which is born of reading one's own mind.

I stood before the mirror and looked *into* myself—seeing there the atavistic memories, the desires, the fears, the self-defeat, the seeds of madness, the lurking filth and cruelty; the slimy, crawling, secret shapes which dare not rise even in dreams. I saw the unutterable foulness beneath all the veneer of consciousness and intellect, and knew it for my true nature. Every man's nature. Perhaps it can be suppressed and controlled, if one remains unaware. But merely to realize that *it is there* is a horror which must not be permitted.

When I conclude this account I shall take the "cheaters," as Joe Henshaw so appropriately called them, and destroy them forever. I shall use a revolver for that purpose; aiming it quite steadily and deliberately at these accursed instruments, and shattering them with a single shot.

And I shall be wearing them at the time . . .

Hungarian Rhapsody

Right after Labor Day the weather turned cold and all the summer cottage people went home. By the time ice began to form on Lost Lake there was nobody around but Solly Vincent.

Vincent was a big fat man who had purchased a year-round home on the lake early that spring. He wore loud sports-shirts all summer long, and although nobody ever saw him hunting or fishing, he entertained a lot of weekend guests from the city at his place. The first thing he did when he bought the house was to put up a big sign in front which read SONOVA BEACH. Folks passing by got quite a bang out of it.

But it wasn't until fall that he took to coming into town and getting acquainted. Then he started dropping into Doc's Bar one or two evenings a week, playing cards with the regulars in the back room.

Even then, Vincent didn't exactly open up. He played a good game of poker and he smoked good cigars, but he never said anything about himself. Once, when Specs Hennessey asked him a direct question, he told the gang he came from Chicago, and that he was a retired business man. But he never mentioned what business he had retired from.

The only time he opened his mouth was to ask questions, and he didn't really do that until the evening Specs Hennessey brought out the gold coin and laid it on the table.

"Ever see anything like that before?" he asked the gang. Nobody said anything, but Vincent reached over and picked it up.

"German, isn't it?" he mumbled. "Who's the guy with the beard—the Kaiser?"

Specs Hennessey chuckled. "You're close," he said. "That's old Franz Joseph. He used to be boss of the Austro-Hungarian Empire, forty-fifty years ago. That's what they told me down at the bank."

"Where'd you get it, in a slot-machine?" Vincent wanted to know.

Specs shook his head. "It came in a bag, along with about a thousand others."

That's when Vincent really began to look interested. He picked up the coin again and turned it in his stubby fingers. "You gonna tell what happened?" he asked.

Specs didn't need any more encouragement. "Funniest damn thing," he said. "I was sitting in the office last Wednesday when this dame showed up and asked if I was the real-estate man and did I have any lake property for sale. So I said sure, the Schultz cottage over at Lost Lake. A mighty fine bargain, furnished and everything, for peanuts to settle the estate.

"I was all set to give her a real pitch but she said never mind that, could I show it to her? And I said, of course, how about tomorrow, and she said why not right now, tonight?

"So I drove her out and we went through the place and she said she'd take it, just like that. I should see the lawyer and get the papers ready and she'd come back Monday night and close the deal. Sure enough, she showed up, lugging this big bag of coins. I had to call Hank Felch over from the bank to find out what they were and if they were any good. Turns out they are, all right. Good as gold." Specs grinned. "That's how come I know about Franz Joseph." He took the coin from Vincent and put it back in his pocket. "Anyway, it looks like you're going to have a new neighbor out there. The Schultz place is only about a half-mile down the line from yours. And if I was you, I'd run over and borrow a cup of sugar."

Vincent blinked. "You figure she's loaded, huh?"

Specs shook his head. "Maybe she is, maybe she isn't. But the main thing is, she's stacked." He grinned again. "Name's Helene Esterhazy. Helene, with an *e* on the end. I saw it when she signed. Talks like one of them Hungarian refugees—figure that's what she is, too. A countess, maybe, some kind of nobility. Probably busted out from behind the Iron Curtain and decided to hole up some place where the Commies couldn't find her. Of course I'm only guessing, because she didn't have much to say for herself."

Vincent nodded. "How was she dressed?" he asked.

"Like a million bucks." Specs grinned at him. "What's the idea, you figuring on marrying for money, or something? I tell you, one look at this dame and you'll forget all about dough. She talks something like this ZaZa Gabor. Looks something like her, too, only she has red hair. Boy, if I wasn't a married man, I'd—"

"When she say she was moving in?" Vincent interrupted.

"She didn't say. But I figure right away, in a day or so."

Vincent yawned and stood up.

"Hey, you're not quitting yet, are you? The game's young—"

"Tired," Vincent said. "Got to hit the sack."

And he went home, and he hit the sack, but not to sleep. He kept thinking about his new neighbor.

Actually, Vincent wasn't too pleased with the idea of having anyone for a neighbor, even if she turned out to be a beautiful redheaded refugee. For Vincent was something of a refugee himself, and he'd come up north to get away from people; everybody except the few special friends he invited up during summer weekends. Those people he could trust, because they were former business associates. But there was always the possibility of running into former business rivals—and he didn't want to see any of them. Not ever. Some of them might nurse grudges, and in Vincent's former business a grudge could lead to trouble.

That's why Vincent didn't sleep very well at night, and why he always kept a little souvenir of his old business right under the pillow. You never could tell.

Of course, this sounded legitimate enough; the dame probably was a Hungarian refugee, the way Specs Hennessey said. Still, the whole thing might be a very clever plant, a way of moving in on Vincent which wouldn't be suspected.

In any case, Vincent decided he'd keep his eye on the old Schultz cottage down the line and see what happened. So the next morning he went into town again and bought himself a very good pair of binoculars, and the day after that he used them when the moving van drove into the drive of the Schultz place half a mile away.

Most of the leaves had fallen from the trees and Vincent got a pretty clear view from his kitchen window. The moving van was a small one, and there was just the driver and a single helper, carrying in a bunch of boxes and crates. Vincent didn't see any furniture and that puzzled him until he remembered the Schultz cottage had been sold furnished. Still, he wondered about the boxes, which seemed to be quite heavy. Could the whole story be on the up-and-up and the boxes maybe filled with more gold coins? Vincent couldn't make up his mind. He kept waiting for the woman to drive in, but she didn't show, and after a while the men climbed into their van and left.

Vincent watched most of the afternoon and nothing happened. Then he fried himself a steak and ate it, looking out at the sunset over the lake. It was then that he noticed the light shining from the cottage window. She must have sneaked in while he was busy at the stove.

He got out his binoculars and adjusted them. Vincent was a big man, and he had a powerful grip, but what he saw nearly caused the binoculars to drop from his fingers.

The curtain was up in her bedroom, and the woman was lying on the bed. She was naked, except for a covering of gold coins.

Vincent steadied himself and propped both hands up on the sill as he squinted through the binoculars.

There was no mistake about it—he saw a naked woman, wallowing in a bed strewn with gold. The light reflected from the coins, it danced and dazzled across her bare body, it radiated redly from her long auburn hair. She was pale, wide-eyed, and voluptuously lovely, and her oval face with its high cheekbones and full lips seemed transformed into a mask of wanton ecstasy as she caressed her nakedness with handfuls of shimmering gold.

Then Vincent knew that it wasn't a plant, she wasn't a phoney. She was a genuine refugee, all right, but that wasn't important. What was important was the way the blood pounded in his temples, the way his throat tightened up until he almost choked as he stared at her, stared at all that long, lean loveliness and the white and the red and the gold.

He made himself put down the binoculars, then. He made himself pull the shade, and he made himself wait until the next morning even though he got no rest that night.

But bright and early he was up, shaving close with his electric razor, dressing in the double-breasted gab that hid his paunch, using the lotion left over from summer when he used to bring the tramps up from the city. And he put on his new tie and his big smile, and he walked very quickly over to the cottage and knocked on the door.

No answer.

He knocked a dozen times, but nothing happened. The shades were all down, and there wasn't a sound.

Of course he could have forced the lock. If he'd thought she was a plant, he'd have done so in a moment, because he carried the souvenir in his coat-pocket, ready for action. And if he'd had any idea of just getting at the coins he would have forced the lock, too. That would be the ideal time, when she was away.

Only he wasn't worried about plants, and he didn't give a damn about the money. What he wanted was the woman. Helene Esterhazy. Classy name. Real class. A countess, maybe. A writhing redhead on a bed of golden coins—

Vincent went away after a while, but all day long he sat in the window and watched. Watched and waited. She'd probably gone into town to stock up on supplies. Maybe she visited the beauty parlor, too. But she ought to be back. She had to come back. And when she did—

This time he missed her because he finally had to go to the bathroom, along about twilight. But when he returned to his post and saw the light in the front room, he didn't hesitate. He made the half-mile walk in about five minutes, flat, and he was puffing a little. Then he forced himself to wait on the doorstep for a moment before knocking. Finally his ham-fist rapped, and she opened the door.

She stood there, staring startled into the darkness, and the lamplight from behind shone through the filmy transparency of her long hostess-gown, then flamed through the long red hair that flowed loosely across her shoulders.

"Yes?" she murmured.

Vincent swallowed painfully. He couldn't help it. She looked like a hundred-a-night girl; hell, make it a thousand-a-night, make it a million. A million in gold coins, and her red hair like a veil. That was all he could think of, and he couldn't remember the words he'd rehearsed, the line he'd so carefully built up in advance.

"My name's Solly Vincent," he heard himself saying. "I'm your neighbor, just down the lake a ways. Heard about you moving in and I thought I ought to, well, introduce myself."

"So."

She stared at him, not smiling, not moving, and he got a sick hunch that she knew just what he'd been thinking.

"Your name's Esterhazy, isn't it? Tell me you're Hungarian, something like that. Well, I figured maybe you're a stranger here, haven't got settled yet, and—"

"I'm quite satisfied here." Still she didn't smile or move. Just stared like a statue; a cold, hard, goddam beautiful statue.

"Glad to hear it. But I just meant, maybe you'd like to stop in at my place, sort of get acquainted. I got some of that Tokay wine and a big record-player, you know, classic stuff. I think I even have that piece, that *Hungarian Rhapsody* thing, and—"

Now what had he said?

Because all at once she was laughing. Laughing with her lips, with her throat, with her whole body, laughing with everything except those ice-green eyes.

Then she stopped and spoke, and her voice was ice-green too. "No thank you," she said. "As I say, I am quite satisfied here. All I require is that I am not disturbed."

"Well, maybe some other time—"

"Let me repeat myself. I do not wish to be disturbed. Now or at any time. Good evening, Mr. —" The door closed.

She didn't even remember his name. The stuckup bitch didn't even remember his name. Unless she'd pretended to forget on purpose. Just like she slammed the door in his face, to put him down.

Well, nobody put Solly Vincent down. Not in the old days, and not now, either.

He walked back to his place and by the time he got there he was himself again. Not the damfool square who'd come up to her doorstep like a brush salesman with his hat in his hand. And not the jerk who had looked at her through the binoculars like some kid with hot pants.

He was Solly Vincent, and she didn't have to remember his name if she didn't want to. He'd show her who he was. And damned soon.

In bed that night he figured everything out. Maybe he'd saved himself a lot of grief by not getting involved. Even if she was a real disheroo, she was nuttier'n a fruitcake. Crazy foreigner, rolling around in a pile of coins. All these Hunky types, these refugees, were nuts. God knows what might have happened if he'd gotten mixed up with her. He didn't need a woman, anyway. A guy could always have himself a woman, particularly if he had money.

Money. That was the important thing. She had money. He'd seen it. Probably those crates were full of dough. No wonder she was hiding out here; if the Commies knew about her haul, they'd be right on the spot. That's the way he figured it, that's the way Specs Hennessey, the real-estate man, had figured it.

So why not?

The whole plan came to him at once. Call a few contacts in the city—maybe Carney and Fromkin, they could fence anything, including gold coins. Why the setup was perfect! She was all alone, there was nobody else around for three miles, and when it was over there wouldn't be any questions. It would look like the Commies had showed up and knocked the joint over. Besides, he wanted to see the look on her face when he came busting in—

He could imagine it now.

He imagined it all the next day, when he called Carney and Fromkin and told them to come up about nine. "Got a little deal for you," he said. "Tell you when I see you."

And he was still imagining it when they arrived. So much so that both Fromkin and Carney noticed something was wrong.

"What's it all about?" Carney wanted to know.

He just laughed. "Hope you got good springs in your Caddy," he said. "You may be hauling quite a load back to town."

"Give," Fromkin urged.

"Don't ask any questions. I've got some loot to peddle."

"Where is it?"

"I'm calling for it now."

And that's all he would say. He told them to sit tight, wait there at the house until he came back. They could help themselves to drinks if they liked. He'd only be a half-hour or so.

Then he went out. He didn't tell them where he was going,

and he deliberately circled around the house in case they peeked out. But he doubled back and headed for the cottage down the way. The light was shining in the bedroom window, and it was time for the wandering boy to come home.

Now he could really let himself go, imagining everything. The way she'd look when she answered the door, the way she'd look when he grabbed her gown and ripped it away, the way she'd look when—

But he was forgetting about the money. All right, might as well admit it. The hell with the money. He'd get that too, yes, but the most important thing was the other. He'd show her who he was. She'd know, before she died.

Vincent grinned. His grin broadened as he noticed the light in the bedroom flicker and expire. She was going to sleep now. She was going to sleep in her bed of gold. So much the better. Now he wouldn't even bother to knock. He'd merely force the door, force it very quietly, and surprise her.

As it turned out, he didn't even have to do that. Because the door was unlocked. He tiptoed in very softly, and there was moonlight shining in through the window to help him find his way, and now there was the thickness in the throat again but it didn't come from confusion. He knew just what he was doing, just what he was going to do. His throat was thick because he was excited, because he could imagine her lying in there, naked on the heap of coins.

Because he could *see* her.

He opened the bedroom door, and the shade was up now so that the moonlight fell upon the whiteness and the redness and the golden glinting, and it was even better than he'd imagined because it was real.

Then the ice-green eyes opened and for a moment they stared in the old way. Suddenly there was a change. The eyes were flame-green now, and she was smiling and holding out her arms. Nuts? Maybe so. Maybe making love to all that money warmed her up. It didn't matter. What mattered was her arms, and her hair like a red veil, and the warm mouth open and panting. What mattered was to know that the gold was here and she was here and he was going to have them both, first her and then the money. He tore at his clothes, and then he was panting and sinking down to tear at her. She writhed and wriggled and his hands slipped on the coins and then his nails sank into the dirt beneath.

The dirt beneath—

There was dirt in her bed. And he could feel it and he could smell it, for suddenly she was above and behind him, pressing him down so that his face was rubbing in the dirt, and she'd twisted his hands around behind his back. He heaved, but she was very strong, and her cold fingers were busy at his wrists, knotting something tightly. Too late he tried to sit up, and then she hit him with something. Something cold and hard, something she'd taken from his own pocket; *my own gun*, he thought.

Then he must have passed out for a minute, because when he came to he could feel the blood trickling down the side of his face, and her tongue, licking it.

She had him propped up in the corner now, and she had tied his hands and legs to the bedpost, very tightly. He couldn't move. He knew because he tried, God how he tried. The earth-smell was everywhere in the room. It came from the bed, and it came from her, too. She was naked, and she was licking his face. And she was laughing.

"You came anyway, eh?" she whispered. "You had to come, is that it? Well, here you are. And here you shall stay. I will keep you for a pet. You are big and fat. You will last a long, long time."

Vincent tried to move his head away. She laughed again.

"It isn't what you planned, is it? I know why you came back. For the gold. The gold and the earth I brought with me to sleep upon, as I did in the old country. All day I sleep upon it, but at night I awake. And when I do, you shall be here. No one will ever find or disturb us. It is good that you are strong. It will take many nights before I finish."

Vincent found his voice. "No," he croaked. "I never believed— you must be kidding, you're a refugee—"

She laughed again. "Yes. I am a refugee. But not a *political* refugee." Then she retracted her tongue and Vincent saw her teeth. Her long white teeth, moving against the side of his neck in the moonlight . . .

Back at the house Carney and Fromkin got ready to climb into the Cadillac.

"He's not showing up, that's for sure," Carney said. "We'll blow before there's any trouble. Whatever he had cooked up, the deal went sour. I knew it the minute I saw his face. He had a funny look, you know, like he'd flipped."

"Yeah," Fromkin agreed. "Something wrong with old Vincent, all right. I wonder what's biting him lately."

The Light-House

Note: This story is the result of a suggestion from Professor T. O. Mabbott, the distinguished Poe scholar, who wrote me following publication of my *The Man Who Collected Poe*. He had been instrumental in publishing the unfinished version of Poe's last story, *The Light-House*, in its definitive form, and was kind enough to suggest I try my hand at completing the tale. Poe's manuscript covers four leaves and ends with the notation from "January 3", and it is here that my collaboration begins. Here, then, is the last story from the pen of Poe, with the humble apologies of yours truly—

Robert Bloch

Jan. 1, 1796. This day—my first on the lighthouse—I make this entry in my Diary, as agreed on with DeGrät. As regularly as I *can* keep the journal, I will—but there is no telling what may happen to a man all alone as I am—I may get sick or worse . . .

So far well! The cutter had a narrow escape—but why dwell on that, since I am *here*, all safe? My spirits are beginning to revive already, at the mere thought of being—for once in my life at least—thoroughly *alone*; for, of course, Neptune, large as he is, is not to be taken into consideration as "society". Would in Heaven I had ever found in "society" one half as much *faith* as in this poor dog;—in such case I and "society" might never have parted—even for a year . . .

What most surprises me, is the difficulty DeGrät had in getting me the appointment—and I a noble of the realm! It could not be that the Consistory had any doubt of my ability to manage the light. *One* man has attended it before now—and got on quite as well as the three that are usually put in. The duty is a mere nothing; and the printed instructions are as plain as possible. It would never have done to let Orndoff accompany me. I should never have made any way with my book as long as he was within reach of me, with his intolerable gossip—not to mention that everlasting meerschaum. Besides, I wish to be *alone* ...

It is strange that I never observed, until this moment, how dreary a sound that word has—"alone"! I could half fancy there was some peculiarity in the echo of these cylindrical walls—but oh, no!—that is all nonsense. I do believe I am going to get nervous about my insulation. *That* will never do. I have not forgotten DeGrät's prophecy. Now for a scramble to the lantern and a good look around to "see what I can see." ... To see what I can see indeed!—not very much. The swell is subsiding a little, I think—but the cutter will have a rough passage home, nevertheless. She will hardly get within sight of the Norland before noon tomorrow—and yet it can hardly be more than 190 or 200 miles.

Jan. 2. I have passed this day in a species of ecstasy that I find it impossible to describe. My passion for solitude could scarcely have been more thoroughly gratified. I do not say *satisfied;* for I believe I should never be satiated with such delight as I have experienced today ...

The wind lulled after day-break, and by the afternoon the sea had gone down materially ... Nothing to be seen with the telescope even, but ocean and sky, with an occasional gull.

Jan. 3. A dead calm all day. Towards evening, the sea looked very much like glass. A few sea-weeds came in sight; but besides them absolutely *nothing* all day—not even the slightest speck of cloud ... Occupied myself in exploring the light-house ... It is a very lofty one—as I find to my cost when I have to ascend its interminable stairs—not quite 160 feet, I should say, from the low-water mark to the top of the lantern. From the bottom *inside* the shaft, however, the distance to the summit is 180 feet at least:—thus the floor is 20 feet below the surface of the sea, even at low-tide ...

It seems to me that the hollow interior at the bottom should have been filled in with solid masonry. Undoubtedly the whole would have been thus rendered more *safe*:—but what am I thinking about. A structure such as this is safe enough under any circumstances. I should feel myself secure in it during the fiercest hurricane that ever raged—and yet I have heard seamen say that, occasionally, with a wind at South-West, the sea has been known to run higher here than anywhere with the single exception of the Western opening of the Straits of Magellan.

No mere sea, though, could accomplish anything with this solid iron-riveted wall—which, at 50 feet from high-water mark, is four feet thick, if one inch . . . The basis on which the structure rests seems to me to be chalk . . .

Jan. 4. I am now prepared to resume work on my book, having spent this day in familiarizing myself with a regular routine.

My actual duties will be, I perceive, absurdly simple—the light requires little tending beyond a periodic replenishment of the oil for the six-wick burner. As to my own needs, they are easily satisfied, and the exertion of an occasional trip down the stairs is all I must anticipate.

At the base of the stairs is the entrance room; beneath that is twenty feet of empty shaft. Above the entrance room, at the next turn of the circular iron staircase, is my store-room which contains the casks of fresh water and the food supplies, plus linens and other daily needs. Above that—again another spiral of those interminable stairs!—is the oil room, completely filled with the tanks from which I must feed the wicks. Fortunately, I perceive that I can limit my descent to the storeroom to once a week if I choose, for it is possible for me to carry sufficient provisions in one load to supply both myself and Neptune for such a period. As to the oil supply, I need only to bring up two drums every three days and thus insure a constant illumination. If I choose, I can place a dozen or more spare drums on the platform near the light and thus provide for several weeks to come.

So it is that in my daily existence I can limit my movements to the upper half of the light-house; that is to say, the three spirals opening on the topmost three levels. The lowest is my "living room"—and it is here, of course, that Neptune is confined the greater part of the day; here, too, that I plan to write at a desk near the wall-slit that affords a view of the sea without. The second highest level is my bedroom and kitchen combined. Here the weekly rations of food and water are contained in cupboards for that purpose; at hand is the ingenious stove fed by the self-same oil that lights the beacon above. The topmost level is the service room giving access to the light itself and to the platform surrounding it. Since the light is fixed, and its reflectors set, there is no need for me ever to ascend to the platform save when replenishing the oil supply or making a repair or adjustment as per the written instructions—a circumstance which may well never arise during my stay here.

Already I have carried enough oil, water and provender to the upper levels to last me for an entire month—I need stir from my two rooms only to replenish the wicks.

For the rest, I am free! utterly free—my time is my own, and in this lofty realm I rule as King. Although Neptune is my only living subject I can well imagine that I am sovereign o'er all I see—ocean below and stars above. I am master of the sun that rises in rubicund radiance from the sea at dawn, emperor of wind and monarch of the gale, sultan of the waves that sport or roar in roiling torrents about the base of my palace pinnacle. I command the moon in the heavens, and the very ebb and flow of the tide does homage to my reign.

But enough of fancies—DeGrät warned me to refrain from morbid or from grandiose speculation—now I shall take up in all earnestness the task that lies before me. Yet this night, as I sit before the window in the starlight, the tides sweeping against these lofty walls can only echo my exultation; I am free—and, at last, alone!

Jan. 11. A week has passed since my last entry in this diary, and as I read it over, I can scarce comprehend that it was I who penned those words.

Something has happened—the nature of which lies unfathomed. I have worked, eaten, slept, replenished the wicks twice. My outward existence has been placid. I can ascribe the alteration in my feelings to naught but some inner alchemy; enough to say that a disturbing change has taken place.

"Alone!" I, who breathed the word as if it were some mystic incantation bestowing peace, have come—I realize it now—to loathe the very sound of the syllables. And the ghastliness of meaning I know full well.

It is a dismaying, it is a dreadful thing, to be alone. Truly alone, as I am, with only Neptune to exist beside me and by his breathing presence remind me that I am not the sole inhabitant of a blind and insensate universe. The sun and stars that wheel overhead in their endless cycle seem to rush across the horizon unheeding—and, of late, unheeded, for I cannot fix my mind upon them with normal constancy. The sea that swirls or ripples below me is naught but a purposeless chaos of utter emptiness.

I thought myself to be a man of singular self-sufficiency, beyond the petty needs of a boring and banal society. How wrong I was!—for I find myself longing for the sight of another face, the sound of another voice, the touch of other hands whether they offer caresses or blows. Anything, anything for reassurement that my dreams are indeed false and that I am *not*, actually, alone.

And yet I *am*. I am, and I will be. The world is two hundred miles away; I will not know it again for an entire year. And it in turn—but no more! I cannot put down my thoughts while in the grip of this morbid mood.

Jan. 13. Two more days—two more centuries!—have passed. Can it be less than two weeks since I was immured in this prison tower? I mount the turret of my dungeon and gaze at the horizon; I am not hemmed in by bars of steel but by columns and pillars and webs of wild and raging water. The sea has changed; grey skies have wrought a wizardry so that I stand surrounded by a tumult that threatens to become a tempest.

I turn away, for I can bear no more, and descend to my room. I seek to write—the book is bravely begun, but of late I can bring myself to do nothing constructive or creative—and in a moment I fling aside my pen and rise to pace. To endlessly pace the narrow, circular confines of my tower of torment.

Wild words, these? And yet I am not alone in my affliction—Neptune, Neptune the loyal, the calm, the placid—he feels it too.

Perhaps it is but the approach of the storm that agitates him so—for Nature bears closer kinship with the beast. He stays constantly at my side, whining now, and the muffled roaring of the waves without our prison causes him to tremble. There is a chill in the air that our stove cannot dissipate, but it is not cold that oppresses him . . .

I have just mounted to the platform and gazed out at the spectacle of gathering storm. The waves are fantastically high; they sweep against the light-house in titanic tumult. These solid walls of stone shudder rhythmically with each onslaught. The churning sea is gray no longer—the water is black, black as basalt and as heavy. The sky's hue has deepened so that at the moment no horizon is visible. I am surrounded by a billowing blackness thundering against me from all sides . . .

Back below now, as lightning flickers. The storm will break soon, and Neptune howls piteously. I stroke his quivering flanks, but the poor animal shrinks away. It seems that he fears even my presence; can it be that my own features betray an equal agitation? I do not know—I only feel that I am helpless, trapped here and awaiting the mercy of the storm. I cannot write much longer.

And yet I will set down a further statement. I must, if only to prove to myself that reason again prevails. In writing of my venture up to the platform—my viewing of the sea and sky—I omitted to mention the meaning of a single moment. There came upon me, as I gazed down at the black and boiling madness of the waters below, a wild and wilful craving to become one with it. But why should I disguise the naked truth?—I felt an insane impulse to hurl myself into the sea!

It has passed now; passed, I pray, forever. I did not yield to this perverse prompting and I am back here in my quarters, writing calmly once again. Yet the fact remains—the hideous urge to destroy myself came suddenly, and with the force of one of those monstrous waves.

And what—I force myself to realize—was the meaning of my demented desire? It was that I sought escape, escape from loneliness. It was as if by mingling with the sea and the storm I would no longer be *alone*.

But I defy the elements. I defy the powers of the earth and of the heavens. Alone I am, alone I *must* be—and come what may, I shall survive! My laughter rises above all your thunder!

So—ye spirits of the storm—blow, howl, rage, hurl your watery weight against my fortress—I am greater than you in all

your powers. But wait! Neptune ... something has happened to
the creature ... I must attend him ...

Jan. 16. The storm is abated. I am back at my desk now, alone—
truly alone. I have locked poor Neptune in the store-room below;
the unfortunate beast seems driven out of his wits by the forces
of the storm. When last I wrote he was worked into a frenzy,
whining and pawing and wheeling in circles. He was incapable of
responding to my commands and I had no choice but to literally
drag him down the stairs by the scruff of his neck and incarcerate
him in the store-room where he could not come to harm. I own
that concern for *my* safety was involved—the possibility of being
imprisoned in this light-house with a mad dog must be avoided.

His howls, throughout the storm, were pitiable indeed, but
now he is silent. When last I ventured to gaze into the room I
perceived him sleeping, and I trust that rest and calm will restore
him to my full companionship as before.

Companionship!

How shall I describe the horrors of the storm I faced *alone?*

In this diary entry I have prefaced a date—*January 16th*—but
that is merely a guess. The storm has swept away all track of
Time. Did it last a day, two days, three—as I now surmise?—a
week, or a century? I do *not* know.

I know only an endless raging of waters that threatened, time
and again, to engulf the very pinnacle of the light-house. I know
only an eternity of ebony, an aeon of billowing black composed
of sea and sky commingled. I only know that there were times
when my own voice out-roared the storm—but how can I convey
the cause of *that?* There was a time, perhaps a full day, perhaps
much longer, when I could not bear to rise from my couch but lay
with my face buried in the pillows, weeping like a child. But mine
were not the pure tears of childhood innocence—call them,
rather, the tears of Lucifer upon the realization of his eternal
fall from grace. It seemed to me that I was truly the victim of an
endless damnation; condemned forever to remain a prisoner in a
world of thunderous chaos.

There is no need to write of the fancies and fantasies which
assailed me through those unhallowed hours. At times I felt that

the light-house was giving way and that I would be swept into the sea. At times I knew myself to be a victim of a colossal plot—I cursed DeGrät for sending me, knowingly, to my doom. At times (and these were the worst moments of all) I felt the full force of loneliness, crashing down upon me in waves higher than those wrought by water.

But all has passed, and the sea—and myself—are calm again. A peculiar calmness, this; as I gaze out upon the water there are certain phenomena I was not aware of until this very moment.

Before setting down my observations, let me reassure myself that I am, indeed, *quite* calm; no trace of my former tremors or agitation yet remains. The transient madness induced by the storm has departed and my brain is free of phantasms—indeed, my perceptive faculties seem to be sharpened to an unusual acuity.

It is almost as though I find myself in possession of an additional sense, an ability to analyze and penetrate beyond former limitations superimposed by Nature.

The water on which I gaze is placid once more. The sky is only lightly leaden in hue. But wait—low on the horizon creeps a sudden flame! It is the sun, the Arctic sun in sullen splendour, emerging momentarily from the pall to incarnadine the ocean. Sun and sky, sea and air about me, turn to blood.

Can it be I who but a moment ago wrote of returned, regained sanity? I, who have just shrieked aloud, "Alone!"—and half-rising from my chair, heard the muffled booming echo reverberate through the lonely light-house, its sepulchral accent intoning "*Alone!*" in answer? It may be that I am, despite all resolution, going mad; if so, I pray the end comes soon.

Jan. 18. There will be no end! I have conceived a notion, a theory which my heightened faculties soon will test. I shall embark upon an experiment . . .

Jan. 26. A week has passed here in my solitary prison. Solitary?—perhaps, but not for long. The experiment is proceeding. I must set down what has occurred.

The sound of the echo set me to thinking. One sends out one's voice and it comes back. One sends out one's thoughts and—can it be that there is a response? Sound, as we know, travels in waves and patterns. The emanations of the brain, perhaps, travel similarly. And they are not confined by physical laws of time, space, or *duration*.

Can one's thoughts produce a reply that *materializes*, just as one's voice produces an echo? An echo is a product of a certain vacuum. A thought . . .

Concentration is the key. I have been concentrating. My supplies are replenished, and Neptune—visited during my venture below—seems rational enough, although he shrinks away when I approach him. I have left him below and spent the past week here. Concentration, I repeat, is the key to my experiment.

Concentration, by its very nature, is a difficult task: I addressed myself to it with no little trepidation. Strive but to remain seated quietly with a mind "empty" of all thought, and one finds in the space of a very few minutes that the errant body is engaged in all manner of distracting movement—foot tapping, finger twisting, facial grimacing.

This I managed to overcome after a matter of many hours— my first three days were virtually exhausted in an effort to rid myself of nervous agitation and assume the inner and outer tranquillity of the Indian *fakir*. Then came the task of "filling" the empty consciousness—filling it completely with *one* intense and concentrated effort of will. What echo would I bring forth from nothingness? What companionship would I seek here in my loneliness? What was the sign or symbol I desired? What symbolized to me the whole absent world of life and light?

DeGrät would laugh me to scorn if he but knew the concept that I chose. Yet I, the cynical, the jaded, the decadent, searched my soul, plumbed my longing, and found that which I most desired—a simple sign, a token of all the earth removed: a fresh and growing flower, a *rose!*

Yes, a simple rose is what I have sought—a rose, torn from its living stem, perfumed with the sweet incarnation of life itself. Seated here before the window I have dreamed, I have mused, I have then concentrated with every fibre of my being upon a *rose*.

My mind was filled with redness—not the redness of the sun

upon the sea, or the redness of blood, but the rich and radiant redness of the rose. My soul was suffused with the scent of a rose: as I brought my faculties to bear exclusively upon the image these walls fell away, the walls of my very flesh fell away, and I seemed to merge in the texture, the odour, the color, the actual *essence* of a rose.

Shall I write of this, the seventh day, when heated at the window as the sun emerged from the sea, I felt the commanding of my consciousness? Shall I write of rising, descending the stairs, opening the iron door at the base of the light-house and peering out at the billows that swirled at my very feet? Shall I write of stooping, of grasping, of holding?

Shall I write that I have indeed descended those iron stairs and returned here with my wave-borne trophy—*that this very day, from waters two hundred miles distant from any shore, I have reached down and plucked a fresh rose?*

Jan. 28. It has not withered! I keep it before me constantly in a vase on this table, and it is a priceless ruby plucked from dreams. It is real—as real as the howls of poor Neptune, who senses that something odd is afoot. His frantic barking does not disturb me; nothing disturbs me, for I am master of a power greater than earth or space or time. And I shall use this power, now, to bring me the final boon. Here in my tower I have become quite the philosopher: I have learned my lesson well and realize that I do not desire wealth, or fame, or the trinkets of society. My need is simply this—Companionship. And now, with the power that is mine to control, I shall have it!

Soon, quite soon, I shall no longer be alone!

Jan. 30. The storm has returned, but I pay it no heed; nor do I mark the howlings of Neptune, although the beast is now literally dashing himself against the door of the store-room. One might fancy that his efforts are responsible for the shuddering of the very light-house itself; but no, it is the fury of the northern gale. I pay it no heed, as I say, but I fully realize that this storm surpasses in extent and intensity anything I could imagine as witness to its predecessor.

Yet it is unimportant; even though the light above me flickers and threatens to be extinguished by the sheer velocity of wind that seeps through these stout walls; even though the ocean sweeps against the foundations with a force that makes solid stone seem flimsy as straw; even though the sky is a single black roaring mouth that yawns low upon the horizon to engulf me.

These things I sense but dimly, as I address myself to the appointed task. I pause now only for food and a brief respite—and scribble down these words to mark the progress of resolution towards an inevitable goal.

For the past several days I have bent my faculties to my will, concentrating utterly and to the uttermost upon the summoning of a Companion.

This Companion will be—I confess it!—a woman; a woman far surpassing the limitations of common mortality. For she is, and must be fashioned, of dreams and longing, of desire and delight beyond the bounds of flesh.

She is the woman of whom I have always dreamed, the One I have sought in vain through what I once presumed, in my ignorance, was the world of reality. It seems to me now that I have always known her, that my soul has contained her presence forever. I can visualize her perfectly—I know her hair, each strand more precious than a miser's gold; the riches of her ivory and alabaster brow, the perfection of her face and form are etched forever in my consciousness. DeGrät would scoff that she is but the figment of a dream—but DeGrät did not see the rose.

The rose—I hesitate to speak of it—has gone. It was the rose which I set before me when first I composed myself to this new effort of will. I gazed at it intently until vision faded, senses stilled, and I lost myself in the attempt of conjuring up my vision of a Companion.

Hours later, the sound of rising waters from without aroused me. I gazed about, my eyes sought the reassurance of the rose and rested only upon a *foulness*. Where the rose had risen proudly in its vase, red crest rampant upon a living stem, I now perceived only a noxious, utterly detestable strand of ichorous decay. No rose this, but only seaweed; rotted, noisome and putrescent. I flung it away, but for long moments I could not banish a wild presentiment—was it true that I had deceived myself? Was it a weed, and only a weed I plucked from the ocean's breast? Did the force of my thought momentarily invest it with the attributes of a rose? Would anything I called up from the depths—the depths of sea or the depths of consciousness— be *truly* real?

The blessed image of the Companion came to soothe these fevered speculations, and I knew myself saved. There *was* a rose; perhaps my thought had created it and nourished it—only when my entire concentration turned to other things did it depart, or resume another shape. And with my Companion, there will be no need for focussing my faculties elsewhere. She, and she alone, will be the recipient of everything my mind, my heart, my soul possesses. If will, if sentiment, if love are needed to preserve her, these things she shall have in entirety. So there is nothing to fear. Nothing to fear . . .

Once again now I shall lay my pen aside and return to the great task—the task of "creation", if you will—and I shall not fail. The fear (I admit it!) of loneliness is enough to drive me forward to unimaginable brinks. She, and she alone, can save me, shall save me, *must* save me! I can see her now—the golden glitter of her— and my consciousness calls to her to rise, to appear before me in radiant reality. Somewhere upon these storm-tossed seas she *exists*, I know it—and wherever she may be, my call will come to her and she will respond.

Jan. 31. The command came at midnight. Roused from the depths of the most profound innermost communion by a thunderclap, I rose as though in the grip of somnambulistic compulsion and moved down the spiral stairs.

The lantern I bore trembled in my hand; its light wavered in the wind, and the very iron treads beneath my feet shook with the furious force of the storm. The booming of the waves as they struck the lighthouse walls seemed to place me within the center of a maelstrom of ear-shattering sound, yet over the demoniacal din I could detect the frenzied howls of poor Neptune as I passed the door behind which he was confined. The door shook with the combined force of the wind and of his still desperate efforts to free himself—but I hastened on my way, descending to the iron door at the base of the light-house.

To open it required the use of both hands, and I set the lantern down at one side. To open it, moreover, required the summoning of a resolution I scarcely possessed—for beyond that door was the force and fury of the wildest storm that ever shrieked across these seething seas. A sudden wave might dash me from the doorway, or, conversely, enter and inundate the light-house itself.

But consciousness prevailed; consciousness drove me forward.

I *knew*. I thrilled to the certainty that *she* was without the iron portal—I unbolted the door with the urgency of one who rushes into the arms of his beloved.

The door swung open—blew open—roared open—and the storm burst upon me; a ravening monster of black-mouthed waves capped with white fangs. The sea and sky surged forward as if to attack, and I stood enveloped in Chaos. A flash of lightning revealed the immensity of utter Nightmare.

I saw it not, for the same flash illumined the form, the lineaments of *she* whom I sought.

Lightning and lantern were unneeded—her golden glory outshone all as she stood there, pale and trembling, a goddess arisen from the depths of the sea!

Hallucination, vision, apparition? My trembling fingers sought, and found, their answer. Her flesh was real—cold as the icy waters from whence she came, but palpable and permanent. I thought of the storm, of doomed ships and drowning men, of a girl cast upon the waters and struggling towards the succor of the light-house beacon. I thought of a thousand explanations, a thousand miracles, a thousand riddles or reasons beyond rationality. Yet only one thing mattered—my Companion was here, and I had but to step forward and take her in my arms.

No word was spoken, nor could one be heard in all that Inferno. No word was needed, for she smiled. Pale lips parted as I held out my arms, and she moved closer. Pale lips parted—and I saw the pointed teeth, set in rows like those of a shark. Her eyes, fishlike and staring, swam closer. As I recoiled, her arms came up to cling, and they were cold as the waters beneath, cold as the storm, cold as death.

In one monstrous moment I *knew*, knew with uttermost certainty, that the power of my will had indeed summoned, the call of my consciousness *had* been answered. But the answer came not from the living, for nothing lived in this storm. I had sent my will out over the waters, but the will penetrates all dimensions, and my answer had come from *below* the waters. *She* was from below, where the drowned dead lie dreaming, and I had awakened her and clothed her with a horrid life. A life that thirsted, and must drink . . .

I think I shrieked, then, but I heard no sound. Certainly, I did not hear the howls from Neptune as the beast, burst from his prison, bounded down the stairs and flung himself upon the creature from the sea.

His furry form bore her back and obscured my vision; in an instant she was falling backwards, away, into the sea that spawned her. Then, and only then, did I catch a glimpse of the final moment of animation in that which my consciousness had summoned. Lightning seared the sight inexorably upon my soul—the sight of the ultimate blasphemy I had created in my pride. The rose had wilted . . .

The rose had wilted and become seaweed. And now, the golden one was gone and in its place was the bloated, swollen obscenity of a thing long-drowned and dead, risen from the slime and to that slime returning.

Only a moment, and then the waves overwhelmed it, bore it back into the blackness. Only a moment, and the door was slammed shut. Only a moment, and I raced up the iron stairs, Neptune yammering at my heels. Only a moment, and I reached the safety of this sanctuary.

Safety? There is no safety in the universe for me, no safety in a consciousness that could create such horror. And there is no safety here—the wrath of the waves increases with every moment, the anger of the sea and its creatures rises to an inevitable crescendo.

Mad or sane, it does not matter, for the end is the same in either case. I know now that the light-house will shatter and fall. I am already shattered, and must fall with it.

There is time only to gather these notes, strap them securely in a cylinder and attach it to Neptune's collar. It may be that he can swim, or cling to a fragment of debris. It may be that a ship, passing by this toppling beacon, may stay and search the waters for a sign—and thus find and rescue the gallant beast.

That ship shall not find me. I go with the light-house and go willingly, down to the dark depths. Perhaps—is it but perverted poetry?—I shall join my Companion there forever. Perhaps . . .

The light-house is trembling. The beacon flickers above my head and I hear the rush of waters in their final onslaught. There is—yes—a wave, bearing down upon me. It is higher than the tower, it blots out the sky itself, everything . . .

The Hungry House

At first there were two of them—he and she, together. That's the way it was when they bought the house.

Then *it* came. Perhaps it was there all the time, waiting for them in the house. At any rate, it was there now. And nothing could be done.

Moving was out of the question. They'd taken a five-year lease, secretly congratulating themselves on the low rental. It would be absurd to complain to the agent, impossible to explain to their friends. For that matter, they had nowhere else to go; they had searched for months to find a home.

Besides, at first neither he nor she cared to admit awareness of its presence. But both of them knew it was there.

She felt it the very first evening, in the bedroom. She was sitting in front of the high, oldfashioned mirror, combing her hair. The mirror hadn't been dusted yet and it seemed cloudy; the light above it flickered a bit, too.

So at first she thought it was just a trick of shadows or some flaw in the glass. The wavering outline behind her seemed to blur the reflection oddly, and she frowned. Then she began to experience what she often thought of as her "married feeling"—the peculiar awareness which usually denoted her husband's unseen entrance into a room she occupied.

He must be standing behind her, now. He must have come in quietly, without saying anything. Perhaps he was going to put his arms around her, surprise her, startle her. Hence the shadow on the mirror.

She turned, ready to greet him.

The room was empty. And still the odd reflection persisted, together with the sensation of a presence at her back.

She shrugged, moved her head, and made a little face at her-

158

self in the mirror. As a smile it was a failure, because the warped glass and the poor light seemed to distort her grin into something alien—into a smile that was not altogether a composition of her own face and features.

Well, it had been a fatiguing ordeal, this moving business. She flicked a brush through her hair and tried to dismiss the problem.

Nevertheless she felt a surge of relief when he suddenly entered the bedroom. For a moment she thought of telling him, then decided not to worry him over her "nerves".

He was more outspoken. It was the following morning that the incident occurred. He came rushing out of the bathroom, his face bleeding from a razor-cut on the left cheek.

"Is that your idea of being funny?" he demanded, in the petulant little-boy fashion she found so engaging. "Sneaking in behind me and making faces in the mirror? Gave me an awful start—look at this nick I sliced on myself."

She sat up in bed.

"But darling, I haven't been making faces at you. I didn't stir from this bed since you got up."

"Oh." He shook his head, his frown fading into a second set of wrinkles expressing bewilderment. "Oh, I see."

"What is it?" She suddenly threw off the covers and sat on the edge of the bed, wriggling her toes and peering at him earnestly.

"Nothing," he murmured. "Nothing at all. Just thought I saw you, or somebody, looking over my shoulder in the mirror. All of a sudden, you know. It must be those damned lights. Got to get some bulbs in town today."

He patted his cheek with a towel and turned away. She took a deep breath.

"I had the same feeling last night," she confessed, then bit her lip.

"You did?"

"It's probably just the lights, as you said, darling."

"Uh huh." He was suddenly preoccupied. "That must be it. I'll make sure and bring those new bulbs."

"You'd better. Don't forget, the gang is coming down for the housewarming on Saturday."

Saturday proved to be a long time in coming. In the interim

both of them had several experiences which served to upset their minds much more than they cared to admit.

The second morning, after he had left for work, she went out in back and looked at the garden. The place was a mess—half an acre of land, all those trees, the weeds everywhere, and the dead leaves of autumn dancing slowly around the old house. She stood off on a little knoll and contemplated the grave gray gables of another century. Suddenly she felt lonely here. It wasn't only the isolation, the feeling of being half a mile from the nearest neighbor, down a deserted dirt road. It was more as though she were an intruder here—an intruder upon the past. The cold breeze, the dying trees, the sullen sky were welcome; they belonged to the house. She was the outsider, because she was young, because she was alive.

She felt it all, but did not think it. To acknowledge her sensations would be to acknowledge fear. Fear of being alone. Or, worse still, fear of *not* being alone.

Because, as she stood there, the back door closed.

Oh, it was the autumn wind, all right. Even though the door didn't bang, or slam shut. It merely closed. But that was the wind's work, it had to be. There was nobody in the house, nobody to close the door.

She felt in her housedress pocket for the door key, then shrugged as she remembered leaving it on the kitchen sink. Well, she hadn't planned to go inside yet anyway. She wanted to look over the yard, look over the spot where the garden had been and where she fully intended a garden to bloom next spring. She had measurements to make, and estimates to take, and a hundred things to do here outside.

And yet, when the door closed, she knew she had to go in. Something was trying to shut her out, shut her out of her own house, and that would never do. Something was fighting against her, fighting against all idea of change. She had to fight back.

So she marched up to the door, rattled the knob, found herself locked out as she expected. The first round was lost. But there was always the window.

The kitchen window was eye-level in height, and a small crate served to bring it within easy reach. The window was open a good four inches and she had no trouble inserting her hands to raise it further.

She tugged.

Nothing happened. The window must be stuck. But it wasn't stuck; she'd just opened it before going outside and it opened quite easily; besides, they'd tried all the windows and found them in good operating condition.

She tugged again. This time the window raised a good six inches and then—something slipped. The window came down like the blade of a guillotine, and she got her hands out just in time. She bit her lip, sent strength through her shoulders, raised the window once more.

And this time she stared into the pane. The glass was transparent, ordinary window glass. She'd washed it just yesterday and she knew it was clean. There had been no blur, no shadow, and certainly no movement.

But there was movement now. Something cloudy, something obscenely opaque, peered out of the window, peered out of itself and pressed the window down against her. Something matched her strength to shut her out.

Suddenly, hysterically, she realized that she was staring at her own reflection through the shadows of the trees. Of course, it had to be her own reflection. And there was no reason for her to close her eyes and sob as she tugged the window up and half-tumbled her way into the kitchen.

She was inside, and alone. Quite alone. Nothing to worry about. Nothing to worry him about. She wouldn't tell him.

He wouldn't tell her either. Friday afternoon, when she took the car and went into town for groceries and liquor in preparation for tomorrow's party, he stayed home from the office and arranged the final details of settling down.

That's why he carried up all the garment bags to the attic—to store the summer clothes, get them out of the way. And that's how he happened to open the little cubicle under the front gable. He was looking for the attic closet; he'd put down the bags and started to work along the wall with a flashlight. Then he noticed the door and the padlock.

Dust and rust told their own story; nobody had come this way for a long, long time. He thought again of Hacker, the glib real-estate agent who'd handled the rental of the place. "Been vacant several years and needs a little fixing up," Hacker had said. From the looks of it, nobody had lived here for a coon's age. All the better; he could force the lock with a common file.

He went downstairs for the file and returned quickly, noting as he did so that the attic dust told its own story. Apparently the former occupants had left in something of a hurry—debris was scattered everywhere, and swaths and swirls scored the dust to indicate that belongings had been dragged and hauled and swept along in a haphazard fashion.

Well, he had all winter to straighten things out, and right now he'd settle for storing the garment bags. Clipping the flashlight to his belt, he bent over the lock, file in hand, and tried his skill at breaking and entering.

The lock sprung. He tugged at the door, opened it, inhaled a gust of mouldy dampness, then raised the flash and directed the beam into the long, narrow closet.

A thousand silver slivers stabbed at his eyeballs. Golden, gleaming fire seared his pupils. He jerked the flashlight back, sent the beam upwards. Again, lances of light entered his eyes.

Suddenly he adjusted his vision and comprehension. He stood peering into a room full of mirrors. They hung from cords, lay in corners, stood along the walls in rows.

There was a tall, stately full-length mirror, set in a door; a pair of plate-glass ovals, inset in oldfashioned dresser-tops; a panel glass, and even a complete, dismantled bathroom medicine cabinet similar to the one they had just installed. And the floor was lined with hand-mirrors of all sizes and shapes. He noted an ornate silver-handled mirror straight from a woman's dressing-table; behind it stood the vanity-mirror removed from the table itself. And there were pocket mirrors, mirrors from purse-compacts, mirrors of every size and shape. Against the far wall stood a whole series of looking-glass slabs that appeared to have been mounted at one time in a bedroom wall.

He gazed at half a hundred silvered surfaces, gazed at half a hundred reflections of his own bewildered face.

And he thought again of Hacker, of their inspection of the

house. He had noted the absence of a medicine cabinet at the time, but Hacker had glossed over it. Somehow he hadn't realized that there were no mirrors of any sort in the house—of course, there was no furniture, but still one might expect a door panel in a place this old.

No mirrors? Why? And why were they all stacked away up here, under lock and key?

It was interesting. His wife might like some of these—that silver-handled beauty mirror, for example. He'd have to tell her about this.

He stepped cautiously into the closet, dragging the garment bags after him. There didn't seem to be any clothes-pole here, or any hooks. He could put some up in a jiffy, though. He piled the bags in a heap, stooping, and the flashlight glittered on a thousand surfaces, sent facets of fire into his face.

Then the fire faded. The silver surfaces darkened oddly. Of course, his reflection covered them now. His reflection, and something darker. Something smoky and swirling, something that was a part of the mouldy dampness, something that choked the closet with its presence. It was behind him—no, at one side—no, in front of him—all around him—it was growing and growing and blotting him out—it was making him sweat and tremble and now it was making him gasp and scuttle out of the closet and slam the door and press against it with all his waning strength, and its name was—

Claustrophobia. That was it. Just claustrophobia, a fancy name for nerves. A man gets nervous when he's cooped up in a small space. For that matter, a man gets nervous when he looks at himself too long in a mirror. Let alone fifty mirrors!

He stood there, shaking, and to keep his mind occupied, keep his mind off what he had just half-seen, half-felt, half-known, he thought about mirrors for a moment. About looking into mirrors. Women did it all the time. Men were different.

Men, himself included, seemed to be self-conscious about mirrors. He could remember going into a clothing-store and seeing himself in one of the complicated arrangements that afforded a side and rear view. What a shock that had been, the first time—and every time, for that matter! A man looks different in a mirror.

Not the way he imagines himself to be, knows himself to be. A mirror distorts. That's why men hum and sing and whistle while they shave. To keep their minds off their reflections. Otherwise they'd go crazy. What was the name of that Greek mythological character who was in love with his own image? Narcissus, that was it. Staring into a pool for hours.

Women could do it, though. Because women never saw themselves, actually. They saw an idealization, a vision. Powder, rouge, lipstick, mascara, eye-shadow, brilliantine, or merely an emptiness to which these elements must be applied. Women were a little crazy to begin with, anyway. Hadn't she said something the other night about seeing him in her mirror when he wasn't there?

Perhaps he'd better not tell her, after all. At least, not until he checked with the real-estate agent, Hacker. He wanted to find out about this business, anyway. Something was wrong, somewhere. Why had the previous owners stored all the mirrors up here?

He began to walk back through the attic, forcing himself to go slowly, forcing himself to think of something, anything, except the fright he'd had in the room of reflections.

Reflect on something. Reflections. Who's afraid of the big bad reflection? Another myth, wasn't it?

Vampires. They had no reflections. "Tell me the truth now, Hacker. The people who built this house—were they vampires?"

That was a pleasant thought. That was a pleasant thought to carry downstairs in the afternoon twilight, to hug to your bosom in the gloom while the floors creaked and the shutters banged and the night came down in the house of shadows where something peered around the corners and grinned at you in the mirrors on the walls.

He sat there waiting for her to come home, and he switched on all the lights, and he put the radio on too and thanked God he didn't have a television set because there was a screen and the screen made a reflection and the reflection might be something he didn't want to see.

But there was no more trouble that evening, and by the time she came home with her packages he had himself under control. So they ate and talked quite naturally—oh, quite naturally, and if it was listening it wouldn't know they were both afraid.

They made their preparations for the party, and called up a few people on the phone, and just on the spur of the moment he suggested inviting Hacker, too. So that was done and they went to bed. The lights were all out and that meant the mirrors were dark, and he could sleep.

Only in the morning it was difficult to shave. And he caught her, yes he caught her, putting on her makeup in the kitchen, using the little compact from her purse and carefully cupping her hands against reflections.

But he didn't tell her and she didn't tell him, and if it guessed their secrets, it kept silent.

He drove off to work and she made canapes, and if at times during the long, dark, dreary Saturday the house groaned and creaked and whispered, that was only to be expected.

The house was quiet enough by the time he came home again, and somehow, that was worse. It was as though something were waiting for night to fall. That's why she dressed early, humming all the while she powdered and primped, swirling around in front of the mirror (you couldn't see too clearly if you swirled). That's why he mixed drinks before their hasty meal and saw to it that they both had several stiff ones (you couldn't see too clearly if you drank).

And then the guests tumbled in. The Teters, complaining about the winding back road through the hills. The Valliants, exclaiming over the antique panelling and the high ceilings. The Ehrs, whooping and laughing, with Vic remarking that the place looked like something designed by Charles Addams. That was a signal for a drink, and by the time Hacker and his wife arrived the blaring radio found ample competition from the voices of the guests.

He drank, and she drank, but they couldn't shut it out altogether. That remark about Charles Addams was bad, and there were other things. Little things. The Talmadges had brought flowers, and she went out to the kitchen to arrange them in a cut-glass vase. There were facets in the glass, and as she stood in the kitchen, momentarily alone, and filled the vase with water from the tap, the crystal darkened beneath her fingers, and something peered, reflected from the facets. She turned, quickly, and she was all alone. All alone, holding a hundred naked eyes in her hands.

So she dropped the vase, and the Ehrs and Talmadges and Hackers and Valliants trooped out to the kitchen, and he came too. Talmadge accused her of drinking and that was reason enough for another round. He said nothing, but got another vase for the flowers. And yet he must have known, because when somebody suggested a tour of the house, he put them off.

"We haven't straightened things out upstairs yet," he said. "It's a mess, and you'd be knocking into crates and stuff."

"Who's up there now?" asked Mrs. Teters, coming into the kitchen with her husband. "We just heard an awful crash."

"Something must have fallen over," the host suggested. But he didn't look at his wife as he spoke, and she didn't look at him.

"How about another drink?" she asked. She mixed and poured hurriedly, and before the glasses were half empty, he took over and fixed another round. Liquor helped to keep people talking and if they talked it would drown out other sounds.

The strategem worked. Gradually the group trickled back into the living room in twos and threes, and the radio blared and the laughter rose and the voices babbled to blot out the noises of the night.

He poured and she served, and both of them drank, but the alcohol had no effect. They moved carefully, as though their bodies were brittle glasses—glasses without bottom—waiting to be shattered by some sudden strident sound. Glasses hold liquor, but they never get drunk.

Their guests were not glasses; they drank and feared nothing, and the drinks took hold. People moved about, and in and out, and pretty soon Mr. Valliant and Mrs. Talmadge embarked on their own private tour of the house upstairs. It was irregular and unescorted, but fortunately nobody noticed either their departure or their absence. At least, not until Mrs. Talmadge came running downstairs and locked herself in the bathroom.

Her hostess saw her pass the doorway and followed her. She rapped on the bathroom door, gained admittance, and prepared to make discreet inquiries. None were necessary. Mrs. Talmadge, weeping and wringing her hands, fell upon her.

"That was a filthy trick!" she sobbed. "Coming up and sneaking in on us. The dirty louse—I admit we were doing a little smooching, but that's all there was to it. And it isn't as though he didn't make enough passes at Gwen Hacker himself. What I want to know is, where did he get the beard? It frightened me out of my wits."

"What's all this?" she asked—knowing all the while what it was, and dreading the words to come.

"Jeff and I were in the bedroom, just standing there in the dark, I swear it, and all at once I looked up over my shoulder at the mirror because light began streaming in from the hall. Somebody had opened the door, and I could see the glass and this face. Oh, it was my husband all right, but he had a beard on and the way he came slinking in, glaring at us—"

Sobs choked off the rest. Mrs. Talmadge trembled so that she wasn't aware of the tremors which racked the frame of her hostess. She, for her part, strained to hear the rest. "—sneaked right out again before we could do anything, but wait till I get him home—scaring the life out of me and all because he's so crazy jealous—the look on his face in the mirror—"

She soothed Mrs. Talmadge. She comforted Mrs. Talmadge. She placated Mrs. Talmadge. And all the while there was nothing to soothe or calm or placate her own agitation.

Still, both of them had restored a semblance of sanity by the time they ventured out into the hall to join the party—just in time to hear Mr. Talmadge's agitated voice booming out over the excited responses of the rest.

"So I'm standing there in the bathroom and this old witch comes up and starts making faces over my shoulder in the mirror. What gives here, anyway? What kind of a house you running here?"

He thought it was funny. So did the others. Most of the others. The host and hostess stood there, not daring to look at each other. Their smiles were cracking. Glass is brittle.

"I don't believe you!" Gwen Hacker's voice. She'd had one, or perhaps three, too many. "I'm going up right now and see for myself." She winked at her host and moved towards the stairs.

"Hey, hold on!" He was too late. She swept, or wobbled, past him.

"Halloween pranks," said Talmadge, nudging him. "Old babe

in a fancy hairdo. Saw her plain as day. What you cook up for us here, anyhow?"

He began to stammer something, anything, to halt the flood of foolish babbling. She moved close to him, wanting to listen, wanting to believe, wanting to do anything but think of Gwen Hacker upstairs, all alone upstairs looking into a mirror and waiting to see—

The screams came then. Not sobs, not laughter, but screams. He took the stairs two at a time. Fat Mr. Hacker was right behind him, and the others straggled along, suddenly silent. There was the sound of feet clubbing the staircase, the sound of heavy breathing, and over everything the continuing high-pitched shriek of a woman confronted with terror too great to contain.

It oozed out of Gwen Hacker's voice, oozed out of her body as she staggered and half-fell into her husband's arms in the hall. The light was streaming out of the bathroom, and it fell upon the mirror that was empty of all reflection, fell upon her face that was empty of all expression.

They crowded around the Hackers—he and she were on either side and the others clustered in front—and they moved along the hall to her bedroom and helped Mr. Hacker stretch his wife out on the bed. She had passed out, somebody mumbled something about a doctor, and somebody else said no, never mind, she'll be all right in a minute, and somebody else said well, I think we'd better be getting along.

For the first time everybody seemed to be aware of the old house and the darkness, and the way the floors creaked and the windows rattled and the shutters banged. Everyone was suddenly sober, solicitous, and extremely anxious to leave.

Hacker bent over his wife, chafing her wrists, forcing her to swallow water, watching her whimper her way out of emptiness. The host and hostess silently procured hats and coats and listened to expressions of polite regret, hasty farewells, and poorly formulated pretenses of, "had a marvelous time, darling."

Teters, Valliants, Talmadges were swallowed up in the night. He and she went back upstairs, back to the bedroom and the Hackers. It was too dark in the hall, and too light in the bedroom. But there they were, waiting. And they didn't wait long.

Mrs. Hacker sat up suddenly and began to talk. To her husband, to them.

"I saw her," she said. "Don't tell me I'm crazy, I saw her! Standing on tiptoe behind me, looking right into the mirror. With the same blue ribbon in her hair, the one she wore the day she—"

"Please, dear," said Mr. Hacker.

She didn't please. "But I saw her. Mary Lou! She made a face at me in the mirror, and she's dead, you know she's dead, she disappeared three years ago and they never did find the body—"

"Mary Lou Dempster." Hacker was a fat man. He had two chins. Both of them wobbled.

"She played around here, you know she did, and Wilma Dempster told her to stay away, she knew all about this house, but she wouldn't and now—oh, her face!"

More sobs. Hacker patted her on the shoulder. He looked as though he could stand a little shoulder-patting himself. But nobody obliged. He stood there, she stood there, still waiting. Waiting for the rest.

"Tell them," said Mrs. Hacker. "Tell them the truth."

"All right, but I'd better get you home."

"I'll wait. I want you to tell them. You must, now."

Hacker sat down heavily. His wife leaned against his shoulder. The two waited another moment. Then it came.

"I don't know how to begin, how to explain," said fat Mr. Hacker. "It's probably my fault, of course, but I didn't know. All this foolishness about haunted houses—nobody believes that stuff any more, and all it does is push property values down, so I didn't say anything. Can you blame me?"

"I saw her face," whispered Mrs. Hacker.

"I know. And I should have told you. About the house, I mean. Why it hasn't rented for twenty years. Old story in the neighborhood, and you'd have heard it sooner or later anyway, I guess."

"Get on with it," said Mrs. Hacker. She was suddenly strong again and he, with his wobbling chins, was weak.

Host and hostess stood before them, brittle as glass, as the words poured out; poured out and filled them to overflowing. He and she, watching and listening, filling up with the realization, with the knowledge, with that for which they had waited.

It was the Bellman house they were living in, the house Job Bellman built for his bride back in the sixties; the house where his bride had given birth to Laura and taken death in exchange. And Job Bellman had toiled through the seventies as his daughter grew to girlhood, rested in complacent retirement during the eighties as Laura Bellman blossomed into the reigning beauty of the county—some said the state, but then flattery came quickly to men's lips in those days.

There were men aplenty, coming and going through that decade; passing through the hall in polished boots, bowing and stroking brilliantined mustachios, smirking at old Job, grinning at the servants, and gazing in moonstruck adoration at Laura.

Laura took it all as her rightful due, but land's sakes, she'd never think of it, no, not while Papa was still alive, and no, she couldn't, she was much too young to marry, and why, she'd never heard of such a thing, she'd always thought it was so much nicer just being friends—

Moonlight, dances, parties, hayrides, sleighrides, candy, flowers, gifts, tokens, cotillion balls, punch, fans, beauty spots, dressmakers, curlers, mandolins, cycling, and the years that whirled away. And then, one day, old Job dead in the four-poster bed upstairs, and the Doctor came and the Minister, and then the Lawyer, hack-hack-hacking away with his dry, precise little cough, and his talk of inheritance and estate and annual income.

Then she was alone, just she and the servants and the mirrors. Laura and her mirrors. Mirrors in the morning, and the careful inspection, the scrutiny that began the day. Mirrors at night before the caller arrived, before the carriage came, before she whirled away to another triumphal entry, another fan-fluttering, pirouetting descent of the staircase. Mirrors at dawn, absorbing the smiles, listening to the secrets, the tale of the evening's triumph.

"Mirror, mirror on the wall, who is the fairest of them all?"

Mirrors told her the truth, mirrors did not lie, mirrors did not paw or clutch or whisper or demand in return for acknowledgement of beauty.

Years passed, but mirrors did not age, did not change. And Laura did not age. The callers were fewer and some of them were oddly altered. They seemed older, somehow. And yet how could that be? For Laura Bellman was still young. The mirrors said so, and they always told the truth. Laura spent more and more time with the mirrors. Powdering, searching for wrinkles, tinting and curling her long hair. Smiling, fluttering eyelashes, making deliciously delicate little *moues*. Swirling daintily, posturing before her own perfection.

Sometimes, when the callers came, she sent word that she was not at home. It seemed silly, somehow, to leave the mirrors. And after a while, there weren't many callers to worry about. Servants came and went, some of them died, but there were always new ones. Laura and the mirrors remained. The nineties were truly gay, but in a way other people wouldn't understand. How Laura laughed, rocking back and forth on the bed, sharing her giddy secrets with the glass!

The years fairly flew by, but Laura merely laughed. She giggled and tittered when the servants spoke to her, and it was easier now to take her meals on a tray in her room. Because there was something wrong with the servants, and with Doctor Turner who came to visit her and who was always being tiresome about going away for a rest to a lovely home.

They thought she was getting old, but she wasn't—the mirrors didn't lie. She wore the false teeth and the wig to please the others, the outsiders, but she didn't really need them. The mirrors told her she was unchanged. They talked to her now, the mirrors did, and she never said a word. Just sat nodding and swaying before them in the room reeking of powder and *patchouli*, stroking her throat and listening to the mirrors telling her how beautiful she was and what a belle she would be if she would only waste her beauty on the world. But she'd never leave here, never; she and the mirrors would always be together.

And then came the day they tried to take her away, and they actually laid hands upon her—upon her, Laura Bellman, the most exquisitely beautiful woman in the world! Was it any wonder that she fought, clawed and kicked and whined, and struck out so that one of the servants crashed headlong into the beautiful glass and struck his foolish head and died, his nasty blood staining the image of her perfection?

Of course it was all a stupid mistake and it wasn't her fault, and Doctor Turner told the magistrate so when he came to call. Laura didn't have to see him, and she didn't have to leave the house. But they always locked the door to her room now, and they took away all her mirrors.

They *took away* all her mirrors!

They left her alone, caged up, a scrawny, wizened, wrinkled old woman with no reflection. They took the mirrors away and made her old; old, and ugly, and afraid.

The night they did it, she cried. She cried and hobbled around the room, stumbling blindly in a tearsome tour of nothingness.

That's when she realized she was old, and nothing could save her. Because she came up against the window and leaned her wrinkled forehead against the cold, cold glass. The light came from behind her and as she drew away she could see her reflection in the window.

The window—it was a mirror, too! She gazed into it, gazed long and lovingly at the tear-streaked face of the fantastically rouged and painted old harridan, gazed at the corpse-countenance readied for the grave by a mad embalmer.

Everything whirled. It was her house, she knew every inch of it, from the day of her birth onwards the house was a part of her. It was her room, she had lived here for ever and ever. But *this*—this obscenity—was not her face. Only a mirror could show her that, and there would never be a mirror for her again. For an instant she gazed at the truth and then, mercifully, the gleaming glass of the windowpane altered and once again she gazed at Laura Bellman, the proudest beauty of them all. She drew herself erect, stepped back, and whirled into a dance. She danced forward, a prim self-conscious smile on her lips. Danced into the windowpane, half-through it, until razored splinters of glass tore her scrawny throat.

That's how she died and that's how they found her. The Doctor came, and the servants and the Lawyer did what must be done. The house was sold, then sold again. It fell into the hands of a rental agency. There were tenants, but not for long. They had troubles with mirrors.

A man died—of a heart attack, they said—while adjusting his

necktie before the bureau one evening. Grotesque enough, but he had complained to people in the town about strange happenings, and his wife babbled to everyone.

A school-teacher who rented the place in the twenties "passed away" in circumstances which Doctor Turner had never seen fit to relate. He had gone to the rental agency and begged them to take the place off the market; that was almost unnecessary, for the Bellman home had its reputation firmly established by now.

Whether or not Mary Lou Dempster had disappeared here would never be known. But the little girl had last been seen a year ago on the road leading to the house and although a search had been made and nothing discovered, there was talk aplenty.

Then the new heirs had stepped in, briskly, with their pooh-poohs and their harsh dismissals of advice, and the house had been cleaned and put up for rental.

So he and she had come to live here—with it. And that was the story, all of the story.

Mr. Hacker put his arm around Gwen, harrumphed, and helped her rise. He was apologetic, he was shame-faced, he was deferential. His eyes never met those of his tenant.

He barred the doorway. "We're getting out of here, right now," he said. "Lease or no lease."

"That can be arranged. But—I can't find you another place tonight, and tomorrow's Sunday—"

"We'll pack and get out of here tomorrow," she spoke up. "Go to a hotel, anywhere. But we're leaving."

"I'll call you tomorrow," said Hacker. "I'm sure everything will be all right. After all, you've stayed here through the week and nothing, I mean nobody has—"

His words trailed off. There was no point in saying any more. The Hackers left and they were all alone. Just the two of them.

Just the *three* of them, that is.

But now they—he and she—were too tired to care. The inevitable letdown, product of overindulgence and over-excitement, was at hand.

They said nothing, for there was nothing to say. They heard nothing, for the house—and it—maintained a sombre silence.

She went to her room and undressed. He began to walk around

the house. First he went to the kitchen and opened a drawer next to the sink. He took a hammer and smashed the kitchen mirror.

Tinkle-tinkle! And then a crash! That was the mirror in the hall. Then upstairs, to the bathroom. Crash and clink of broken glass in the medicine cabinet. Then a smash as he shattered the panel in his room. And now he came to her bedroom and swung the hammer against the huge oval of the vanity, shattering it to bits.

He wasn't cut, wasn't excited, wasn't upset. And the mirrors were gone. Every last one of them was gone.

They looked at each other for a moment. Then he switched off the lights, tumbled into bed beside her, and sought sleep.

The night wore on.

It was all a little silly in the daylight. But she looked at him again in the morning, and he went into his room and hauled out the suitcases. By the time she had breakfast ready he was already laying his clothes out on the bed. She got up after eating and took her own clothing from the drawers and hangars and racks and hooks. Soon he'd go up to the attic and get the garment bags. The movers could be called tomorrow, or as soon as they had a destination in mind.

The house was quiet. If it knew their plans, it wasn't acting. The day was gloomy and they kept the lights off without speaking—although both of them knew it was because of the window-panes and the story of the reflection. He could have smashed the window glass of course, but it was all a little silly. And they'd be out of here shortly.

Then they heard the noise. Trickling, burbling. A splashing sound. It came from beneath their feet. She gasped.

"Water-pipe—in the basement," he said, smiling and taking her by the shoulders.

"Better take a look." She moved towards the stairs.

"Why should you go down there? I'll tend to it."

But she shook her head and pulled away. It was her penance for gasping. She had to show she wasn't afraid. She had to show him—and it, too.

"Wait a minute," he said. "I'll get the pipe-wrench. It's in the trunk in the car." He went out the back door. She stood irreso-lute, then headed for the cellar stairs. The splashing was getting

louder. The burst pipe was flooding the basement. It made a
funny noise, like laughter.

He could hear it even when he walked up the driveway and
opened the trunk of the car. These old houses always had something wrong with them; he might have known it. Burst pipes and—

Yes. He found the wrench. He walked back to the door, listening to the water gurgle, listening to his wife scream.

She *was* screaming! Screaming down in the basement, screaming down in the dark.

He ran, swinging the heavy wrench. He clumped down the
stairs, down into the darkness, the screams tearing up at him.
She was caught, it had her, she was struggling with it but it was
strong, too strong, and the light came streaming in on the pool
of water beside the shattered pipe and in the reflection he saw
her face and the blackness of other faces swirling around her and
holding her.

He brought the wrench up, brought it down on the black blur,
hammering and hammering and hammering until the screaming
died away. And then he stopped and looked down at her. The dark
blur had faded away into the reflection of the water—the reflection that had evoked it. But she was still there, and she was still,
and she would be still forever now. Only the water was getting
red, where her head rested in it. And the end of the wrench was
red, too.

For a moment he started to tell her about it, and then he realized she was gone. Now there were only the two of them left. He
and it.

And he was going upstairs. He was walking upstairs, still carrying the bloody wrench, and he was going over to the phone to
call the police and explain.

He sat down in a chair before the phone, thinking about what
he'd tell them, how he'd explain. It wouldn't be easy. There was
this madwoman, see, and she looked into mirrors until there
was more of her alive in her reflection than there was in her own
body. So when she committed suicide she lived on, somehow, and
came alive in mirrors or glass or anything that reflected. And she
killed others or drove them to death and their reflections were
somehow joined with hers so that this thing kept getting stronger

and stronger, sucking away at life with that awful core of pride that could live beyond death. Woman, thy name is vanity! And that, gentlemen, is why I killed my wife.

Yes, it was a fine explanation, but it wouldn't hold water. *Water*—the pool in the basement had evoked it. He might have known it if only he'd stopped to think, to reflect. *Reflect*. That was the wrong word, now. Reflect. The way the windowpane before him was reflecting.

He stared into the glass now, saw it behind him, surging up from the shadows. He saw the bearded man's face, the peering, pathetic, empty eyes of a little girl, the goggling grimacing stare of an old woman. It wasn't there, behind him, but it was alive in the reflection, and as he rose he gripped the wrench tightly. It wasn't there, but he'd strike at it, fight at it, come to grips with it somehow.

He turned, moving back, the ring of shadow-faces pressing. He swung the wrench. Then he saw *her* face coming up through all the rest. Her face, with shining splinters where the eyes should be. He couldn't smash it down, he couldn't hit her again.

It moved forward. He moved back. His arm went out to one side. He heard the tinkle of window glass behind him and vaguely remembered that this was how the old woman had died. The way he was dying now—falling through the window, and cutting his throat, and the pain lanced up and in, tearing at his brain as he hung there on the jagged spikes of glass, bleeding his life away.

Then he was gone.

His body hung there, but he was gone.

There was a little puddle on the floor, moving and growing. The light from outside shone on it, and there was a reflection.

Something emerged fully from the shadows now, emerged and capered demurely in the darkness.

It had the face of an old woman and the face of a child, the face of a bearded man, and *his* face, and *her* face, changing and blending.

It capered and postured, and then it squatted, dabbling. Finally, all alone in the empty house, it just sat there and waited. There was nothing to do now but wait for the next to come. And meanwhile, it could always admire itself in that growing, growing red reflection on the floor . . .

Sleeping Beauty

"New Orleans," said Morgan. "The land of dreams."

"That's right," the bartender nodded. "That's the way the song goes."

"I remember Connee Boswell singing it when I was just a kid," Morgan told him. "Made up my mind to hit this town some day and see for myself. But what I want to know is, where is it?"

"It?"

"The land of dreams," Morgan murmured. "Where'd it all disappear to?" He leaned forward and the bartender refilled his glass. "Take Basin Street, for instance. It's just a lousy railroad track. And the streetcar named Desire is a bus."

"Used to be a streetcar, all right," the bartender assured him. "Then they took 'em out of the Quarter and made all the streets one way. That's progress, Mac."

"Progress!" Morgan swallowed his drink. "When I got down here today I did the Quarter. Museum, Jackson Square, Pirate's Alley, Antoine's, Morning Call, the works. It's nothing but a tourist trap."

"Now wait a minute," the bartender said. "What about all the old buildings with the balconies and grillwork, stuff like that?"

"I saw them," Morgan admitted. "But you pass one of those fine old green-shuttered jobs and what do you see sitting right next door? A laundromat, that's what. Laundromats in the *Vieux Carre*. They've killed off your old Southern mammy and installed an automatic washer in her place. All the quaint, picturesque atmosphere that's left is hidden behind the walls of a private patio. What's left to see are the antique shops on Royal Street, filled with precious items imported from far-away Brooklyn."

The bartender shrugged. "There's always Bourbon Street."

Morgan made a face. "I hit Bourbon tonight, before I came here. A big neon nothing. Clipjoints and stripjoints. Imitation Dixieland played for visiting Swedes from Minnesota."

"Careful, Mac," said the bartender. "I'm from Duluth myself."

"You would be." Morgan tackled a fresh drink. "There isn't a genuine native or a genuine spot in the whole place. What's the song say about Creole babies with flashing eyes? All I saw was a bunch of B-girls out of exotic, mysterious old Cincinnati."

The bartender tipped the bottle again without being asked. "Now I get the drift, Mac," he muttered. "Maybe you're looking for a little action, huh? Well, I know a place—"

Morgan shook his head. "I'll bet you do. Everybody knows a place. Walking north, before I crossed Rampart, I was stopped three times. Cab-drivers. They wanted to haul me to a place. And what was their big sales-pitch? Air-conditioning, that's what! Man waits half his life, saves his dough for a trip down here, and the land of dreams turns out to be air-conditioned!"

He stood up, knocking against the bar-stool.

"Tell you a secret," Morgan said. "If Jean LaFitte was around today, he'd be a cab-driver."

He lurched out of the tavern and stood on the sidewalk outside, inhaling the damp air. It had turned quite foggy. Fog in the streets. Fog in his brain.

He knew where he was, though—north of Rampart, east of Canal and the Jung Hotel. In spite of the fog, he wasn't lost.

All at once Morgan wished he *was* lost. Lost on this crazy, winding little side street where the grass pushed up between the brick paving-stones and all the houses were shuttered against the night. There were no cars, no passersby, and if it wasn't for the street-lamps he could easily imagine himself to be in the old New Orleans. The *real* New Orleans of the songs and stories, the city of Bolden and Oliver and a kid named Satch.

It had been that way once, he knew. Then World War I came along and they closed down Storeyville. And World War II came along and they turned Bourbon Street into a midway for service-men and conventioneers. The tourists liked it fine; they came to the Mardi Gras parades and they ate at Arnaud's and they sampled a Sazerac at the Old Absinthe House and went home happy.

But Morgan wasn't a tourist. He was a romantic, looking for the land of dreams.

Forget it, he told himself.

So he started to walk and he tried to forget it, but he couldn't. The fog grew thicker—both fogs. Out of the internal fog came phrases of the old songs and visions of the old legends. Out of the external fog loomed the crumbling walls of the St. Louis Cemetery. St. Louis Number One, the guidebooks called it.

Well, to hell with the guidebooks. This was what Morgan had been looking for. The real New Orleans was inside these walls. Dead and buried, crumbling away in decayed glory.

Morgan found the grilled gate. It was locked. He peered through the bars, squinting at foggy figures. There were ghosts inside, real ghosts. He could see them standing silently within—white, looming figures pointing and beckoning to him. They wanted Morgan to join them there, and that's where he belonged. Inside, with the other dead romantics—

"Mister, what you doing?"

Morgan turned, stumbling back against the gateway. A small man peered up at him, a small whitehaired man whose open mouth exuded a curious, sickish-sweet odor.

One of the ghosts, Morgan told himself. *The odor of corruption*—

But it was only alcohol. And the old man was real, even though his face and his eyes seemed filled with fog.

"Can't get in there, Mister," he was saying. "Place is closed for the night."

Morgan nodded. "You the watchman?" he asked.

"No. Just happened I was wandering around."

"So was I." Morgan gestured at the vista beyond the gateway. "First damned thing I've hit in this town that looked real."

The old man smiled, and again Morgan caught the sickish-sweet odor. "You're right," he said. "All the real things are dead. Notice the angels?"

"I thought they were ghosts," Morgan admitted.

"Maybe so. Lots of things inside there besides statues. See the tombs? Everybody's buried above ground, on account of the swamps. Them as couldn't afford a tomb, why they just rented a crypt in the cemetery wall. You could rent by the month if you liked. But if you didn't pay up—out came Grandpa! That is, if the snatchers didn't get him first."

The old man chuckled. "See the bars and chains on the doors?"

he asked. "Rich folk put them up. Had to protect their dead from the bodysnatchers. Some say the grave-robbers were after jewels and such. Others claim the darkies needed the bones for voodoo. I could tell you stories—"

Morgan took a deep breath. "I'd like to hear some of those stories," he said. "How about going somewhere for a drink?"

"A pleasure." The old man bowed.

Under ordinary circumstances, Morgan would have found the spectacle slightly ridiculous. Now it seemed appropriate. And it was appropriate that the little man led him down twisting streets into ever-thickening fog. It was appropriate that he steered him at last into a small, dingy bar with a single dim light burning in its curtained window. It was appropriate that the stranger ordered for them both without inquiring what Morgan would have.

The bartender was a fat man with a pockmarked face which bore no expression at all as he set glasses down before them. Morgan stared at the cloudy greenish liquor. It looked like a condensation of the fog, but it gave off the odd, sickish-sweet smell he had come to recognize.

"Absinthe," the old man murmured. "Not supposed to serve it, but they know me here." He raised his glass. "To the old days," he said.

"The old days."

The drink tasted of licorice and fire.

"Everybody used to know me then," the stranger told him. "Came to Storeyville in nineteen-and-two. Never did pick up the accent, but I've been a professional Southerner ever since. A real professional, you might say." He started a chuckle that ended up as a wheeze. "Throat's dry," he explained.

Morgan beckoned to the bartender. The green liquor climbed in the glasses, then descended. It rose and fell several times during the next hour. And the old man's voice rose and fell, and Morgan felt himself rising and falling, too.

It wasn't a panicky feeling, though. Somehow it seemed quite natural for him to be sitting here in this lonely little bar with a shabbily-dressed old lush who gazed at him with eyes of milky marble.

And it was natural for Morgan to talk about how disappointed he was in New Orleans, about wishing he'd been here to see the Mahogany Hall and the Ivory Palace—

"Storeyville," the old man said. "I can tell you all you want to know about that. Said I was a *professional* Southerner." He wheezed again, then recovered himself. "Had six chickens on the block," he said. "Wouldn't think it to look at me now, but I was a mighty handsome lad. And I made out. Had my own rig, nigger coachman and all. When autos came along, I got me a *chauffeur*. Wore spats every day of the week." He lifted his glass. "Six chickens, a high-class house. Professor in the parlor, mirrors all over the walls in every room upstairs. Bartender on duty twenty-four hours a day, and the biggest call was for champagne. Customers came from far away as Memphis, just to see the oil paintings."

"No air-conditioning?" Morgan mumbled.

"What's that?"

"Never mind. Go on."

"Called it the Palace," the old man murmured. "And it was. When the girls came down in their evening-dresses, with their hair done up and their eyes kind of sparkling behind their fans, they looked like queens. And we treated our customers like kings. Things were a lot different in the trade, then. Us fancy operators, we knew how to show a man a good time. We didn't hustle 'em in for a quick trick and push 'em out again. Gave a sociable evening, a little refinement, a little refreshment, a little romance."

He sighed. "But the army closed Storeyville. Jazz bands went north, Professors got jobs in shoe-shine parlors, and I sold the oil-paintings. Still, I was luckier than most. I'd made my pile. Even hung onto the Palace, but closed everything up except for my own room downstairs. Nobody around today except me and the Red Queen."

"The Red Queen?"

"Told you I was a professional. Just because the lid clamped down, that didn't mean all us old-timers got squashed. I've kept going, on the q.t., understand? Sort of a sentimental gesture, if you follow me. Never more than one chicken now, but that's enough. Enough for the few who still appreciate it, who still want a taste of the old days, the old ways—"

Morgan burned his throat on the drink. "You mean to tell me

you're still—in business?" he asked. "You've got a girl, the same kind who used to work in Storeyville in the old days?"

His companion nodded solemnly. "Trained her myself," he murmured. "Wears the old dresses, oldfashioned stuff, not like the chippies over in the big houses. Got her room fixed up like it was forty-five, fifty years ago. Like stepping into the past, and she treats you right, you know? I'm pretty careful who I let in these days, but there was something about you, I said to myself when I saw you—"

Morgan stood up. "Come on," he said. He produced his wallet, flung a bill on the table. "I've got dough. Been saving it up just for this trip. How much is this going to cost me?"

"She'll set the price," the old man told him. "For me this is only—well, you might call it a hobby."

Then they were out in the night again, and it seemed to Morgan that the fog was thicker, the streets darker and narrower than before. And the absinthe burned, and he alternately stumbled forward and hung back; eager for the past recaptured and wondering why he was seeking a nameless destination with a drunken old pimp.

Then they came to the house, and it looked like any other ancient house in the fog, in the absinthe haze. The old man unlocked the door, and he stood in the dark, high-ceilinged, mahogany-panelled hallway while the gas-jet sputtered on. The old man's room was off to the right; the big double-doors of what used to be the parlor were tightly closed. But the huge staircase loomed ahead, and Morgan blinked as his companion reeled over to it and cupped his hands, shouting, "Company!"

His voice echoed and reechoed down the long hall, reverberating off the walls and the doorways, and Morgan got the feeling they were all alone in the dim circle of light from the gas-jet, that the old man was crazy, that this was indeed the land of dreams.

But, "Company!" the old man shouted again, his face contorted, his voice angry and insistent. "Damned woman," he shrilled. "Sleeps her life away. I've had trouble with her before about this. Thought I'd taught her a lesson, but maybe I'll have to teach her again"—and once more he shouted up the stairway.

"Company!"

"Send him up."

The voice was soft, musical and thrilling. The moment Morgan heard it, he knew he hadn't made a mistake. Crazy old man, crazy old house, crazy errand—but there was the voice, the warm and wanton invitation.

"Go ahead," the little man urged. "Right at the head of the stairs, her room is. You won't need a light."

Then he went into his room and Morgan climbed the stairs, feet moving over frayed carpeting, eyes intent on the doorway looming above the landing. When Morgan reached the door he fumbled for the knob in the darkness, standing there for a long moment as he tried to enter.

Quite suddenly the door opened inward, and there he was in the big bedroom, with twenty crystal chandeliers tinkling their welcome, twenty velvet carpets offering cushioned caresses to his feet, twenty ornate vanities spreading a pungent powder-and-patchouli perfume from their littered tops.

Twenty great canopied beds straddled the center of the room, and twenty occupants waved him forward. The light blazed down on the redness; the rich, reflected radiance of twenty Red Queens. They had red hair and red lips and red garters and red nipples. Twice twenty white arms opened to enfold him in an embrace that was all illusion.

Morgan reeled forward through a thousand rippling reflections from the mirrored walls and ceiling, trying to find the real bed and the real Red Queen. She laughed at him then, because he was drunk, and she held out her hand to guide him, draw him down beside her. And her touch was fire, and her mouth was a furnace, and her body was a volcano gushing lava, and the mirrors whirled wildly in a long red dream of laughter and delight.

He must have put on his clothes again and tiptoed downstairs around dawn; he couldn't remember. He didn't recall saying goodbye or paying the girl or seeing the old man again, either, nor could he recollect walking back into the Quarter. The absinthe had left him with a splitting headache and a bitter aftertaste in his mouth, and now he moved like an automaton, turning into the first place he saw.

It was a small Oyster Bar, but he didn't want the traditional dozen raws—he needed coffee. The fog was gone from the morning streets, but it lingered inside his skull, and Morgan wondered vaguely how he'd managed to find his way back to familiar surroundings. He stepped up to the counter and reached for his wallet.

His pocket was empty.

His hand began a search, up and down, forward and back. But his wallet was gone. His wallet, his identification, his license, his three hundred dollars in cash.

Morgan couldn't remember what had happened, but one thing was obvious. He'd been rolled. Rolled in the good oldfashioned way by a bad oldfashioned girl.

In a way it was almost funny, and in a way it served him right. He knew that, but somehow he failed to see either the humor or the justice of it all. And when it came to justice—

Morgan gave up all thoughts of coffee and went to the police. He started to tell his story to a desk sergeant, told a little more of it to a polite lieutenant, and ended up telling the whole thing over again to a plain-clothes detective as he walked with him down Rampart Street, heading east.

The detective, whose name was Belden, didn't seem to be polite at all.

Morgan freely admitted he'd been drinking last night, and even found the first little bar he had patronized. The bartender Morgan had talked to was off-duty, but the day-man gave the detective his home phone, and Belden called him from the tavern and talked to him. The bartender remembered seeing Morgan, all right.

"He said you were drunk as a skunk," the impolite Belden reported. "Now, where did you go from there?"

"St. Louis Cemetery," Morgan said. But to his chagrin, he couldn't find his way. In the end, Belden led him there.

"Then what?" Belden demanded.

"Then I met this old man—" Morgan began.

But when Belden asked for an exact description, Morgan couldn't give it to him. And Belden wanted to know the old man's name, and where they'd gone together, and why. Morgan tried to explain how he'd felt, why he had agreed to drink with a stranger; the detective wasn't interested.

"Take me to the tavern," he said.

They prowled the side streets, but Morgan couldn't find the tavern. Finally he had to admit as much. "But I was there," he insisted. "And then we went to this house—"

"All right." Belden shrugged. "Take me to the house."

Morgan tried. For almost an hour he trudged up and down the winding streets, but all the houses looked alike, and their sameness in the sunlight was different than their distinctiveness in darkness. There was nothing romantic about these shabby old buildings, nothing that savoured of a midnight dream.

Morgan could see that the detective didn't believe him. And then, when he told him the whole story once again—about the old man training his girl in the Storeyville tradition, about the mirrored room upstairs and the red garters and all the rest of it—he knew the detective would never believe. Standing here in the bright street, with the sun sending splinters into his reddened eyes, Morgan found it hard to believe himself. Maybe it *had* been the liquor; maybe he'd made up the part about the old man and all the rest. He could have passed out in front of the cemetery, someone might have come along and lifted his wallet. That made sense. More sense than a journey to the land of dreams.

Apparently Belden thought so too, because he advanced just that theory as they started walking back.

Morgan found himself nodding in agreement, and then he turned his head suddenly and said, "There it is—that's the tavern we went into, I'm sure of it!"

And it *was* the tavern. He recognized the pockmarked man who had served them, and the pockmarked man recognized him. And, "Yes," he told Belden. "He came with the old one, with Louie."

The detective had his notebook out. "Louie who? What's his last name?"

"This I cannot tell you," the bartender said. "He is just old man, he has been a long time in the neighborhood. Harmless but—" The bartender made a twirling gesture close to his forehead.

"Do you know where he lives?" Belden asked.

Surprisingly enough, the bartender nodded. "Yes." He muttered an address and Belden wrote it down.

"Come on," he said to Morgan. "Looks as if you were giving me a straight story after all." He uttered a dry chuckle. "Thought we knew what was going on down here, but I guess the old boy fooled us. Imagine, running a panel house undercover in this day and age! That's one for the books."

A surprisingly short walk led them to the building, on a street scarcely two blocks away. The house was old, and looked untenanted; some of the front windows were caved in and the drawn green shades flapped listlessly in the hot morning breeze. Morgan didn't recognize the place even when he saw it, and he stood on the doorstep while Belden rang the bell.

For a long while there was no answer, and then the door opened just a crack. Morgan saw the old man's face, saw his rheumy red eyes blinking out at them.

"What you want?" the old man wheezed. "Who are you?"

Belden told him who he was and what he wanted. The old man opened the door a bit wider and stared at Morgan.

"Hello," Morgan said. "I'm back again. Looks like I mislaid my wallet." He'd already made up his mind not to enter charges—the old boy was in enough hot water already.

"Back?" the little whitehaired man snapped. "What do you mean, you're back? Never set eyes on you before in my life."

"Last night," Morgan said. "I think I left my wallet here."

"Nonsense. Nobody here last night. Nobody ever comes here any more. Not for over forty years. I'm all alone. All alone—"

Belden stepped forward. "Suppose we have a look around?" he asked. Morgan wondered if the old man would try to stop him, ask for a search warrant. Instead, he merely laughed and opened the door wide.

"Sure," he said. "Come on in. Welcome to the Palace." He chuckled again, then wheezed. "Throat is dry," he explained.

"It wasn't so dry last night," Morgan told him. "When we drank together."

The old man shook his head. "Don't listen to him, Mister," he told Belden. "Never saw him before."

They stepped into the hall and Morgan recognized it. The dark panelling looked dingy in the daylight, and he could see the dust on the floor. There was dust everywhere, a thick coating on the wood of the double-doors and lighter deposit on the small door leading to the old man's room.

They went in there, and Belden began his search. It didn't take long, because there weren't many places to look. The old man's furniture consisted of a single chair, a small brass bed, and a battered bureau. There wasn't even a closet. Belden went over the bed and mattress, then examined the contents of the bureau drawers. Finally, he frisked old Louie.

"One dollar and fourteen cents," he announced.

The old man snatched the coins from the detective's hand. "See, what'd I tell you?" he muttered. "I got no wallet. And I don't know anything about the mark, either. I'm clean, I am. Ask down at the station-house. Ask Captain Leroux."

"I don't know any Captain Leroux," Belden said. "What's his detail?"

"Why, Storeyville, of course. Where do you think you are?"

"Storeyville's been closed for almost forty-five years," Belden answered. "Where do you think *you* are?"

"Right here. Where I always been. In the Palace. I'm a professional man, I am. Used to have six chickens on the block. Then the heat came on strong, and all I had left was the Red Queen. She sleeps too much, but I can fix that. I fixed it once and I can fix it again—"

Belden turned to Morgan and repeated the twirling gesture the pockmarked bartender had made.

But Morgan shook his head. "Of course," he said. "The wallet's upstairs. She has it. Come on!"

The old man put his hand on Morgan's shoulder. His mouth worked convulsively. "Mister, don't go up there. I was only fooling—she's gone, she beat it out on me this morning, I swear it! Sure, she copped your leather all right. Up to her old tricks. But she did a Dutch on me, you won't find her—"

"We'll see for ourselves." Belden was already pounding up the stairs, and Morgan followed him. The dust rising from the stair-treads and Morgan started to choke. His ears began to hurt, because Belden hammered on the door at the head of the stairs.

"You sure this was the one?" he panted.

Morgan nodded.

"But it couldn't be, man—this door isn't locked, it's sealed. Sealed tight."

Morgan didn't answer him. His head throbbed, and his stomach was beginning to churn, but he knew what he must do. Shouldering the detective aside, he thrust the full weight of his body against the door.

The ancient wood groaned, then splintered around the rotten doorframe. With a rasp of hinges, the door tottered and fell inward.

A cloud of dust billowed out, filling Morgan's lungs, blinding him. He coughed, he choked, but he groped forward and stepped into the room.

The twenty chandeliers were gone, and the twenty carpets and the twenty vanities and the twenty beds. That's because the mirrors hung cracked and broken in their frames. Now there was only one of everything—one cobwebbed chandelier, one ragged and mouldering patch of carpet, one vanity whose littered top gave off a scent of dead perfume and musty decay, and one canopy bed with its yellowed hangings mildewed and shredded.

And the bed had only one occupant. She was sleeping, just as the old man whined now while he peered over Morgan's shoulder. Always sleeping, and maybe he'd have to fix her again like he did once years ago. Morgan saw that she was still wearing the red garters, but aside from that he wouldn't have recognized her. One skeleton looks just like another.

"What the hell kind of a joke is this?" Belden wanted to know.

The old man couldn't tell him, because he was alternately whining and complaining, and then he was weeping in a high, shrill voice—something about the Red Queen and the old days and how he hadn't meant to do it, and only he could awaken her on the nights when Company came calling.

Morgan couldn't tell him, either. He couldn't tell him about the land of dreams, or the land of nightmares either.

All he could do was walk over to the bed, lift the rotting skull from the rotting pillow, reach his hand underneath and pull out his brand new, shiny leather wallet.

Sweet Sixteen

Everything was peaceful the night before the trouble came. Ben Kerry perched on the porch rail outside his cottage, blinking like an owl in the twilight. He peered across the wide rolling expanse of the Kettle Moraine country and flapped his arms as if he were about to take off.

"There's gold in them thar hills," he muttered. "I never knew it, but I could have gotten in on the ground floor, too."

Ted Hibbard grinned at him. "You mean, when the glacier swept down and made them? You're not *that* old."

Kerry chuckled and lit his pipe. "That's right, son. And I wasn't here when the glacier rolled back and the Indians came, either. They used the hills for signalling posts or for their ceremonial rituals. No money in that, I grant you."

"I know," Hibbard said. "I read your book about it."

Kerry chuckled again. "No money in *that*, either. If it wasn't for the university presses, we anthropologists would starve to death waiting for a publisher. Because we never see what's right under our noses." He stared out at the hills again, far into deepening dusk.

"Of course the farmers didn't see, either, when they arrived here. They preferred to settle on level land. And their sons and grandsons sought still better soil, down around the waterways. So all these rock-strewn hills with their boulder out-croppings, stood deserted until maybe thirty years ago. Then the automobile brought the first hunters and fishermen from the cities. They put up cheap cabins on cheap land. And they didn't see the gold any more than I did, when I came here just before the War. All I wanted was a summer place where I could get away from people."

Ted Hibbard chuckled, now. "Strikes me as funny," he said. "An anthropologist who hates people."

"Don't hate 'em," Kerry insisted. "At least, not most of 'em.

Even today, we know, the majority of the inhabitants of the earth are still savages. I've always gotten along with *them* very well. It's the civilized who frighten me."

"Such as your students and former students?" Hibbard smiled up at him. "I thought I was welcome here."

"You are, believe me. But you're an exception. You aren't like the others. You didn't move out here for a fast buck."

"Oh," Hibbard said. "So that's what you mean by the gold, is it?"

"Of course. What you see out there isn't hill country any more. It's real-estate. Development property. Right after the War the city people came. Not the hunters and the fishermen now, but the exurbanites. The supper de-luxe exurbanites, who could afford to move forty miles out of town instead of just fifteen. They've been pouring in ever since, putting up their ranch-houses and their double garages for the station wagons."

"Still looks like a pretty lonely region to me," Hibbard mused. "Too damned lonely, after dark."

"The Indians were afraid of the hills at night," Kerry told him. "They used to huddle inside their tepees around the fire. Just like today's citizens huddle inside their ranch-houses around the TV set."

"I suppose you have a right to be resentful," Hibbard said. "All these property-values going up. If you'd anticipated the boom you might have picked up choice locations years ago and made a fortune."

Kerry shrugged. "Wouldn't need a fortune. Just enough to move on. By now I could have a little *cabana* down along the barren stretches of the Florida Keys. I'd call it the *Key Pout*."

A white face popped around the corner of the porch.

"Hey, Dad! Mom says it's almost time for supper."

"Okay," Hibbard answered. "Tell her I'll be along soon."

The face disappeared.

"Nice boy you have there," Kerry said.

"Hank? We think so. Crazy about math, all that sort of thing. Can't wait to start school in the fall. I guess he's a lot more serious about things than I was at his age. A lot more than most kids are, nowadays."

"That's why I like him." Kerry tapped his pipe against the porch-rail. "You know, I'm not really such a misanthrope. This hermit pose of mine is mostly pretense. But some of it is defense, too. Defense against the mobs taking over our cities, our culture. I saw it coming, fifteen years ago. That's why I got out. It's bad enough having to stay in town during the school year, to teach. Once that's over, I come back to the cottage here. Now even this little bit of privacy is being invaded. The hot-dog stands are taking over Walden Pond, I guess."

Hibbard stood up. "I hope you don't resent my hanging around this way," he said.

"Good heavens, no! When you bought your place last month I was mighty pleased to see you. I'm still a member of the human race, remember, even though I find the average rural resident as much of an alien as I do the city troglodyte or his suburbanite cousin. You're more than welcome here, at any time. I like your wife, and I like that boy of yours. They're real people."

"Meaning that the rest are not?"

"Don't bait me," Kerry said. "You understand very well what I'm talking about. That's why you moved out here yourself, isn't it?"

Hibbard moved to the edge of the porch. "Well, I guess so. Actually, we came out here because of Hank, mostly. Didn't like the city schools. Didn't like the kind of kids he ran around with back in town. They're—I don't know—different. All these juvenile delinquents. You know."

Kerry nodded. "Indeed I do. As a matter of fact, I've been spending most of the summer taking notes for a little monograph. Nothing pretentious, understand—sociology's out of my line—but it's an interesting study. And this happens to be an ideal spot for anthropological field-trips."

"You mean there's a lot of rural delinquence around here?" Hibbard looked distressed. "We were hoping to get away from that."

"Don't worry," Kerry reassured him. "From what I've seen, the farm areas are still pretty well untouched. Of course, we have the usual percentage of barnyard sadists, truants, maladjusted types. But Hank won't run into too many; at his age most of them have either gone off to the armed services or the Industrial Home for Boys. It's the city youngsters I've been investigating."

"You're talking about exurbanite kids like mine? Or is there some kind of boy's camp around here?"

"Neither. I'm speaking about our weekend visitors. Don't tell me you haven't seen them in town during the summer."

"No, I haven't. Actually, I've been so busy getting our place straightened out that I don't get into town very often. About once a week I stock up on supplies, usually on a Wednesday. I heard it's pretty crowded, weekends."

"You heard correctly," Kerry told him. "But perhaps you might be interested in seeing just what I'm talking about. I plan to take a run in tomorrow morning, about nine or so. And you're welcome to ride along."

"Will do." Hibbard waved his hand in salute.

Kerry stood on the porch and watched his guest walk down the hillside path, his shoulders silhouetted against the sunset.

From the far horizon came a low, rumbling sound. It might have been the mutter of distant thunder—at least, that is what both men mistook it for at the time.

Neither of them knew that it heralded the arrival of the trouble. They must have been coming in all through the night, and they were still gathering around ten the following morning when Ben Kerry drove Hibbard into town in his old Ford.

Their first encounter occurred on the highway just outside the town limits, between the *Welcome To Hilltop* sign and the notice which read *Speed Limit 25 m.p.h.*

It came in the form of a rumbling again, but this time there was no mistaking it for thunder. The motorcycle roared along the road behind them, then swerved past without slackening speed. As it zoomed by, Hibbard caught a glimpse of a squat figure in a black leather jacket, with a monkey on his back. At least, it looked like a monkey in the dusty passing blur; not until a moment later did he realize that what he had seen was a girl with cropped hair who was clinging with arms entwined about the cyclist.

As they speeded ahead, Hibbard saw the girl raise her right hand as though in a gesture of greeting. Automatically he started to return her wave, then froze as Kerry gripped his shoulder.

"Look out!" he shouted, and ducked his head.

At that instant something struck the windshield of the car and bounced off with a clatter. It fell in a silvery arc to the side of the road, and Hibbard understood. The girl had not been waving. She had hurled an empty beer-can at them.

"Why, she could have broken the windshield!" he exclaimed.

Kerry nodded. "Happens all the time. By tonight you'll find the roadside paved with empties."

"But they aren't even supposed to *buy* beer, are they? Isn't there a state law?"

Kerry jerked his finger over his shoulder. "Sign says you cut down to twenty-five miles an hour when you enter town, too," he muttered. "But they're doing close to fifty."

"You talk as if you expected such things."

"I do. It's like this every weekend, all summer long. Everyone knows what to expect around here."

"And nobody tries to do anything about it?"

"Wait and see," Kerry told him.

They were entering town now, passing a row of motels. Although it was still mid-morning, a surprising number of cars were parked before the various units. Hibbard gazed at them curiously, noting a strange incongruity. Virtually none of the vehicles were cognizable as standard units. Painted junkers, restyled hot-rods, ancient sports cars predominated. And there were dozens of motorcycles.

"I see you notice our weekend visitors' choice of transportation," Kerry said. "I'm afraid it's apt to strike you as a bit unconventional. As a group they seem to dislike what I believe is called 'Detroit iron'—you might gather from that that they utilize the motor car as a symbol of protest. As I remark in my notes, there seems to be an automotive in their madness."

He slowed to a snail's pace as they proceeded up the short thoroughfare known, inevitably, as Main Street. The sidewalks were jammed with the usual Saturday throng of farm-folk, but intermingling with them was the unusual throng of teen-age visitants.

There was no difficulty in separating them from the local youngsters; not these swaggering, guffawing figures in their metal-studded jackets and skintight jeans. Their booted feet thudded along the pavement, their visored caps bobbed. Some of them were bareheaded, choosing to display shaven skulls, crew-cuts, and the more outlandish coiffures known as "Mohawks" or—for polite abbreviation—the "d.a." An occasional older lad in the crowd was more apt to affect the other extreme; long, greasy locks and exaggerated sideburns. Several of the latter youths wore spade beards, which gave them an oddly goatish appearance. The resemblance to satyrs was perhaps increased by the presence, and the attitudes, of their female companions. Virtually all of them were indistinguishable from the girl on the motorcycle; the cropped hair, overpainted face, and tight sweater and jodhpurs seemed to be standard equipment.

Their boisterous babble rose and echoed from the artificial amphitheatre created by the store-fronts lining either side of the narrow street; from the end of the block came the sound of a juke-box blaring away at full volume inside the root-beer stand and drive-in.

A large crowd of juveniles congregated before it, and several couples were dancing on the sidewalk, oblivious of those who had to step out into the street in order to pass by. The sun's rays reflected from a score of beer-cans held in a score of hands.

Hibbard turned to his companion. "I think I get it now," he said. "I remember reading something about this a couple of years back. Wasn't there a motorcycle convention in some small town in California? A gang took over, almost started a riot?"

"There was," the older man confirmed. "And it happened again, last year, in another state. Then I read of another instance, this summer. If you wanted to check on such things, I imagine you'd find the phenomenon has become commonplace all over."

"Is this what you wanted to show me?" Hibbard asked. "That cyclist gangs are coming in here and terrorizing the citizens?"

Kerry shook his head.

"Don't be melodramatic," he murmured. "In the first place, this isn't a 'cyclist gang'. Any more than it's a 'hot-rod crowd' or a 'sports car mob' or a congregation of Elvis Presley fans. These youngsters come from all over; the big city, the outlying suburbs, the smaller industrial communities nearby. There's no outward indication that they belong to any formal group, club, or organization. They just congregate, apparently. And if you look closely, you'll see they're not terrorizing the citizens, as you put it. In fact most of the local merchants are delighted to have them here." He waved his arm in the direction of the beer-drinkers. "They're good customers. They leave a lot of money in town over a weekend."

"But you said yourself that they break the laws. They must stir up trouble, get into fights, do damage."

"They pay for it, I guess.'

"What about the local authorities? What do they think?"

Kerry smiled. "You mean the mayor? He's a plumber here in town, gets a hundred dollars a year to hold the title as a part-time job. He doesn't worry much."

"But the police—"

"We have a local sheriff, that's all. The place isn't even big enough to have its own jail. That's over at the county seat."

"Don't the citizens who aren't merchants do any complaining? Are they willing to sit back and just let a bunch of strange young hoodlums run wild?"

"I guess they complain. But so far there hasn't been any action taken. For my selfish purposes, it's just as well. You'd be surprised what I've managed to observe during this summer alone. What I want to do now is get over and see one of their race meetings."

"Race meetings?"

"That's right. You didn't think they come here just to walk up and down Main Street, did you? Saturday or Sunday afternoons you'll generally find them off in the hills, on one of those little side roads back behind the county trunk highways. They rent a spot from a local farmer and hold drag races, hill-climbing contests, that sort of thing. This week there'll be a gathering in our neighborhood, I think. They were always west of town before this, but I guess something happened and they got run off from their usual spot. Now old Lautenshlager is going to let them use the big hill behind his property. We ought to be able to see the bonfire tonight."

"Bonfire?"

Kerry nodded. "They usually have them."

"What do they think they are, Indians?" Hibbard stared at a trio on the nearby corner; a skinny boy epileptically contorted over a guitar and a writhing couple who seemed to be executing an impromptu war-dance. He had to grin at the sight. "Maybe they are, at that," he admitted. "They sure sound like savages."

"Rock-and-roll," Kerry shrugged.

Suddenly Hibbard's grin faded. "Look at that," he snapped, pointing up the street ahead.

A beat-up convertible was screeching down the avenue towards them, loaded with youngsters whose voices competed more than successfully with the mechanical din. As the car moved forward, a cat moved quickly out of its path. But not quickly enough, for the car swerved purposefully to the side. There was a jarring thump and a louder screech, followed by howls of laughter.

"Did you see what they did?" Hibbard demanded. "They deliberately went out of their way to run it down! Let me out of here! I'm going to—"

"Oh no you're not." Kerry put his foot down on the accelerator and the Ford moved on. "The poor thing's dead. You can't help it now. No sense starting trouble."

"What's the matter with you?" Hibbard's voice was shrill. "You aren't going to let them get away with this, are you?" He stared as the convertible skidded to a halt and its inmates poured out across the sidewalk. "It's bad enough when small boys torture an animal out of childish curiosity, but these aren't children. They're old enough to know what they're doing."

"That's right," Kerry agreed. "Like you say, they're savages. Remember the riots. You can't win." Kerry drove in silence, turning off at the end of the street and cutting back along a sideroad which circled the edge of town and joined the highway once again. Even at a distance it was possible to hear the blare of music, the cough of exhaust pipes, the yammer of horns and the snarl of the cycles.

"They must have noise wherever they go," Kerry said, at last. "I suppose it's what the psychiatrists call oral aggression."

Hibbard didn't reply.

"Rock-and-roll is another manifestation. But then again, there was swing in your salad days and jazz in mine. In fact you can see a lot of parallels if you look for them. Eccentric dress and hair styles, the drinking—the whole pattern of rebellion against authority."

Hibbard stirred restlessly. "But not the senseless cruelty," he said. "Sure, I remember frat initiations and how wild we got after football games. But there was nothing like this. There were a few bullies or maladjusted kids with mean streaks—now they all behave like a pack of psychos."

"Your boy isn't like that," Kerry answered. "Lots of them are normal."

"Yes. But there seem to be so many of the other sort. More and more each year. Don't tell me you haven't noticed. You told me you've been studying these kids. And just now, back in town, you were afraid."

Kerry sighed. "Yes, I've studied them. And I am afraid." He paused. "How about coming home for lunch with me? I think I ought to show you a few things."

Hibbard nodded. The noonday countryside was silent, or almost silent. It was only by listening very closely that they could hear the faint rumbling, moving along the roads in the direction of the distant hills.

Kerry spread the scrapbooks on the table after lunch. "Started these myself some time ago," he said. "But recently I've signed up with a clipping service."

He riffled the pages of the topmost book. "Here's your motorcycle riots, and a section on gang fights. Rumbles, they call them. A report from the Police Commissioner of New York on the rise of delinquency. A list of weapons taken from a group of high-school freshmen in Detroit—switch-blade knives, straight razors, brass knuckles, two pistols, a hatchet. All of them used in a street battle. A section on narcotics, one on armed robbery, quite a few stories of arson. I've tried to eliminate what seem to be run-of-the-mill occurrences, so the clippings involving sex-crimes mostly concern forcible rape, gang assaults, and sadistic perversion. Even so, you can see there's a frightening assortment. This second book is devoted exclusively to news stories of torture and murder. I warn you, it's not pleasant reading."

It wasn't. Hibbard found his gorge rising. He'd noticed such items, of course, while skimming through his daily paper, but had never paid too much attention to their frequency. Here, for the first time, he encountered a mass accumulation, and it was an anthology of horror.

He read about the teen-age kidnappers in Chicago who mutilated and then killed an infant; the youngster down South who butchered his sister; the boy who blew off the head of his mother with a shotgun. Case after case of parricide, fratricide, infanticide; instance after instance of apparently senseless slaughter.

Kerry glanced over his shoulder and sighed.

"Truth is stranger than fiction, isn't it?" he muttered. "You'll look a long time before discovering any Penrods or Willie Baxters in those news-clippings. This isn't a Booth Tarkington world any more. For that matter, you'll search in vain for an Andy Hardy."

"I believe it," said Hibbard. "But I can't understand it. Of course, there were always juvenile delinquents, Dead End Kids, that sort of thing. Only they seemed to be the exceptions, the victims of the Depression. And the zoot-suiters during the War were supposed to be the result of lack of parental supervision. The youngsters in these cases seem to be the products of normal upbringing; I notice the stories make quite a point out of the fact that most of them come from nice homes, prosperous backgrounds. What's happened to our kids?"

"You'll still find nice children around. Hank isn't that way, remember."

"But what's influencing the majority? Why has there been such a terrible change in the last few years?"

Kerry puffed on his pipe. "Lots of explanations, if you want them. Dr. Wertham, for example, blames a lot of it on the comic books. Some psychotherapists say television is the villain. Others think the War left its mark; kids live in the shadow of military service, so they rebel. They've taken new heroes in their own image— James Dean, Marlon Brando, the torn-shirt totem rules their clan. Oh, there's already a most impressive literature on the subject."

"Well, it doesn't impress me," Hibbard declared. "Maybe it sounds good, but how does one of those fancy theories explain a thing like this? Listen." He jabbed his finger at one of the clippings pasted on the page opened before them. "Here's a case from just last month. A fourteen-year-old boy, down South. He got up out of bed in the middle of the night and killed his parents in cold blood, while they slept. No rhyme or reason for it, he admits he had no reason to hate them, and the alienists' reports seem to show he's perfectly normal, had an ordinary home-life. His story is that he just woke up out of a sound sleep and felt a sudden 'urge to kill somebody.' So he did." Hibbard thumbed through the book. "Come to think of it, that's what a lot of them say. They just get an 'impulse,' or 'something comes over them,' or they 'want to see what it's like.' And the next day the cops are beating the bushes for the bodies of missing babies, or digging up fragments of dismembered corpses in gravel-pits. I tell you, it doesn't make sense!"

He closed the scrap-book and stared at Kerry. "You've gone to a lot of trouble to collect these clippings," he said. "And you say you've been studying this juvenile delinquent problem all summer. You must have come to some conclusions."

Kerry shrugged. "Perhaps. But I'm not quite ready to commit myself. I need further data before presenting a hypothesis." He gave Hibbard a long look. "You were a pretty fair student, as I recall. Let's see what you make of it all."

"Well, there's a couple of things that occur to me. First, this insistence, in case after case, over and over again, that a youngster suddenly experiences an irresistible impulse to commit murder. Generally, in such examples, the child is alone and not part of any gang. Come to think of it, he's often an only child, isn't he, or lives an isolated life?"

Kerry's eyes narrowed. "Go on."

"That seems to take care of one group. But there's another— the gangs. The ones that go in for the uniforms, and the regalia. I notice there's quite a bit of reference to initiations and secret society mumbo-jumbo. They've got a jive-talk language of their own, and fancy names, that sort of thing. And they seem to be premeditated in their crimes." He hesitated. "On the face of it, we're dealing with two totally different types. No, wait a minute— there's one thing all these kids seem to have in common."

Kerry leaned forward. "What's that?"

"They don't *feel* anything—no shame, no guilt, no remorse.

There's no empathy towards their victims, none at all. Time after time the stories bring that point out. They kill for kicks, but it doesn't really touch them at all. In other words, they're psychopaths."

"Now we're getting somewhere," Kerry said. "You call them psychopaths. And just what *is* a psychopath?"

"Why, like I said—somebody who doesn't have normal feeling, who lacks responsibility. You've studied up on psychology, you ought to know."

Kerry gestured towards the row of bookshelves lining the sides of his fireplace. "That's right. I've got quite a collection of psychotherapy texts up there. But you can search through them in vain for a satisfactory definition of the so-called psychopathic personality. He isn't considered a psychotic. He doesn't respond to any form of treatment. No psychiatric theory presently offers a demonstrable explanation of how a psychopath evolves, and for lack of contrary evidence it's often assumed that he's born that way."

"Do you believe that?"

"Yes. But unlike orthodox therapists, I have a reason. I think I know what a psychopath is. And—"

"Dad!"

Both of them turned at the cry.

Hibbard's son stood in the doorway, the rays of the late afternoon sun reflecting redly from the bright blood streaming down the side of his face.

"Hank! What happened? Did you have an accident?" He moved towards the boy.

"No, I'm all right. Honest I am. I just didn't want to go home and scare Mom."

"Sit down." Kerry led him to a chair. "Let me get some hot water, clean you off." He went over to the sink and returned with a cloth and a basin. Skillfully he sponged the blood away, revealing the lacerations on the scalp.

"Not too deep," he told Hibbard. "A little peroxide and a bandage, now."

The boy winced, then subsided as Kerry finished his ministrations.

"Better?"

"I'm all right," Hank insisted. "It's just that they hit me with the tire-chain—"

"Who hit you?"

"I don't know. Some guys. I went for a walk this afternoon, and I heard all this racket up on the hill behind old Lautenshlager's place, you know. And I saw all these guys, and some dames, too. They were riding motorcycles up and down, making a lot of noise. I wanted to see what was going on, that's all, I just wanted to see what was going on—"

His lower lip trembled and Hibbard patted his shoulder. "Sure, I understand. So you went up there, eh? And then what happened?"

"Well, I started to go up. But before I could get very close, these big guys jumped me. There must have been five or six of them; they just came out from around some bushes and grabbed me. And one of them had a stick and another one had this tire-chain, and he swung it at me and hit me alongside of the head, here. The others let go of me to get out of the way, and that's how I got loose. I started to run, and they were chasing me, only I got across the fence and then I ducked down behind Lautenshlager's barn so they couldn't see me."

"Did you get a good look at the fellows?"

"Well, one of them had a beard. And they were all wearing these black leather jackets and some kind of boots."

"It's the gang, all right. Our friends, the psychopaths." Hibbard stood up. "You can walk, can't you? Then come on."

"Where are we going?"

"Home, of course. I'm going to see to it that you get to bed. You got quite a knock, there. And then I think I'll hop in the car and take a little run over to the county seat. Seems to me this is a matter for the State police."

Kerry put down his pipe. "Are you sure it's wise to stir up trouble?" he asked, quietly. "No telling what might happen."

"Something has happened already," Hibbard answered. "When a bunch of hoodlums knock my son over the head with a tire-chain, that's trouble enough for me. Come on, Hank."

He led the boy out of the door and down the path, without a backward look.

Kerry grimaced, then shook his head. For a moment he opened his mouth to call after them, then closed it. After that he just stood there, his eyes intent on the far hills. No smoke rose from them in the waning horizon-light, but the sound of racing exhausts was plainly audible. Kerry stood there listening for a long time. Then, slowly, wearily, he walked into the front room. He kindled a fire in the fireplace and sat down before it, balancing a notebook on his lap. From time to time he scribbled a few words, sitting stiffly, head poised as though listening for an unexpected sound. His face bore the tight, strained look of a man who had been waiting for trouble—and found it.

It must have been almost an hour before the sound came. Even though he'd been tensed and alert, Kerry jumped when he heard the footsteps. He rushed to the door, reaching it just as Hibbard burst in.

"Oh, it's you!" His voice rose in relief. "So dark I didn't recognize who it was at first."

Hibbard didn't respond for a moment. He stood there, panting, waiting to regain his breath.

"Ran all the way," he wheezed.

"What's the matter? Is it Hank?"

"No. The kid's all right, I guess. We put him to bed when I got him home, and my wife doesn't think there's any concussion. She used to be a nurse, you know. So I decided to grab a sandwich before I drove in for the police. We had the door shut, so I guess that's why I didn't hear anything. They must have sneaked in and out of the yard again very quietly."

"Who?"

"Our young friends. Guess they figured out where Hank lived and decided I might be going after them. Anyway, they weren't taking any chances. They slashed all my tires."

Hibbard's voice rose. "They could see there are no telephone wires around our place, and I suppose they thought if they fixed the car I couldn't do anything. But I'll show them!"

"Take it easy, now."

"I am taking it easy. I'm just here to borrow your car, that's all."

"You still intend to get the police?"

"What do you mean, *still?* After what just happened, nothing could stop me. I made sure everything was locked good and tight when I left, but even that's no guarantee. For all I know, they'll be around to burn the house down before the night is over."

Kerry shook his head. "I don't think so. I think if you just go back home and stay there quietly there won't be any more trouble. All they want now is to be left alone."

"Well what they want and what they're going to get is two different things. I'm going to round up every police officer, every trooper in this part of the state. We're going to put an end to this sort of thing—"

"No. You won't end it. Not that way."

"Look, I'm not here to argue with you. Give me your car-keys."

"Not until you listen to me, first."

"I listened to you long enough. I should have got tough the minute I saw those kids run over the cat." Hibbard wiped his forehead. "All right, what is it you wanted to say?"

Kerry walked over and stood next to the bookshelves.

"We were talking about psychopaths this afternoon. I told you that psychiatrists didn't understand them, but that I did. Sometimes it takes an anthropologist to know these things. In my time I've studied a great deal concerning the so-called 'gang-spirit' and the secret societies of many cultures. You find them in all regions, and there are certain similarities. For example, did you know that in some places, even the young women have their own groups? Lips says—"

"I'm not interested in a lecture."

"You will be. Lips says there are hundreds of such societies in Africa alone. The Bundu group, in Nigeria, wears special masks and costumes for their secret rituals. The male adventurer who dares to spy on them is disciplined, or even killed."

"Listen, a gang of crazy kids around a bonfire isn't any secret lodge!"

"You noted the similarity yourself, this afternoon."

"I said some kids ran in gangs, yes. But others don't. What about the 'loners,' the ones who just get the urge to kill?"

"They don't know what they are, that's all. They haven't recognized themselves. For that matter, I don't think the gangs do, not consciously. They think they're just out for thrills. And I only pray that they go on that way, that they don't realize what brings them together."

"We know what brings them together. They're all psycho."

"And what *is* a psychopath?" Kerry's voice was soft. "A psycho-therapist couldn't tell you, but an anthropologist can. A psychopath is a fiend."

"What?"

"A fiend. A devil. A creature known in all religions, at all times, to all men. The spawn of a union between a demon and a mortal woman." Kerry forced a smile. "Yes, I know how it sounds. But think a moment. Think of when all this started—this wave of sudden, unnatural juvenile crime, of psychopathic cruelty. Only a few years ago, wasn't it? Just about the time when the babies born in the early years of the War started to enter their teens. Because that's when it happened, during the War, when the men were away. And the women had nightmares—the kind of nightmares some women have had throughout the ages. The nightmare of the incubus, the carnal demon who visits them in sleep. It happened before in the history of our culture, during the Crusades. And then followed the rise of the witch-cults all over Europe— the witch-cults presided over and attended by the spawn of the night-fiends; the half-human offspring of a blasphemous union. Don't you see how it all fits into the pattern? The unholy love of cruelty for its own sake, the strange, sudden maniacal urge to torture and destroy which comes in sleep, the hideous inability to respond to normal sentiment and normal feelings, the seemingly irrational way in which certain youngsters are irresistibly drawn together into groups who thrive on violence? As I said, I don't think that even the gangs realize the truth about themselves yet— but if they ever do, you'll see a wave of Satanism and Black Magic which will put the Middle Ages to shame. Even now, they gather about fires in the summer night, seeking the hilltop haunts—"

"You're batty!" Hibbard grabbed Kerry by the shoulder and shook him roughly. "They're just kids, that's all. What they need is a damned good beating, the whole lot of them, and maybe a couple of years in reform school."

Kerry shook him off. "Now you're talking like the authorities—the truant officers and the police and the get-tough school of welfare workers. Don't you see, that's just the way they've tried to handle the problem, and it never works? Any more than psychotherapy can work? Because you're dealing with something you're no longer conditioned to believe in. You're dealing with fiends. What we need is exorcism. I can't let you go up there, tonight. The police will just start a riot, it will be murder—"

Hibbard hit him, then, and he went down. His head struck the edge of the fireplace and he lay silent, an ugly bruise rising along the side of his right temple. Hibbard stooped, felt his pulse, then gasped in relief. Quickly he explored the contents of Kerry's jacket-pockets. His hands closed over the car-keys.

Then he rose, turned, and ran from the cottage.

Kerry came to with a start. There was a throbbing in his head. He grasped the mantel, pulled himself erect. The throbbing intensified. But it wasn't all in his head; part of it pounded in rhythm from a distance. He recognized the sound, the roaring that came from the hills.

He rubbed his forehead, then walked slowly in the direction of the porch. The distant darkness was dissolved in a reddish glow, and he could see the flames rising now from the far hilltop.

Kerry felt in his pockets, then swore and started for the door. He hesitated in the doorway, then returned to the living-room and stooped over his desk. His hand scrabbled in the right top drawer; closed over a small revolver. He slipped it into his jacket-pocket and headed for the door once again.

It was dark on the path, but the faint flicker of flames guided his descent. When he reached the bottom of the hill and made sure that his car was gone, he swore again, then squatted until he discerned the fresh tire-tracks and the direction in which they led. Hibbard had chosen to take the back road, the nearest approach to the highway which led to the county seat. The road was rough and it skirted directly behind the big hill on the Lautenshlager property, but it would be the fastest route. Kerry wondered if he'd reach the highway in time to head off the police. He hadn't been able to convince Hibbard, but he was willing to try again.

The police weren't going to solve the situation. There'd just be more violence. If he only had time to work on the problem *his* way, to talk to those who still retained faith in the age-old remedy of exorcism, the casting-out of demons—

Kerry lengthened his stride, smiling wryly to himself. He couldn't blame Hibbard for his reaction. Most men were of the same mind today. Most *civilized* men—that is to say, the small minority of our western culture who go their way blindly, ignoring the other billion and a half who still know, as they have always known, that the forces of darkness exist and are potent. Potent, and able to spawn.

Perhaps it was just as well they didn't believe. He'd told Hibbard the truth—the only immediate hope lay in the fact that the changelings themselves weren't fully aware of their own nature. The fiends didn't know they were fiends. Once they came to learn, and united—

He put the thought away as he worked around behind the hill where the fire flared. Kerry sought the shadows at the side of the road for concealment; the noise of racing motors and the sound of shouts muffled his passing.

Then he rounded a sharp turn and saw the car looming drunkenly in the ditch. Through narrowing eyes he recognized the vehicle as his own. Had there been an accident? He started forward, calling softly. "Hibbard—where are you?"

The figure emerged from the edge of darkness. "Kind of thought you'd be along."

Kerry had just time enough to wonder about the oddly altered voice; time enough for that and no more. Because then they were all around him, some of them holding and some of them striking, and he went down.

When he came to he was already on top of the hill; yes, he must be, because the big brush-fire was leaping and roaring right before him, and the figures were leaping and roaring around it.

Why it was like the old woodcuts, the ones showing the Sabbat and the Adoration of the Master. Only there was no Master in the center of the fire—just this burned and blackening figure, a charred dummy of some sort, thrust upright against a post. And the youngsters were dancing and capering, somebody was plucking the guts of a guitar, it was rock-and-roll, just a gang of kids having a good time. Some of them were drinking beer and a few had even started up their motorcycles to race in a circle about the flames.

Sure, they'd panicked and hit him, but they were only teen-agers, he told himself, it had to be that way. And he'd explain, he'd tell them. He had to thrust the other thought from his mind, had to. Now they were pulling him into the circle and the big kid, the one with the beaver-tails dangling from his cap, was grinning at him.

"We found the other one," he called. "Clobbered him before he got away."

"Man, he's all shook up."

"Must be hip. He was on his way to town."

"If he got there, we'd really have a gasser."

"Ungood."

"What'll it be?"

Kerry whirled, seeking the source of the voices. He stared at the circle of goatish, grinning faces in the firelight. A girl danced past, bop-fashion, her eyes wild.

"How about the sacrifice bit?"

And then they were all shouting. "The sacrifice bit, that's it! Yeah, Man!"

Sacrifice. Man. The *Black Man* of the Sabbat.

Kerry fought the association, he had to fight it, he couldn't believe that. And then they were pushing him closer to the fire, and he could see the blackened dummy, see that it wore glasses.

When he recognized what was burning there he couldn't fight the knowledge any more, and it was too late to fight the hands which gripped him, held him, then thrust him forward into the flames.

It was the Sabbat, he knew it now; the olden ways with new celebrants and a new tongue for the rituals. Kerry winced in pain, the smoke was suffocating him, in a moment he'd fall.

A mighty shout went up and he made one last effort to retain his faculties. If only he could hear what they were screaming—at least then he'd learn the final truth. *Did they or did they not know what they really were?*

But he fell forward, fainting, as the motorcycles began to race around and around the fire.

Their roaring drowned out every other sound, so even at the end, Kerry never heard the chanting.

That Hell-Bound Train

When Martin was a little boy, his Daddy was a Railroad Man. He never rode the high iron, but he walked the tracks for the *CB&Q*, and he was proud of his job. And when he got drunk (which was every night) he sang this old song about *That Hell-Bound Train*.

Martin didn't quite remember any of the words, but he couldn't forget the way his Daddy sang them out. And when Daddy made the mistake of getting drunk in the afternoon and got squeezed between a Pennsy tank-car and an *AT&SF* gondola, Martin sort of wondered why the Brotherhood didn't sing the song at his funeral.

After that, things didn't go so good for Martin, but somehow he always recalled Daddy's song. When Mom up and ran off with a traveling salesman from Keokuk (Daddy must have turned over in his grave, knowing she'd done such a thing, and with a *passenger*, too!) Martin hummed the tune to himself every night in the Orphan Home. And after Martin himself ran away, he used to whistle the song at night in the jungles, after the other bindlestiffs were asleep.

Martin was on the road for four-five years before he realized he wasn't getting anyplace. Of course he'd tried his hand at a lot of things—picking fruit in Oregon, washing dishes in a Montana hash-house—but he just wasn't cut out for seasonal labor or pearl-diving, either. Then he graduated to stealing hub-caps in Denver, and for a while he did pretty well with tires in Oklahoma City, but by the time he'd put in six months on the chain-gang down in Alabama he knew he had no future drifting around this way on his own.

So he tried to get on the railroad like his Daddy had, but they told him times were bad; and between the truckers and the airlines and those fancy new fintails General Motors was making, it looked as if the days of the highballers were just about over.

But Martin couldn't keep away from the railroads. Wherever he traveled, he rode the rods; he'd rather hop a freight heading north in sub-zero weather than lift his thumb to hitch a ride with a Cadillac headed for Florida. Because Martin was loyal to the memory of his Daddy, and he wanted to be as much like him as possible, come what may. Of course, he couldn't get drunk every night, but whenever he did manage to get hold of a can of Sterno, he'd sit there under a nice warm culvert and think about the old days.

Often as not, he'd hum the song about *That Hell-Bound Train*. That was the train the drunks and the sinners rode; the gambling men and the grifters, the big-time spenders, the skirt-chasers, and all the jolly crew. It would be fun to take a trip in such good company, but Martin didn't like to think of what happened when that train finally pulled into the Depot Way Down Yonder. He didn't figure on spending eternity stoking boilers in Hell, without even a Company Union to protect him. Still, it would be a lovely ride. If there *was* such a thing as a Hell-Bound Train. Which, of course, there wasn't.

At least Martin didn't *think* there was, until that evening when he found himself walking the tracks heading south, just outside of Appleton Junction. The night was cold and dark, the way November nights are in the Fox River Valley, and he knew he'd have to work his way down to New Orleans for the winter, or maybe even Texas. Somehow he didn't much feel like going, even though he'd heard tell that a lot of those Texas automobiles had solid gold hub-caps.

No sir, he just wasn't cut out for petty larceny. It was worse than a sin—it was unprofitable, too. Bad enough to do the Devil's work, but then to get such miserable pay on top of it! Maybe he'd better let the Salvation Army convert him.

Martin trudged along, humming Daddy's song, waiting for a rattler to pull out of the Junction behind him. He'd have to catch it—there was nothing else for him to do.

Too bad there wasn't a chance to make a better deal for himself, somewhere. Might as well be a rich sinner as a poor sinner.

Besides, he had a notion that he could strike a pretty shrewd bargain. He'd thought about it a lot, these past few years, particularly when the Sterno was working. Then his ideas would come on strong, and he could figure a way to rig the setup. But that was all nonsense, of course. He might as well join the gospel-shouters and turn into a working-stiff like all the rest of the world. No use dreaming dreams; a song was only a song and there was no Hell-Bound Train.

There was only *this* train, rumbling out of the night, roaring towards him along the track from the south.

Martin peered ahead, but his eyes couldn't match his ears, and so far all he could recognize was the sound. It *was* a train, though; he felt the steel shudder and sing beneath his feet.

And yet, how could it be? The next station south was Neenah-Menasha, and there was nothing due out of there for hours.

The clouds were thick overhead, and the field-mists roll like a cold fog in a November midnight. Even so, Martin should have been able to see the headlights as the train rushed on. But there were no lights.

There was only the whistle, screaming out of the black throat of the night. Martin could recognize the equipment of just about any locomotive ever built, but he'd never heard a whistle that sounded like this one. It wasn't signalling; it was screaming like a lost soul.

He stepped to one side, for the train was almost on top of him now, and suddenly there it was, looming along the tracks and grinding to a stop in less time than he'd ever believed possible. The wheels hadn't been oiled, because they screamed too, screamed like the damned. But the train slid to a halt and the screams died away into a series of low, groaning sounds, and Martin looked up and saw that this was a passenger train. It was big and black, without a single light shining in the engine cab or any of the long string of cars, and Martin couldn't read any lettering on the sides, but he was pretty sure this train didn't belong on the Northwestern Road.

He was even more sure when he saw the man clamber down out of the forward car. There was something wrong about the way he walked, as though one of his feet dragged. And there was something even more disturbing about the lantern he carried, and what he did with it. The lantern was dark, and when the man alighted, he held it up to his mouth and blew. Instantly the lantern glowed redly. You don't have to be a member of the Railway Brotherhood to know that this is a mighty peculiar way of lighting a lantern.

As the figure approached, Martin recognized the conductor's cap perched on his head, and this made him feel a little better for a moment—until he noticed that it was worn a bit too high, as though there might be something sticking up on the forehead underneath it.

Still, Martin knew his manners, and when the man smiled at him, he said, "Good evening, Mr. Conductor."

"Good evening, Martin."

"How did you know my name?"

The man shrugged. "How did you know I was the Conductor?"

"You *are*, aren't you?"

"To you, yes. Although other people, in other walks of life, may recognize me in different roles. For instance, you ought to see what I look like to the folks out in Hollywood." The man grinned. "I travel a great deal," he explained.

"What brings you here?" Martin asked.

"Why, you ought to know the answer to that, Martin. I came because you needed me."

"I did?"

"Don't play the innocent. Ordinarily, I seldom bother with single individuals any more. The way the world is going, I can expect to carry a full load of passengers without soliciting business. Your name has been down on the list for several years already—I reserved a seat for you as a matter of course. But then, tonight, I suddenly realized you were backsliding. Thinking of joining the Salvation Army, weren't you?"

"Well—" Martin hesitated.

"Don't be ashamed. To err is human, as somebody-or-other once said. *Reader's Digest*, wasn't it? Never mind. The point is, I felt you needed me. So I switched over and came your way."

"What for?"

"Why, to offer you a ride, of course. Isn't it better to travel comfortably by train than to march along the cold streets behind a Salvation Army band? Hard on the feet, they tell me, and even harder on the ear-drums."

"I'm not sure I'd care to ride your train, sir," Martin said. "Considering where I'm likely to end up."

"Ah, yes. The old argument." The Conductor sighed. "I suppose you'd prefer some sort of bargain, is that it?"

"Exactly," Martin answered.

"Well, I'm afraid I'm all through with that sort of thing. As I mentioned before, times have changed. There's no shortage of prospective passengers any more. Why should I offer you any special inducements?"

"You must want me, or else you wouldn't have bothered to go out of your way to find me."

The Conductor sighed again. "There you have a point. Pride was always my besetting weakness, I admit. And somehow I'd hate to lose you to the competition, after thinking of you as my own all these years." He hesitated. "Yes, I'm prepared to deal with you on your own terms, if you insist."

"The terms?" Martin asked.

"Standard proposition. Anything you want."

"Ah," said Martin.

"But I warn you in advance, there'll be no tricks. I'll grant you any wish you can name—but in return, you must promise to ride the train when the time comes."

"Suppose it never comes?"

"It will."

"Suppose I've got the kind of a wish that will keep me off forever?"

"There is no such wish."

"Don't be too sure."

"Let me worry about that," the Conductor told him. "No matter what you have in mind, I warn you that I'll collect in the end. And there'll be none of this last-minute hocus-pocus, either. No last-hour repentances, no blonde *frauleins* or fancy lawyers showing up to get you off. I offer a clean deal. That is to say, you'll get what you want, and I'll get what I want."

"I've heard you trick people. They say you're worse than a used-car salesman."

"Now wait a minute—"

"I apologize," Martin said, hastily. "But it *is* supposed to be a fact that you can't be trusted."

"I admit it. On the other hand, you seem to think you have found a way out."

"A sure-fire proposition."

"Sure-fire? Very funny!" The man began to chuckle, then halted. "But we waste valuable time, Martin. Let's get down to cases. What do you want from me?"

"A single wish."

"Name it and I shall grant it."

"Anything, you said?"

"Anything at all."

"Very well, then." Martin took a deep breath. "I want to be able to stop Time."

"Right now?"

"No. Not yet. And not for everybody. I realize that would be impossible, of course. But I want to be able to stop Time for myself. Just once, in the future. Whenever I get to a point where I know I'm happy and contented, that's where I'd like to stop. So I can just keep on being happy forever."

"That's quite a proposition," the Conductor mused. "I've got to admit I've never heard anything just like it before—and believe me, I've listened to some lulus in my day." He grinned at Martin. "You've really been thinking about this, haven't you?"

"For years," Martin admitted. Then he coughed. "Well, what do you say?"

"It's not impossible, in terms of your own *subjective* time-sense," the Conductor murmured. "Yes, I think it could be arranged."

"But I mean *really* to stop. Not for me just to *imagine* it."

"I understand. And it can be done."

"Then you'll agree?"

"Why not? I promised you, didn't I? Give me your hand."

Martin hesitated. "Will it hurt very much? I mean, I don't like the sight of blood, and—"

"Nonsense! You've been listening to a lot of poppycock. We already have made our bargain, my boy. No need for a lot of childish rigamarole. I merely intend to put something into your hand. The ways and means of fulfilling your wish. After all, there's no telling at just what moment you may decide to exercise the agreement, and I can't drop everything and come running. So it's better if you can regulate matters for yourself."

"You're going to give me a Time-stopper?"

"That's the general idea. As soon as I can decide what would be practical." The Conductor hesitated. "Ah, the very thing! Here, take my watch."

He pulled it out of his vest-pocket; a railroad watch in a silver case. He opened the back and made a delicate adjustment; Martin tried to see just exactly what he was doing, but the fingers moved in a blinding blur.

"There we are," the Conductor smiled. "It's all set, now. When you finally decide where you'd like to call a halt, merely turn the stem in reverse and unwind the watch until it stops. When it stops, Time stops, for you. Simple enough?"

"Sure thing."

"Then here, take it." And the Conductor dropped the watch into Martin's hand.

The young man closed his fingers tightly around the case. "That's all there is to it, eh?"

"Absolutely. But remember—you can stop the watch only once. So you'd better make sure that you're satisfied with the moment you choose to prolong. I caution you in all fairness; make very certain of your choice."

"I will." Martin grinned. "And since you've been so fair about it, I'll be fair, too. There's one thing you seem to have forgotten. It doesn't really matter *what* moment I choose. Because once I stop Time for myself, that means I stay where I am forever. I'll never have to get any older. And if I don't get any older, I'll never die. And if I never die, then I'll never have to take a ride on your train."

The Conductor turned away. His shoulders shook convulsively, and he may have been crying. "And you said *I* was worse than a used-car salesman," he gasped, in a strangled voice.

Then he wandered off into the fog, and the train-whistle gave an impatient shriek, and all at once it was moving swiftly down the track, rumbling out of sight in the darkness.

Martin stood there, blinking down at the silver watch in his hand. If it wasn't that he could actually see it and feel it there, and if he couldn't smell that peculiar odor, he might have thought he'd imagined the whole thing from start to finish—train, Conductor, bargain, and all.

But he had the watch, and he could recognize the scent left by the train as it departed, even though there aren't many locomotives around that use sulphur and brimstone as fuel.

And he had no doubts about his bargain. Better still, he had no doubts as to the advantages of the pact he'd made. That's what came of thinking things through to a logical conclusion. Some fools would have settled for wealth, or power, or Kim Novak. Daddy might have sold out for a fifth of whiskey.

Martin knew that he'd made a better deal. Better? It was foolproof. All he needed to do now was choose his moment. And when the right time came, it was his—forever.

He put the watch in his pocket and started back down the railroad track. He hadn't really had a destination in mind before, but he did now. He was going to find a moment of happiness . . .

Now young Martin wasn't altogether a ninny. He realized perfectly well that happiness is a relative thing; there are conditions and degrees of contentment, and they vary with one's lot in life. As a hobo, he was often satisfied with a warm handout, a double-length bench in the park, or a can of Sterno made in 1957 (a vintage year). Many a time he had reached a state of momentary bliss through such simple agencies, but he was aware that there were better things. Martin determined to seek them out.

Within two days he was in the great city of Chicago. Quite naturally, he drifted over to West Madison Street, and there he took steps to elevate his role in life. He became a city bum, a panhandler, a moocher. Within a week he had risen to the point where happiness was a meal in a regular one-arm luncheon joint, a two-bit flop on a real army cot in a real flophouse, and a full fifth of muscatel.

There was a night, after enjoying all three of these luxuries to the full, when Martin was tempted to unwind his watch at the pinnacle of intoxication. Then he remembered the faces of the honest johns he'd braced for a handout today. Sure, they were squares, but they were prosperous. They wore good clothes, held good jobs, drove nice cars. And for them, happiness was even more ecstatic; they ate dinner in fine hotels, they slept on innerspring mattresses, they drank blended whiskey.

Squares or no, they had something there. Martin fingered his watch, put aside the temptation to hock it for another bottle of muscatel, and went to sleep determining to get himself a job and improve his happiness-quotient.

When he awoke he had a hangover, but the determination was still with him. It stayed long after the hangover disappeared, and before the month was out Martin found himself working for a general contractor over on the South Side, at one of the big rehabilitation projects. He hated the grind, but the pay was good, and pretty soon he got himself a one-room apartment out on Blue Island Avenue. He was accustomed to eating in decent restaurants now, and he bought himself a comfortable bed, and every Saturday night he went down to the corner tavern. It was all very pleasant, but—

The foreman liked his work and promised him a raise in a month. If he waited around, the raise would mean that he could afford a secondhand car. With a car, he could even start picking up a girl for a date now and then. Lots of the other fellows on the job did, and they seemed pretty happy.

So Martin kept on working, and the raise came through and the car came through and pretty soon a couple of girls came through.

The first time it happened, he wanted to unwind his watch immediately. Until he got to thinking about what some of the older men always said. There was a guy named Charlie, for example, who worked alongside him on the hoist. "When you're young and don't know the score, maybe you get a kick out of running around with those pigs. But after a while, you want something better. A nice girl of your own. That's the ticket."

Well, he might have something there. At least, Martin owed it to himself to find out. If he didn't like it better, he could always go back to what he had.

It was worth a try. Of course, nice girls don't grow on trees (if they did, a lot more men would become forest rangers) and almost six months went by before Martin met Lillian Gillis. By that time he'd had another promotion and was working inside, in the office. They made him go to night school to learn how to do simple bookkeeping, but it meant another fifteen bucks extra a week, and it was nicer working indoors.

And Lillian *was* a lot of fun. When she told him she'd marry him, Martin was almost sure that the time was now. Except that she was sort of—well, she was a *nice* girl, and she said they'd have to wait until they were married. Of course, Martin couldn't expect to marry her until he had a little more money saved up, and another raise would help, too.

That took a year. Martin was patient, because he knew it was going to be worth it. Every time he had any doubts, he took out his watch and looked at it. But he never showed it to Lillian, or anybody else. Most of the other men wore expensive wristwatches and the old silver railroad watch looked just a little cheap.

Martin smiled as he gazed at the stem. Just a few twists and he'd have something none of these other poor working slobs would ever have. Permanent satisfaction, with his blushing bride—

Only getting married turned out to be just the beginning. Sure, it was wonderful, but Lillian told him how much better things would be if they could move into a new place and fix it up. Martin wanted decent furniture, a TV set, a nice car.

So he started taking night courses and got a promotion to the front office. With the baby coming, he wanted to stick around and see his son arrive. And when it came, he realized he'd have to wait until it got a little older, started to walk and talk and develop a personality of its own.

About this time the company sent him out on the road as a troubleshooter on some of those other jobs, and now *he* was eating at those good hotels, living high on the hog and the expense-account. More than once he was tempted to unwind his watch. This was the good life. And he realized it could be even better if he just didn't have to *work*. Sooner or later, if he could cut in on one of the company deals, he could make a pile and retire. Then everything would be ideal.

It happened, but it took time. Martin's son was going to high school before he really got up there into the chips. Martin got the feeling that it was now or never, because he wasn't exactly a kid any more.

But right about then he met Sherry Westcott, and she didn't seem to think he was middle-aged at all, in spite of the way he was losing hair and adding stomach. She taught him that a *toupee* could cover the bald spot and a cummerbund could cover the potgut. In fact, she taught him quite a number of things, and he so enjoyed learning that he actually took out his watch and prepared to unwind it.

Unfortunately, he chose the very moment that the private detectives broke down the door of the hotel room, and then there was a long stretch of time when Martin was so busy fighting the divorce action that he couldn't honestly say he was enjoying any given amount.

When he made the final settlement with Lil he was broke again, and Sherry didn't seem to think he was so young, after all. So he squared his shoulders and went back to work.

He made his pile, eventually, but it took longer this time, and there wasn't much chance to have fun along the way. The fancy dames in the fancy cocktail lounges didn't seem to interest him any more, and neither did the liquor. Besides, the Doc had warned him about that.

But there were other pleasures for a rich man to investigate. Travel, for instance—and not riding the rods from one hick burg to another, either. Martin went around the world *via* plane and luxury liner. For a while it seemed as though he would find his moment after all. Visiting the Taj Mahal by moonlight, the moon's radiance was reflected from the back of the battered old watch-case, and Martin got ready to unwind it. Nobody else was there to watch him—

And that's why he hesitated. Sure, this was an enjoyable moment, but he was alone. Lil and the kid were gone, Sherry was gone, and somehow he'd never had time to make any friends. Maybe if he found a few congenial people, he'd have the ultimate happiness. That must be the answer—it wasn't just money or power or sex or seeing beautiful things. The real satisfaction lay in friendship.

So on the boat trip home, Martin tried to strike up a few acquaintances at the ship's bar. But all these people were so much younger, and Martin had nothing in common with them. Also, they wanted to dance and drink, and Martin wasn't in condition to appreciate such pastimes. Nevertheless, he tried.

Perhaps that's why he had the little accident the day before they docked in San Francisco. "Little accident" was the ship's doctor's way of describing it, but Martin noticed he looked very grave when he told him to stay in bed, and he'd called an ambulance to meet the liner at the dock and take the patient right to the hospital.

At the hospital, all the expensive treatment and expensive smiles and the expensive words didn't fool Martin any. He was an old man with a bad heart, and they thought he was going to die.

But he could fool them. He still had the watch. He found it in his coat when he put on his clothes and sneaked out of the hospital before dawn.

He didn't have to die. He could cheat death with a single gesture—and he intended to do it as a free man, out there under a free sky.

That was the real secret of happiness. He understood it now. Not even friendship meant as much as freedom. This was the best thing of all—to be free of friends or family or the furies of the flesh.

Martin walked slowly beside the embankment under the night sky. Come to think of it, he was just about back where he'd started, so many years ago. But the moment was good, good enough to prolong forever. Once a bum, always a bum.

He smiled as he thought about it, and then the smile twisted sharply and suddenly, like the pain twisting sharply and suddenly in his chest. The world began to spin and he fell down on the side of the embankment.

He couldn't see very well, but he was still conscious, and he knew what had happened. Another stroke, and a bad one. Maybe this was it. Except that he wouldn't be a fool any longer. He wouldn't wait to see what was still around the corner.

Right now was his chance to use his power and save his life. And he was going to do it. He could still move, nothing could stop him.

He groped in his pocket and pulled out the old silver watch, fumbling with the stem. A few twists and he'd cheat death, he'd never have to ride that Hell-Bound Train. He could go on forever.

Forever.

Martin had never really considered the word before. To go on forever—but *how?* Did he *want* to go on forever, like this; a sick old man, lying helplessly here in the grass?

No. He couldn't do it. He wouldn't do it. And suddenly he wanted very much to cry, because he knew that somewhere along the line he'd outsmarted himself. And now it was too late. His eyes dimmed, there was this roaring in his ears . . .

He recognized the roaring, of course, and he wasn't at all surprised to see the train come rushing out of the fog up there on the embankment. He wasn't surprised when it stopped, either, or when the Conductor climbed off and walked slowly towards him.

The Conductor hadn't changed a bit. Even his grin was still the same.

"Hello, Martin," he said. "All aboard."

"I know," Martin whispered. "But you'll have to carry me. I can't walk. I'm not even really talking any more, am I?"

"Yes you are," the Conductor said. "I can hear you fine. And you can walk, too." He leaned down and placed his hand on Martin's chest. There was a moment of icy numbness, and then, sure enough, Martin could walk after all.

He got up and followed the Conductor along the slope, moving to the side of the train.

"In here?" he asked.

"No, the next car," the Conductor murmured. "I guess you're entitled to ride Pullman. After all, you're quite a successful man. You've tasted the joys of wealth and position and prestige. You've known the pleasures of marriage and fatherhood. You've sampled the delights of dining and drinking and debauchery, too, and you travelled high, wide and handsome. So let's not have any last-minute recriminations."

"All right," Martin sighed. "I guess I can't blame you for my mistakes. On the other hand, you can't take credit for what happened, either. I worked for everything I got. I did it all on my own. I didn't even need your watch."

"So you didn't," the Conductor said, smiling. "But would you mind giving it back to me now?"

"Need it for the next sucker, eh?" Martin muttered.

"Perhaps."

Something about the way he said it made Martin look up. He tried to see the Conductor's eyes, but the brim of his cap cast a shadow. So Martin looked down at the watch instead, as if seeking an answer there.

"Tell me something," he said, softly. "If I give you the watch, what will you do with it?"

"Why, throw it into the ditch," the Conductor told him. "That's all I'll do with it." And he held out his hand.

"What if somebody comes along and finds it? And twists the stem backwards, and stops Time?"

"Nobody would do that," the Conductor murmured. "Even if they knew."

"You mean, it was all a trick? This is only an ordinary, cheap watch?"

"I didn't say that," whispered the Conductor. "I only said that no one has ever twisted the stem backwards. They've all been like you, Martin—looking ahead to find that perfect happiness. Waiting for the moment that never comes."

The Conductor held out his hand again.

Martin sighed and shook his head. "You cheated me after all."

"You cheated yourself, Martin. And now you're going to ride that Hell-Bound Train."

He pushed Martin up the steps and into the car ahead. As he entered, the train began to move and the whistle screamed. And Martin stood there in the swaying Pullman, gazing down the aisle at the other passengers. He could see them sitting there, and somehow it didn't seem strange at all.

Here they were; the drunks and the sinners, the gambling men and the grifters, the big-time spenders, the skirt-chasers, and all the jolly crew. They knew where they were going, of course, but they didn't seem to be particularly concerned at the moment. The blinds were drawn on the windows, yet it was light inside, and they were all sitting around and singing and passing the bottle and laughing it up, telling their jokes and bragging their brags, just the way Daddy used to sing about them in the old song.

"Mighty nice traveling companions," Martin said. "Why, I've never seen such a pleasant bunch of people. I mean, they seem to be really enjoying themselves!"

"Sorry," the Conductor told him. "I'm afraid things may not be quite so enjoyable, once we pull into that Depot Way Down Yonder."

For the third time, he held out his hand. "Now, before you sit down, if you'll just give me that watch. I mean, a bargain's a bargain—"

Martin smiled. "A bargain's a bargain," he echoed. "I agreed to ride your train if I could stop Time when I found the right moment of happiness. So, if you don't mind, I think I'll just make certain adjustments."

Very slowly, Martin twisted the silver watch-stem.

"No!" gasped the Conductor. "No!"

But the watch-stem turned.

"Do you realize what you've done?" the Conductor panted. "Now we'll never reach the Depot. We'll just go on riding, all of us, forever and ever!"

Martin grinned. "I know," he said. "But the fun is in the trip, not the destination. You taught me that. And I'm looking forward to a wonderful trip."

The Conductor groaned. "All right," he sighed, at last. "You got the best of me, after all. But when I think of spending eternity trapped here riding this train—"

"Cheer up!" Martin told him. "It won't be that bad. Looks like we have plenty to eat and drink. And after all, these are *your* kind of folks."

"But I'm the Conductor! Think of the endless work this means for me!"

"Don't let it worry you," Martin said. "Look, maybe I can even help. If you were to find me another one of those caps, now, and let me keep this watch—"

And that's the way it finally worked out. Wearing his cap and carrying his battered old silver watch, there's no happier person in or out of this world—now and forever—than Martin. Martin, the new Brakeman on That Hell-bound Train.

Enoch

It always starts the same way.

First, there's the feeling.

Have you ever felt the tread of little feet walking across the top of your skull? Footsteps on your skull, back and forth, back and forth?

It starts like that.

You can't see who does the walking. After all, it's on top of your head. If you're clever, you wait for a chance and suddenly brush a hand through your hair. But you can't catch the walker that way. He knows. Even if you clamp both hands flat to your head, he manages to wriggle through, somehow. Or maybe he jumps.

He is terribly swift. And you can't ignore him. If you don't pay any attention to the footsteps, he tries the next step. He wriggles down the back of your neck and whispers in your ear.

You can feel his body, so tiny and cold, pressed tightly against the base of your brain. There must be something numbing in his claws, because they don't hurt—although later, you'll find little scratches on your neck that bleed and bleed. But at the time, all you know is that something tiny and cold is pressing there. Pressing, and whispering.

That's when you try to fight him. You try not to hear what he says. Because when you listen, you're lost. You have to obey him then.

Oh, he's wicked and wise!

He knows how to frighten and threaten, if you dare to resist. But I seldom try, any more. It's better for me if I do listen and then obey.

As long as I'm willing to listen, things don't seem so bad. Because he can be soothing and persuasive, too. Tempting. The things he has promised me, in that little silken whisper!

He keeps his promises, too.

Folks think I'm poor because I never have any money and live in that old shack on the edge of the swamp. But he has given me riches.

After I do what he wants, he takes me away—out of myself—for days. There are other places besides this world, you know; places where I am king.

People laugh at me and say I have no friends; the girls in town used to call me "scarecrow." Yet sometimes—after I've done his bidding—he brings queens to share my bed.

Just dreams? I don't think so. It's the other life that's just a dream; the life in the shack at the edge of the swamp. That part doesn't seem real any more.

Not even the killing . . .

Yes, I kill people.

That's what Enoch wants, you know.

That's what he whispers about. He asks me to kill people, for him.

I don't like that. I used to fight against it—I told you that before, didn't I?—but I can't any more.

He wants me to kill people for him. Enoch. The thing that lives on the top of my head. I can't see him. I can't catch him. I can only feel him, and hear him, and obey him.

Sometimes he leaves me alone for days. Then, suddenly, I feel him there, scratching away at the roof of my brain. I hear his whisper ever so plainly, and he'll be telling me about someone who is coming through the swamp.

I don't know how he knows about them. He couldn't have seen them, yet he describes them perfectly.

"There's a tramp walking down the Aylesworthy Road. A short, fat man, with a bald head. His name is Mike. He's wearing a brown sweater and blue overalls. He's going to turn into the swamp in about ten minutes when the sun goes down. He'll stop under the big tree next to the dump.

"Better hide behind that tree. Wait until he starts to look for firewood. Then you know what to do. Get the hatchet, now. Hurry."

Sometimes I ask Enoch what he will give me. Usually, I just

trust him. I know I'm going to have to do it, anyway. So I might as well go ahead at once. Enoch is never wrong about things, and he keeps me out of trouble.

That is, he always did—until the last time.

One night I was sitting in the shack eating supper when he told me about this girl.

"She's coming to visit you," he whispered. "A beautiful girl, all in black. She has a wonderful quality to her head—fine bones. Fine."

At first I thought he was telling me about one of my rewards. But Enoch was talking about a real person.

"She will come to the door and ask you to help her fix her car. She has taken the side road, planning to go into town by a shorter route. Now the car is well into the swamp, and one of the tires needs changing."

It sounded funny, hearing Enoch talk about things like automobile tires. But he knows about them. Enoch knows everything.

"You will go out to help her when she asks you. Don't take anything. She has a wrench in the car. Use that."

This time I tried to fight him. I kept whimpering, "I won't do it, I won't do it."

He just laughed. And then he told me what he'd do if I refused. He told me over and over again.

"Better that I do it to her and not to you," Enoch reminded me. "Or would you rather I—"

"No!" I said. "No. I'll do it."

"After all," Enoch whispered, "I can't help it. I must be served every so often. To keep me alive. To keep me strong. So I can serve you. So I can give you things. That is why you have to obey me. If not, I'll just stay right here and—"

"No," I said. "I'll do it."

And I did it.

She knocked on my door just a few minutes later, and it was just as Enoch had whispered it. She was a pretty girl—with blonde hair. I like blonde hair. I was glad, when I went out into the swamp with her, that I didn't have to harm her hair. I hit her behind the neck with the wrench.

Enoch told me what to do, step by step.

After I used the hatchet, I put the body in the quicksand.

Enoch was with me, and he cautioned me about heelmarks. I got rid of them.

I was worried about the car, but he showed me how to use the end of a rotten log and pitch it over. I wasn't sure it would sink, too, but it did. And much faster than I would have believed.

It was a relief to see the car go. I threw the wrench in after it. Then Enoch told me to go home, and I did, and at once I felt the dreamy feeling stealing over me.

Enoch had promised me something extra special for this one, and I sank down into sleep right away. I could barely feel the pressure leave my head as Enoch left me, scampering off back into the swamp for his reward . . .

I don't know how long I slept. It must have been a long time. All I remember is that I finally started to wake up, knowing somehow that Enoch was back with me again, and feeling that something was wrong.

Then I woke up all the way, because I heard the banging on my door.

I waited a moment. I waited for Enoch to whisper to me, tell me what I should do.

But Enoch was asleep now. He always sleeps—afterwards. Nothing wakes him for days on end; and during that time I am free. Usually I enjoy such freedom, but not now. I needed his help.

The pounding on my door grew louder, and I couldn't wait any longer.

I got up and answered.

Old Sheriff Shelby came through the doorway.

"Come on, Seth," he said. "I'm taking you up to the jail."

I didn't say anything. His beady little black eyes were peeping everywhere inside my shack. When he looked at me, I wanted to hide, I felt so scared.

He couldn't see Enoch, of course. Nobody can. But Enoch was there; I felt him resting very lightly on top of my skull, burrowed down under a blanket of hair, clinging to my curls and sleeping as peaceful as a baby.

"Emily Robbins' folks said she was planning on cutting through the swamp," the Sheriff told me. "We followed the tire tracks up to the old quicksand."

Enoch had forgotten about the tracks. So what could I say? Besides,

"Anything you say can be used agin you," said Sheriff Shelby. "Come on, Seth."

I went with him. There was nothing else for me to do. I went with him into town, and all the loafers were out trying to rush the car. There were women in the crowd too. They kept yelling for the men to "get" me.

But Sheriff Shelby held them off, and at last I was tucked away safe and sound in back of the jailhouse. He locked me up in the middle cell. The two cells on each side of mine were vacant, so I was all alone. All alone except for Enoch, and he slept through everything.

It was still pretty early in the morning, and Sheriff Shelby went out again with some other men. I guess he was going to try and get the body out of the quicksand, if he could. He didn't try to ask any questions, and I wondered about that.

Charley Potter, now, he was different. He wanted to know everything. Sheriff Shelby had left him in charge of the jail while he was away. He brought me my breakfast after a while, and hung around asking questions.

I just kept still. I knew better than to talk to a fool like Charley Potter. He thought I was crazy. Just like the mob outside. Most people in that town thought I was crazy—because of my mother, I suppose, and because of the way I lived all alone out in the swamp.

What could I say to Charley Potter? If I told him about Enoch he'd never believe me anyway.

So I didn't talk.

I listened.

Then Charley Potter told me about the search for Emily Robbins, and about how Sheriff Shelby got to wondering over some other disappearances a while back. He said that there would be a big trial, and the District Attorney was coming down from the County Seat. And he'd heard they were sending out a doctor to see me right away.

Sure enough, just as I finished breakfast, the doctor came. Charley Potter saw him drive up and let him in. He had to work fast to keep some of the oafs from breaking in with him. They wanted to lynch me, I suppose. But the doctor came in all right—a little man with one of those funny beards on his chin—and he made Charley Potter go up front into the office while he sat down outside the cell and talked to me.

His name was Dr. Silversmith.

Now up to this time, I wasn't really feeling anything. It had all happened so fast I didn't get a chance to think.

It was like part of a dream; the Sheriff and the mob and all this talk about a trial and lynching and the body in the swamp.

But somehow the sight of this Dr. Silversmith changed things.

He was real, all right. You could tell he was a doctor who wanted to send me to the Institution after they found my mother.

That was one of the first things Dr. Silversmith asked me— what had happened to my mother?

He seemed to know quite a lot about me, and that made it easier for me to talk.

Pretty soon I found myself telling him all sorts of things. How my mother and I lived in the shack. How she made the philtres and sold them. About the big pot and the way we gathered herbs at night. About the nights when she went off alone and I would hear the queer noises from far away.

I didn't want to say much more, but he knew, anyway. He knew they had called her a witch. He even knew the way she died—when Santo Dinorelli came to our door that evening and stabbed her because she had made the potion for his daughter who ran away with that trapper. He knew about me living in the swamp alone after that, too.

But he didn't know about Enoch.

Enoch, up on top of my head all the time, still sleeping, not knowing or caring what was happening to me . . .

Somehow, I was talking to Dr. Silversmith about Enoch. I wanted to explain that it wasn't really I who had killed this girl. So I had to mention Enoch, and how my mother had made the bargain in the woods. She hadn't let me come with her—I was only twelve—but she took some of my blood in a little bottle.

Then, when she came back, Enoch was with her. And he was to be mine forever, she said, and look after me and help me in all ways.

I told this very carefully and explained why it was I couldn't help myself when I did anything now, because ever since my mother died Enoch had guided me.

Yes, all these years Enoch had protected me, just as my mother planned. She knew I couldn't get along alone. I admitted this to Dr. Silversmith because I thought he was a wise man and would understand.

That was wrong.

I knew it at once. Because while Dr. Silversmith leaned forward and stroked his little beard and said, "Yes, yes," over and over again, I could feel his eyes watching me. The same kind as the people in the mob. Mean eyes. Eyes that don't trust you when they see you. Prying, peeping eyes.

Then he began to ask me all sorts of ridiculous questions. About Enoch, at first—although I knew he was only pretending to believe in Enoch. He asked me how I could hear Enoch if I couldn't see him. He asked me if I ever heard any other voices. He asked me how I felt when I killed Emily Robbins and whether I—but I won't even think about that question. Why, he talked to me as if I were some kind of—crazy person!

He had only been fooling me all along about not knowing Enoch. He proved that now by asking me how many other people I had killed. And then he wanted to know, where were their heads?

He couldn't fool me any longer.

I just laughed at him, then, and shut up tighter than a clam.

After a while he gave up and went away, shaking his head. I laughed after him because I knew he hadn't found out what he wanted to find out. He wanted to know all my mother's secrets, and my secrets, and Enoch's secrets too.

But he didn't, and I laughed. And then I went to sleep. I slept almost all afternoon.

When I woke up, there was a new man standing in front of my cell. He had a big, fat smiling face, and nice eyes.

"Hello, Seth," he said, very friendly. "Having a little snooze?"

I reached up to the top of my head. I couldn't feel Enoch, but I knew he was there, and still asleep. He moves fast, even when he's sleeping.

"Don't be alarmed," said the man. "I won't hurt you."

"Did that Doctor send you?" I asked.

The man laughed. "Of course not," he told me. "My name's Cassidy. Edwin Cassidy. I'm the District Attorney, and I'm in charge here. Can I come in and sit down, do you suppose?"

"I'm locked in," I said.

"I've got the keys from the Sheriff," said Mr. Cassidy. He took them out and opened my cell; walked right in and sat down next to me on the bench.

"Aren't you afraid?" I asked him. "You know, I'm supposed to be a murderer."

"Why Seth," Mr. Cassidy laughed, "I'm not afraid of you. I know you didn't mean to kill anybody."

He put his hand on my shoulder, and I didn't draw away. It was a nice fat, soft hand. He had a big diamond ring on his finger that just twinkled away in the sunshine.

"How's Enoch?" he said.

I jumped.

"Oh, that's all right. That fool Doctor told me when I met him down the street. He doesn't understand about Enoch, does he, Seth? But you and I do."

"That Doctor thinks I'm crazy," I whispered.

"Well, just between us, Seth, it did sound a little hard to believe, at first. But I've just come from the swamp. Sheriff Shelby and some of his men are still working down there.

"They found Emily Robbins' body just a little while ago. And other bodies, too. A fat man's body, and a small boy, and some Indian. The quicksand preserves them, you know."

I watched his eyes, and they were still smiling, so I knew I could trust this man.

"They'll find other bodies too, if they keep on, won't they, Seth?"

I nodded.

"But I didn't wait any longer. I saw enough to understand that you were telling the truth. Enoch must have made you do these things, didn't he?"

I nodded again.

"Fine," said Mr. Cassidy, pressing my shoulder. "You see, we do understand each other now. So I won't blame you for anything you tell me."

"What do you want to know?" I asked.

"Oh, lots of things. I'm interested in Enoch, you see. Just how many people did he ask you to kill—all together, that is?"

"Nine," I said.

"And they're all buried in the quicksand?"

"Yes."

"Do you know their names?"

"Only a few." I told him the names of the ones I knew. "Sometimes Enoch just describes them for me and I go out to meet them," I explained.

Mr. Cassidy sort of chuckled and took out a cigar. I frowned.

"Don't want me to smoke, eh?"

"Please—I don't like it. My mother didn't believe in smoking; she never let me."

Mr. Cassidy laughed out loud now, but he put the cigar away and leaned forward.

"You can be a big help to me, Seth," he whispered. "I suppose you know what a District Attorney must do."

"He's a sort of lawyer, isn't he—at trials and things?"

"That's right. I'm going to be at your trial, Seth. Now you don't want to have to get up in front of all those people and tell them about—what happened. Right?"

"No, I don't, Mr. Cassidy. Not those mean people here in town. They hate me."

"Then here's what you do. You tell me all about it, and I'll talk for you. That's friendly enough, isn't it?"

I wished Enoch was there to help me, but he was asleep. I looked at Mr. Cassidy and made up my own mind.

"Yes," I said. "I can tell you."

So I told him everything I knew.

After a while he stopped chuckling, but he was just getting so interested he couldn't bother to laugh or do anything but listen.

"One thing more," he said. "We found some bodies in the swamp. Emily Robbins' body we could identify, and several of the others. But it was be easier if we knew something else. You can tell me this, Seth. Where are the heads?"

I stood up and turned away. "I won't tell you that," I said, "because I don't know."

"Don't know?"

"I give them to Enoch," I explained. "Don't you understand—that's why I must kill people for him. Because he wants their heads."

Mr. Cassidy looked puzzled.

"He always makes me cut the heads off and leave them," I went on. "I put the bodies in the quicksand, and then go home. He puts me to sleep and rewards me. After that he goes away—back to the heads. That's what he wants."

"Why does he want them, Seth?"

I told him. "You see, it wouldn't do you any good if you could find them. Because you probably wouldn't recognize anything anyway."

Mr. Cassidy sat up and sighed. "But why do you let Enoch do such things?"

"I must. Or else he'll do it to me. That's what he always threatens. He has to have it. So I obey him."

Mr. Cassidy watched me while I walked the floor, but he didn't say a word. He seemed to be very nervous, all of a sudden, and when I came close, he sort of leaned away.

"You'll explain all that at the trial, of course," I said. "About Enoch, and everything."

He shook his head.

"I'm not going to tell about Enoch at the trial, and neither are you," Mr. Cassidy said. "Nobody is even going to know that Enoch exists."

"Why?"

"I'm trying to help you, Seth. Don't you know what the people will say if you mention Enoch to them? They'll say you're crazy! And you don't want that to happen."

"No. But what can you do? How can you help me?"

Mr. Cassidy smiled at me.

"You're afraid of Enoch, aren't you? Well, I was just thinking out loud. Suppose you gave Enoch to me?"

I gulped.

"Yes. Suppose you gave Enoch to me, right now? Let me take care of him for you during the trial. Then he wouldn't be yours, and you wouldn't have to say anything about him. He probably doesn't want people to know what he does, anyway."

"That's right," I said. "Enoch would be very angry. He's a secret, you know. But I hate to give him to you without asking—and he's asleep now."

"Asleep?"

"Yes. On top of my skull. Only you can't see him, of course."

Mr. Cassidy gazed at my head and then he chuckled again.

"Oh, I can explain everything when he wakes up," he told me. "When he knows it's all for the best, I'm sure he'll be happy."

"Well—I guess it's all right, then," I sighed. "But you must promise to take good care of him."

"Sure," said Mr. Cassidy.

"And you'll give him what he wants? What he needs?"

"Of course."

"And you won't tell a soul?"

"Not a soul."

"Of course you know what will happen to you if you refuse to give Enoch what he wants," I warned Mr. Cassidy. "He will take it—from you—by force?"

"Don't you worry, Seth."

I stood still for a minute. Because all at once I could feel something move towards my ear.

"Enoch," I whispered. "Can you hear me?"

He heard.

Then I explained everything to him. How I was giving him to Mr. Cassidy.

Enoch didn't say a word.

Mr. Cassidy didn't say a word. He just sat there and grinned. I suppose it must have looked a little strange to see me talking to—nothing.

"Go to Mr. Cassidy," I whispered. "Go to him, now."

And Enoch went.

I felt the weight lift from my head. That was all, but I knew he was gone.

"Can you feel him, Mr. Cassidy?" I asked.

"What—oh, sure!" he said, and stood up.

"Take good care of Enoch," I told him.

"The best."

"Don't put your hat on," I warned. "Enoch doesn't like hats."

"Sorry, I forgot. Well, Seth, I'll say good-bye now. You've been a mighty great help to me—and from now on we can just forget about Enoch, as far as telling anybody else is concerned.

"I'll come back again and talk about the trial. That Doctor Silversmith, he's going to try and tell the folks you're crazy. Maybe it would be best if you just denied everything you told him—now that I have Enoch."

That sounded like a fine idea, but then I knew Mr. Cassidy was a smart man.

"Whatever you say, Mr. Cassidy. Just be good to Enoch, and he'll be good to you."

Mr. Cassidy shook my hand and then he and Enoch went away. I felt tired again. Maybe it was the strain, and maybe it was just that I felt a little queer, knowing that Enoch was gone. Anyway, I went back to sleep for a long time.

It was night time when I woke up. Old Charley Potter was banging on the cell door, bringing me my supper.

He jumped when I said hello to him, and backed away.

"Murderer!" he yelled. "They got nine bodies out'n the swamp. You crazy fiend!"

"Why Charley," I said. "I always thought you were a friend of mine."

"Loony! I'm gonna get out of here right now—leave you locked up for the night. Sheriff'll see that nobuddy breaks in to lynch you—if you ask me, he's wasting his time."

Then Charley turned out all the lights and went away. I heard him go out the front door and put the padlock on, and I was all alone in the jail house.

All alone! It was strange to be all alone for the first time in years—all alone, without Enoch.

I ran my fingers across the top of my head. It felt bare and queer. The moon was shining through the window and I stood there looking out at the empty street. Enoch always loved the moon. It made him lively. Made him restless and greedy. I wondered how he felt now, with Mr. Cassidy.

I must have stood there for a long time. My legs were numb

when I turned around and listened to the fumbling at the door.

The lock clicked open, and then Mr. Cassidy came running in.

"Take him off me!" he yelled. "Take him away!"

"What's the matter?" I asked.

"Enoch—that thing of yours—I thought you were crazy—maybe I'm the crazy one—but take him off!"

"Why, Mr. Cassidy! I told you what Enoch was like."

"He's crawling around up there now. I can feel him. And I can hear him. The things he whispers!"

"But I explained all that, Mr. Cassidy. Enoch wants something, doesn't he? You know what it is. And you'll have to give it to him. You promised."

"I can't. I won't kill for him—he can't make me—"

"He can. And he will."

Mr. Cassidy gripped the bars on the cell door. "Seth, you must help me. Call Enoch. Take him back. Make him go back to you. Hurry."

"All right, Mr. Cassidy," I said.

I called Enoch. He didn't answer. I called again. Silence.

Mr. Cassidy started to cry. It shocked me, and then I felt kind of sorry for him. He just didn't understand, after all. I know what Enoch can do to you when he whispers that way. First he coaxes you, and then he pleads, and then he threatens—

"You'd better obey him," I told Mr. Cassidy. "Has he told you who to kill?"

Mr. Cassidy didn't pay any attention to me. He just cried. And then he took out the jail keys and opened up the cell next to mine. He went in and locked the door.

"I won't," he sobbed. "I won't, I won't!"

"You won't what?' I asked.

"I won't kill Doctor Silversmith at the hotel and give Enoch his head. I'll stay here, in the cell, where I'm safe! Oh you fiend, you devil—"

He slumped down sideways and I could see him through the bars dividing our cells, sitting all hunched over while his hands tore at his hair.

"You'd better," I called out. "Or else Enoch will do something. Please, Mr. Cassidy—oh, hurry—"

Then Mr. Cassidy gave a little moan and I guess he fainted. Because he didn't say anything more and he stopped clawing. I called him once but he wouldn't answer.

So what could I do? I sat down in the dark corner of my cell and watched the moonlight. Moonlight always makes Enoch wild.

Then Mr. Cassidy started to scream. Not loud, but deep down in his throat. He didn't move at all, just screamed.

I knew it was Enoch, taking what he wanted—from him.

What was the use of looking? You can't stop him, and I had warned Mr. Cassidy.

I just sat there and held my hands to my ears until it was all over.

When I turned around again, Mr. Cassidy still sat slumped up against the bars. There wasn't a sound to be heard.

Oh yes, there was! A purring. A soft, faraway purring. The purring of Enoch, after he has eaten. Then I heard a scratching. The scratching of Enoch's claws, when he frisks because he's been fed.

The purring and the scratching came from inside Mr. Cassidy's head.

That would be Enoch, all right, and he was happy now.

I was happy, too.

I reached my hand through the bars and pulled the jail keys from Mr. Cassidy's pocket. I opened my cell door and I was free again.

There was no need for me to stay now, with Mr. Cassidy gone. And Enoch wouldn't be staying, either. I called to him.

"Here, Enoch!"

That was as close as I've ever come to really seeing Enoch—a sort of a white streak that came flashing out of the big red hole he had eaten in the back of Mr. Cassidy's skull.

Then I felt the soft, cold, flabby weight landing on my own head once more, and I knew Enoch had come home.

I walked through the corridor and opened the outer door of the jail.

Enoch's tiny feet began to patter on the roof of my brain.

Together we walked out into the night. The moon was shining, everything was still, and I could hear, ever so softly, Enoch's happy chuckling in my ear.

www.ingramcontent.com/pod-product-compliance
Ingram Content Group UK Ltd.
Pitfield, Milton Keynes, MK11 3LW, UK
UKHW040928050225
454710UK00004B/171